In Your Blood I Run

Celebrating
30 Years of Publishing
in India

In Your Blood I Run

Sonia Bhatnagar

HarperCollins *Publishers* India

First published in India by HarperCollins *Publishers* 2023
4th Floor, Tower A, Building No. 10, Phase II, DLF Cyber City,
Gurugram, Haryana – 122002
www.harpercollins.co.in

2 4 6 8 10 9 7 5 3 1

P-ISBN: 978-93-5629-165-2
E-ISBN: 978-93-5629-168-3

Typeset in 11/14 Adobe Caslon Pro at
Manipal Technologies Limited, Manipal

Printed and bound at
Thomson Press (India) Ltd

To Usha and Sachidanand

Simla, British India, 1936

A darkening sky

RATAN FLICKED HIS CIGARETTE ONTO THE WET SNOW AND once again practised the lies he would tell. The moonlight, the smoke from his cigarette, the snow and mud, all mingled together like a giant bowl of ash. It had stopped snowing the day before but the rain continued beating down. He didn't remember the last time he had seen Simla this shade of grey. Or silver.

Ratan looked up at the sky for a fleeting second as he walked up the familiar path. In the distance, a barefoot, liveried *jampaani* pulled a rickshaw with a coat of arms stamped on it, around a steep corner, and disappeared out of sight. A tiny runaway snowflake bounced off Ratan's cheek and rolled onto the lapel of his coat. He lifted the collar of his coat to keep the wind from lashing against his ears. The collar continued to slap against his neck. All else grew quieter and quieter as he climbed the hill.

It never ceased to amaze him how the din from Lower Bazaar below turned melodious as he went higher up the Ridge. If he were to stop walking now and look down, he would catch a cacophony of sounds that could only amount to noise. The clatter of utensils, the pounding and thumping of *hama dastas*, harsh, strained voices, mingled with the wailing of babies, and dogs barking into the night.

If he gazed upwards at the forests, where the mist came and went, only the music wafted through. The notes swirling within the vast gardens of the British summer homes. The tinkling of manicured hands going over the keys of a piano. The rustle and clink of silk gowns and champagne flutes. Soft, gay laughter and the merry prance of dancing feet.

The thing to do, Ratan had long since decided, was to walk upwards. To leave the noise behind with every step. Here, up and up, the music never stopped. If in summer it was louder and the parties incessant, in winter, it became softer. The parties were fewer but there was always something to celebrate.

Never a dull moment in India, Ratan had heard a British officer tell his wife in her first month in Simla. Flustered, she was watching a turbaned man being taken away by the police. He had painted an offensive slogan with *gulaal* on a parked coach at the Mall Road. A small crowd had gathered and Ratan too had lingered to watch the scene. He still remembered how the vermilion on the man's hands had managed to look bloody and joyous at the same time.

Fading into the fog, still shouting 'Jai Hind!', the man's eyes gleamed with hate. He turned back, again and again, straining against the hands that led him away. Of all the people who stood staring, his eyes sought Ratan out. Daring him to look back, and Ratan had. Letting him know that he, Ratan, was a free man looking at someone bound in chains. That image of the man, half in the fog, half out, had stayed with him. Dark bushy eyebrows over grey eyes flashing like the red light on the police jeep behind.

Later that day, he had told Sara about the man. Chewing on a paan, uncaring of the juice from the betel nut trickling down her mouth, she had tucked the flounce of her evening gown under her to sit cross-legged and listen to him. Then she proceeded to ask what it was exactly that was bothering him.

'How dare he judge me? Why must his choices be mine?'

'You judged him back, didn't you? It's equal then.'

'It's not. He judged me *louder* than I judged him.'

She had smiled then. He wasn't amused.

'Ratan, look at me,' Sara said.

He flashed her a look.

'*Louder*, darling, *louder*.'

He flashed more, eyes hurting and laughing all at once.

It was always like that with Sara. She made him laugh when he wanted to hurt.

Sara Davenport. Lady Davenport. Sara. Sa Re Ga Ma. All the classical Hindustani music lessons that his father had wasted his money on, came back with her name.

And yet, he couldn't stay anymore. He had to tell her, hard as it was going to be, he couldn't put it off any longer. Tonight, he would tell her tonight.

He was to pick her up from Wildflower Hall, where Lady Hotz was having an impromptu charity ball. He would seat her next to him in the Benz, drive her somewhere picturesque and tell her his lies. They were good lies. They wouldn't hurt her. They would be just enough for her to take her next step.

Ratan could see Shyam in the distance now. Silver or grey, it was a clear night. Shyam was waiting for him outside the Davenport House with the keys to the Benz Roadster. Shyam was the only other chauffeur the Davenports relied upon. Married just a few weeks back, he hated working nights. Always in a tearing hurry to go back home to Cheeni, his coy new bride. Holding a lantern, Shyam was hopping from one foot to the other as Ratan appeared closer. Ratan slowed down, enjoying the torture he was inflicting on him.

'Ratan, *saaley*!' Shyam hissed into the night.

Ratan grinned and took the keys from him, amused to see a series of accusations in Shyam's fish-like, protruding eyes.

Pinching Shyam's plump cold cheek, he opened the door to the Benz and got in. Leaning back, he settled in and from the corner of his eye, watched Shyam hurriedly shuffle out of sight. For a long moment, he let himself thaw from the warmth of the plush leather upholstery of the car. Before turning on the ignition and climbing the hill.

As the car pierced the rolling mist, he wondered if Sara would believe his reasons for leaving Simla. The last thing he wanted to do was let her down. She had turned his life around. If he hadn't met her when he did, he would still be with Bhai, inches away from serious trouble, every single day.

But the thing about trouble was that Ratan never had to seek it. It announced itself much as a storm did.

He was half an hour late. Sara had given him the night off and then changed her mind. He had rushed to tell his neighbour Anwar that he could no longer babysit Amira that night. But by the time he had reached, the child was alone with a high fever. Luckily for him, Anwar's wife had returned early from the Kitcheners' home where she worked as an ayah. He had left immediately but was running late.

It was true, Ratan didn't know how to be on time. Another reason why trouble was so fond of him—it was easy to catch him by surprise because he was always in a hurry. His eyes were never on the sky darkening.

He could see Wildflower Hall in the distance now. Hear the muffled sounds of an evening spent in high spirits. Ratan hoped Sara had enjoyed an extra half hour of dancing.

Driving inside the hotel grounds, Ratan was going over what he would say when all of a sudden, something blurred his vision, startling him. His feet were on the brakes at once. Somebody had run out of the trees right in front of the car, disappearing in the darkness amidst the thick firs. Ratan sat still, momentarily flustered, wondering what could make a person run with such agility against such icy wind, before he looked back and saw her. A silhouetted figure, a lot like Sara, leaning against a tree, her hand clutching her throat. *It couldn't be Sara.*

Why would Sara be walking on the grounds in this freezing weather? Had she gotten impatient and decided to meet him halfway? He stopped the car at once and sounded the horn so that she would see him. Then he saw her fall, slowly slumping down, and the sound of the horn and the sound of her falling and hitting the ground merged together, reaching his ears like a long drawn-out cry.

He got out of the car to run but his legs felt like lead. He couldn't move as fast as he wanted to. There was not a soul in sight. The grounds were vast and even if he were to call out for help, nobody would hear him. She was lying under a tree of white champas, breathing raggedly. Her large eyes looking at him, trying to say something to explain all the blood on her hands. The fallen champas under her were smeared with blood too. The wind had picked up. It sounded like the endless fluttering pages of a book.

'Sara? What happened? Oh God, Sara!' his words came out tumbling, one on top of the other, they sounded strange even to himself.

She was trying to speak but couldn't form the words. He leaned closer. She opened and shut her mouth again and again as her arm reached out to clutch at his coat. Her eyes blinked like she couldn't believe this was happening to her.

'Sara, oh God, Sara, talk to me!'

Her hand went from his collar to his bare neck, stayed there for a while as her mouth opened and closed. Blood spluttered out, no words came. Then she convulsed twice. He looked around hoping someone would appear.

'Rat ...' she groped for his hand.

'Yes, yes Sara, I'm right beside you. Please hold on ... I'm going to get help ...'

Her grip on his hand tightened. She was shaking her head. Her eyes looked scared, pleading. He had never seen her look like that before.

He tried to lift her with his other hand—if he could only take her to the car—when he felt his hands touch something warm and wet. Whatever it was, there was a lot of it. He stared at his hands, trying to make sense of the dark red liquid on his hands. The ground was damp too, and soon his hands were muddy and bloody. He looked at Sara helplessly, could she make sense of this? She held his gaze for as long as she could before she convulsed again. Her head dropped and she didn't lift it back.

He cast one last desperate look into the vast darkness, a silent scream stuck in his throat. All the silver had gone out of the night.

What he couldn't do, the wind did for him. Howling round and round the pines swaying above his head. He gathered her to him, as he leaned on her one last time. What should he do now? Sara had always known what to do next.

Running away

In Bombay, three days and three nights later, Lavanya's doorbell rang. Inspector Amrit Singh waited outside, looking at the curtained windows around him. The neighbourhood was alive.

Lavanya answered the doorbell. Little did she know that a vicious murder in Simla was about to be linked to her. Or that she was soon going to be reunited with a friend she had all but given up on.

They both felt all their life's sufferings in the calves of their legs. It was one of the many bonds Ratan and Lavanya shared.

Even if it was her heart that was breaking, it would be her legs that did all the hurting. It went all the way back to when she was eight and ill with a burning fever that refused to go away. She had to miss school for many days. The day she went back to St Mary's, her best friend was sitting with the new girl in class. The lead part in the school play was no longer hers and her favourite teacher, Mrs Guthrie, had a new pet. It was the new girl, of course.

Unable to bear it, she ran away from school much before the final bell sounded. She ran all the way home, not stopping to catch her breath. St Mary's was at the furthest end of Malabar Hill and she lived on the other end. In between were roads and lanes, bustling with cars, double-decker buses, and horse-drawn tongas. Her mother, in a tonga herself, was on her way to pick Lavanya up from school, when she saw a girl running across the road. Her eyes wild, her hair all over her face. Not in her wildest dreams could she have imagined it was her own child on the road like that. By the time Lavanya reached home and collapsed at the gate, she had run an hour without stopping.

Dr Irani took one look at the strained calf muscles and said no school for a month. 'All the Rooh Afza you want *beti,* but no playground, no school, no getting up.' Lavanya cried herself to sleep every night and the pain in her legs only worsened.

As she grew up, in her wrought moments, the instinct to run only grew stronger. But the pain in her legs would also strike at the same time and the resultant effect would be that she couldn't move.

So she learned to write. Unable to take flight, she would sit down and write all her grief down. It became her way of feeling better and at the same time, making the pain in her legs go away.

Ratan was older than her by five years, lived next door, and he was the first person she always read her rants out to. He would show no enthusiasm at all to hear them but she wouldn't let him go till she'd read the last word on the page.

Following him from room to room, under the bed, down the staircase. Behind his mother's *pallu*, inside the almirah, behind the curtains, out in the street. Across the terrace, into the neighbour's garden, down the lane, till he finally got on his cycle and rode off to be rid of her.

He would threaten to gag her, to burn every page in her diary in the middle of the night when she was asleep. As he dodged and swerved out of the way of the constant volley of words pouring from her mouth. They'd both be laughing insanely by the end of it. Tears streaming down her face from laughing so hard, she could barely make out the words on the page. But she couldn't stop reading. The words convulsing, quivering, impossible to understand at times, till she finished her story.

There were days he would be a most gracious reader, editor even. Actually asking her to read something new. Then poring over the words on the page and pronouncing some alive, some dead. And when she would see the struck-out words, lines, at times paragraphs, even, she had to agree he had a point. They were 'extra', like he said.

Not only was he her first reader, but he read more than her. Giving her books to read by authors she had never heard of: Faulkner, Virginia Woolf, Dostoevsky, Dickens, Austen, Dickinson, Premchand, Chattopadhyay, Tagore. She had to *read more*, he would taunt, as he sped away on his cycle.

The day Uncle Seth, his father, asked him to leave the house and never come back, it was her sixteenth birthday. She had been looking forward to reading him a story she had finished.

She had waited for him to come back home from Government Law School, where he studied. Then throwing a purple, pink *chanderi* dupatta over a cream-coloured, freshly tailored kurta with pockets, she had slipped out. Dodging the steady stream of relatives arriving with presents for her, climbing over the wall into the garden and onto the mango tree that led to his room.

They lived on a street her father had named 'the forgotten street', located on the farthest side of Malabar Hill called Little Dibbs Road. It was a row of sturdy Goan-style houses on a patch of land bought by a group of senior and influential High Court lawyers. It didn't show on any of the plans and maps of the city, as it was next to the cremation grounds near the sea. Ratan's father, also a prominent lawyer at the Bombay High Court, was the only one to have turned his house into a sprawling Marwari-style mansion with all the new Art Deco trappings, curving balconies and winding staircases, inside the house. The wall between their homes was only four feet high and often preferred to the heavy, clanging gates by both Ratan and Lavanya, to come and go at will.

'Why walk through beautiful, wrought-iron gates when you can scrape your knees on a wall, haan *beta*?' Lavanya's father would say as he saw her emerge, dusting her elbows and knees. Though she had to admit, the garden on Ratan's side of the wall was far easier to land on, compared to the hard cemented ground on hers. From the tree outside his room, it was three practised steps and a jump in.

She heard the entire row from behind the door in his room.

Ghonchu, their loyal, live-in servant, had seen Ratan breaking into his father's safe. Petrified that the blame would fall on him, Ghonchu had run to call Ratan's father. Begging he not be mentioned. Sure enough, the money had been found in Ratan's room. Packed with his clothes and some books in a small tidy suitcase. Ratan had chosen that moment to tell his father he was going away because he had no wish to become a lawyer like him.

Lavanya opened the door an inch to see the top of their heads through the banister below. She arched her head a little more and recoiled. Ratan's father had, just then, reached out and struck him hard across the face. Ratan stood there, looking at his father, then said what his father knew already.

'I'm leaving.'

'*Ehsaanfaramosh!* Make sure you don't come back then,' his father said, shaking with anger.

She saw Ratan turn around and walk towards the stairway that led to his room. He looked most unperturbed, not a hair was out of place. If she wasn't mistaken, he was climbing the steps two at a time as he was wont to do on the breeziest days.

Lavanya was still crouching on her haunches, ears glued to the door, when Ratan walked back to his room and flung open the door. *Ratan was leaving.* She may never see Ratan again. When was he planning to tell her he was going away? Maybe he wasn't going to tell her at all. Who was she anyway? Just the girl next door who had seen him every day of her life for the last ten years since they had moved in. When the door flung open, she was knocked off balance. Hitting the bookshelf behind and causing many precariously balanced books to tumble down on her one after the other.

'Owwwww ...' she yelled, holding her head.

'Lava! What are you doing here, you idiot?' he stood, glaring down at her as she scowled back.

He walked over and sat on the edge of the bed, looking out of the window at the flickering street light, stroking his cheek where he had been slapped.

'It's just as well he found out,' he said. 'He's nothing but a mean-minded jailor! Every time I listen to Jimmy Rodger's

'In the Jailhouse Now', I think of him. I should play it right now at top volume … damn!'

Ratan was rarely this agitated. Lavanya tried to find a way to bring up the throbbing bump on her head.

'I hate studying law. I hate living in this house. If I wake up in this bed one more day, I'll go mad,' he said.

'But don't you want to be a lawyer like your father? That's all you've ever talked about …' She couldn't finish, she had located the bump and rubbing it was vaguely comforting.

'I want to be … free!' He turned to look at her to see if she understood.

'Ah, only you and the rest of this country …'

'Lava, right now, I don't care about this country. I can't. Right now, I feel I am more important than any country, any empire. And in this house, I feel *chained*. He wants to keep me locked up. Like he kept Ma. And she got away, didn't she? I want to be on the road, Lava, I want to feel the wind in my hair and not have a single thought that has to live up to someone's expectations. Definitely not *his* expectations.'

She didn't say anything. Her head felt numb and there was the same sensation in her legs.

Ratan's mother had left home one morning, a year back. She had left behind no note, nothing. His father had deployed all of his influence and a lot of his money to look for her. He had hired the best private detectives to comb the city but couldn't find her. She had done a good job of disappearing.

'You're all packed … I had no idea …' Lavanya's voice trailed off.

'I was going to tell you. Then all this happened. Look, I got you something.' He walked over to his suitcase and pulled out something wrapped in thin pink paper, then flopped down on the floor beside her and put it in her hands.

'Happy Birthday,' he said.

She opened the folds of the thin, crackling pink paper to find a nose ring with a ruby red stone glittering at her. She folded the paper back and handed it back to him.

'I can't take this. It looks expensive. But thank you.'

He took her hand, opened it, and put the now crumpled pink paper back in her palm, closing her fist.

'Shut up. I got Gattu's father to give it to me for peanuts. He makes this stuff by the dozens, every day.'

She wondered if he had used some of the stolen money for the nose ring. It made her feel important. He had kept the paper box right next to his records in the suitcase.

'What are you going to do? Where will you go?'

'Something. Somewhere.'

'All right. Before you go, I've been meaning to read something to you … remember to be kind.'

She grinned as she saw him wince.

'I'm going to *kill you* with kindness,' he said.

'Pay attention!' she said.

That was five years back. She hadn't seen him since. He had given her an address to write to, of a friend from school, which she had used only once, to send him her first published book of short stories. The stories had appeared quietly in *Voices*, a new literary journal in Bombay, and were later surprisingly compiled into a book. For weeks, then months, she had waited and waited to hear from Ratan and then given up.

It was a strange coincidence that when her doorbell rang, Lavanya was putting the ruby nose ring on.

An evil plan

THE INSPECTOR FOLLOWED THE DOORBELL WITH A SERIES of firm knocks.

Lavanya made up her mind to tell off whoever was at the door. Ask them to come back some other time. She had promised her friend Noor, an actor, that she would see her at Bombay Talkies, a new movie studio started by Himanshu Rai and Devika Rani. She was meeting her on the set of *Jeevan Mahal*, a film Noor had recently signed on. Noor and Lavanya had been friends since they had first met in class five. When Noor, on her first day in school, had quite dramatically replaced her in the school annual day play. Lavanya had started out hating her. What was there not to hate? Noor was fairy-tale pretty, with a personality that made her the life of the classroom. She wasn't unintelligent either and that hurt. Her hand kept shooting up as the adoring teachers would point at her, laughing. 'Yes, Noor, do tell the class the answer.' Yes, Noor, the class will *never* know, if you don't tell them the answer, Lavanya would whisper through clenched teeth, to whoever was sitting next to her.

The days went by and as much as Lavanya resisted the famous Noor charm, Noor was determined to be friends. There was nothing Lavanya could do to keep her away. Soon, they were inseparable and they stayed that way through St. Mary's, then the University of Bombay. And even now, when Noor had become one of the more popular actresses of the Bombay film scene while Lavanya remained an 'aspiring' writer.

It was an important meeting today. Lavanya was running out of funds and did not want to ask her brothers for money. If the director liked her story, she would get a signing amount there and then, Noor had said.

Of course, nothing was that simple. She put on her nose ring, deciding against even the pale brown lipstick she usually wore. She didn't want the director staring at her mouth as she narrated the screenplay. Or worse, eyes travelling down and around to see through her khadi *kameez* to find her new Kestos lace-trimmed bra with three neat hooks at the back. She sighed, lingerie would remain her only indulgence. She was about to tie her tan-and-white, low-heeled Oxford brogues when there was another loud and persistent knock on the door.

Too loud for it to be polite, is what Lavanya thought, eyebrows furrowed, patting the wavy curls at the bottom of her bob just above her shoulder. She was still getting used to the idea of living alone. Hardly a day went by without some 'very concerned' neighbour stopping by to tell her how inappropriate it was for a young girl to live alone after the death of her parents. Why not go to live with your brothers, in Delhi or Calcutta, by turns? Or you must get married soon, they would conclude, pursing their lips, and waiting for

Lavanya's reaction. Lavanya would sip her tea and listen to them thinking, *why don't I tell you what I'll do: I'll put your hairy lip, your mean mouth, your large sniffing nose, and your dark, odorous concern in my next story.* That's what I'll do.

She opened the door to find the biggest man she had ever seen in a policeman's uniform outside her door. He carried a small attaché case and was looking at Lavanya like he couldn't imagine she was the person he had come to see.

'Lavanya Shriram?'

'Yes …?'

'Madam, I am Inspector Amrit Singh from Simla Police. I have been sent to meet with you on a most important matter. May I come in?'

Lavanya, trying to make sense of his overwhelming presence at her door, stepped aside to let him in. The neighbours' constant vigil of her front door will pay off today, she thought to herself. She cast a glance at the windows and doors across the street. Doors not quite shut, curtains not quite drawn. Look, look, dear neighbours, not a lover, not a man but a *policeman.*

Like a big bird, he took his time settling down on the diwan. She kept her purse clasped close to her as she sat down next to him on a *moda.*

'Madam, I will come straight to the point. Do you know Ratan Seth?'

That name after so long. That too from a policeman's mouth. It should have felt odd but it didn't.

'Yes, he used to live next door. Is he … all right?'

He was looking at her to see if the concern in her voice was genuine. Then he spoke like he was speaking to a child. That's the only way men knew to speak to women, Lavanya thought.

They have to pretend they are speaking to a nine-year-old, only then can the conversation be understood.

'Madam, I cannot tell you how he is because *we do not know*. We are looking for him. That is one of the reasons I am here. He is wanted for the murder of Mrs Sara Davenport, the wife of a very senior army officer. Would you happen to know where he could be?'

'What? No, of course not. He has been gone a long time.'

This was the worst trouble Ratan had ever got himself into.

'We have of course visited his father before coming here. We are aware the two of you were very close friends. Yes?'

Poor Uncle Seth. It must be devastating to hear Ratan was implicated in such a serious crime. They would often pass by each other on their street. He would look sharply at her and then look away before she could nod at him. Like she was the reason Ratan had left.

'We have not been in touch since he left home, officer. From what I understand, this has nothing to do with me. I must leave now, I have to see a friend in half an hour. I'm sorry, I would have asked you for a cup of tea but I am in a hurry …'

Lavanya had already started moving towards the door, thinking he would follow.

'Madam, a minute, please? Is this familiar to you?'

Lavanya turned around to see he had not budged from the diwan. His attaché case was now open and in his hands was a book. Covered in dusty cellophane, it looked very strange but familiar. It was her book of short stories, the only one published. It felt so strange to see the book in the policeman's big, dry, calloused hands.

In a daze, she walked back the few steps she had taken and sat back down.

He was removing something else from a diary inside the case.

'Is this your handwriting?' Now he was showing her the note she had written to Ratan, slipped inside the book. Wrapped in cellophane too, the note looked tiny in his hands.

Dear Rat
Where's your evil plan?
Here's mine.

That note. That inside joke. It was funny how relationships faded, became something unrecognizable, and yet the inside joke remained. It seemed to have the ability to withstand everything. Lavanya felt the blood rushing to her face. She forced herself to answer the inspector's question.

'Yes. It is. I sent him this book to read. But I don't know if he read it. I never heard from him.'

What was the joke again? Yes, every time Ratan had something nice to say about what she had written, she would look at him, hands clasped. In her best British accent, she would say, 'Oh, you are too kind, Sir, too kind!' And Ratan would say in the same affected accent, eyes small and mean, 'That's the evil plan, darling, to *kill you* with kindness.'

She would play along. 'But why, kind Sir, why?'

'So that I never have to say anything nice about anything you've written ever again.' He would say and laugh some kind of an evil laugh.

Lavanya would pretend to look shocked at this revelation and cup her cheeks in mock horror.

It was such a silly routine but it never failed to amuse them.

Even as she wrote the note and slipped it inside, she imagined him reading it, his eyes crinkling with laughter.

As evil plans go, this too had a shelf life that seemed to have expired.

She looked at the inspector, hoping he would not ask her to explain the note.

It was impossible to explain an inside joke to a third person, let alone a policeman, and get the same reaction.

Amrit Singh's eyes were no longer curious, they had become hard and condemning. Lavanya stiffened.

'Madam, you are aware this book has objectionable material inside?'

'I'm sorry, what? I don't understand what you mean …'

'This book, Madam, was found near the body. We have, therefore, read what is inside. The book has objectionable material that we believe could well have provoked Ratan to commit the crime. These, you will agree are not simple stories. They have been written to provoke, yes?'

'All stories are written to provoke, Inspector.'

Seeing her cellophane-wrapped book cradled in the policeman's hands, Lavanya had a flash. Her mother telling her yet again that her writing was never going to amount to anything good.

'All your stories are written to provoke a crime?' he sounded aghast, despite himself.

'No, of course not, how could my stories have led to a crime?'

'Madam, no woman in these stories, is being fully clothed. That is truc or not?'

Was this person a critic or a policeman? Her head was reeling.

'Inspector, these stories are about very brave women in very difficult circumstances. *If* that is what you are asking.'

It was exactly like talking to her mother.

'So you agree they are about *obscenities*?' he said.

This was what Ma had often struck her head for. Right till her dying day. With a mind like that, why couldn't she have been a boy? Why couldn't she accept she was a 'girl', why couldn't she sew and cook and keep house for some nice boy in a government job? Did she know what they thought of dark-skinned girls like her?

'No, they are about *love and desire*,' she heard herself say.

The inspector seemed to have reached a conclusion of sorts. He was placing the cellophane packages back inside, handling them like they were bombs that might go off at any second. He shut his case and turned to look at her resolutely.

'Madam, I have to ask you to come with me to the police station for questioning. Your publisher has been called too. Superintendent Donald Harper will ask you a few questions regarding this book. It is procedural.'

If Lavanya still wrote in her diary, she would have noted the date. 16 February 1936, the day that started the spinning of a web she would have no control over. What is it they say about webs? They were created to hunt their prey, and hunt they must. Not only because it's the law of the world but because it is the thread of life itself.

A book and a body

WHILE SIMLA SLEPT DURING THE EARLY DAWN, RATAN was wide awake.

There was a rat under his bedding. He just couldn't find the vile creature. He stood beside the lumpy mattress that had been his bed for the last three days, with a stick in his hand. He had been beating away at the mattress, hoping to produce the hurried exit of the rat, but the mattress lay still, no sign of life stirring under it.

After a while, Ratan was no longer sure if he had imagined the rat's slithery presence or if it really did exist. He continued to stand there, ready to bring down his stick as soon as the rat appeared. Tired, he let his arm drop and the stick fell with a clatter on the floor, startling him. What was he doing? The rat was just a momentary distraction compared to what lay before him.

In the shaft of light streaming in from the barred window in the small shed, Ratan loomed larger than life. The light accentuated his broad back which tapered down to a slim waist and thick-set legs. In the shadow that fell across the wall, the figure wielding a stick in his hand looked nothing less than ominous. He looked like he could kill.

He had woken with a start. It was the same chilling thought that would wake him up every morning. What if she wasn't dead? What if he had left her there alive, still breathing, hoping to be rescued? Was it possible he had deserted her when she needed him most?

Clutching his heart, feeling the palpitations increase as he scrambled to get control of his panicking mind, Ratan grabbed an old crumpled *Times of India* from the stack in the corner and started reading aloud.

Gandhi Interviewed in Jail; Asks Full Freedom for India

His Resisters, He says, Will Fill All the Prisons, Making Government by British Impossible—Calls Campaign 'Mad Risk But 'Justifiable One.'

The letters started swimming in front of his eyes. He let go of the paper and held his head in his hands and went over that night again. Then again. The running shadow of a man in the trees. Sara, leaning against the tree, her hand on her throat. His legs barely moving in that cold, cold night. Sara falling across the rose bushes. The thorns digging into her flesh. Sara breathing with great difficulty. Blood all over the fallen white *champa* flowers. Blood all over his hands. Him, running. Dragging his feet but running.

On that foggy winter night, he had been clear-headed enough to know if they caught him with her dead in his arms, it would be the end of him. Nobody would believe he was innocent. He knew what happened to Indians in prisons. The punishment was only the starting point. The jails were designed to break Indian prisoners in a slow and methodical way. The breaking especially wrung out if an Indian had had the temerity to attack a European. There were too many innocent Indians in jails already. He would lie in some godforsaken damp cell, beaten, wasting away forever. For not telling them the 'truth'. There was only one version of the truth they would want to hear. That he had killed Lady Davenport. One lousy Indian had killed a high-ranking army official's wife. There was no doubt in his mind. It would be the end of him.

He had run. He had left the car there and run. He hadn't known where to go. He was afraid to go back to his quarters, so he had started walking down to where the fields were. Further and further down, past the Ridge where all the wealthy, distinguished British officers lived, past the tier below where the Anglo Indians lived, past the Mall Road and finally past the Lower Bazaar, which stank of the sewage runoff from above, even in the dead of night. This was where he lived, along with the rest of the working class—coolies, labourers, rickshaw pullers, maids and dhobis. He didn't look in the direction of his room. He didn't stop till he could see where the town ended and the fields began. It was a blur how long he walked, ran, stumbled, fell, on and on for hours before the fields come into view.

Shyam came from a family of farmers. They lived on the outskirts of Simla, next to their fields. The last time Ratan had visited Shyam in his house was when his marriage festivities were on. The house had been lit up through the night with lights, music and dance. Now it was dead still and sombre, as if the winds had carried the grimness of the moment ahead of Ratan's arrival. When Ratan finally staggered up and raised the iron knocker on the ancient wooden door, the sound shattered the quiet of the night, carrying with it all the dread that was in Ratan's heart as he knelt against the door. After what seemed an eternity, he heard feet approaching. The door opened a crack and Ratan saw Shyam looking at him with alarm and fear in his eyes. He held the door open and Ratan stumbled in and collapsed on the charpai in the courtyard.

A while later, Shyam had heard Ratan out, his plump cheeks hanging in shock. Every now and then, he'd dart a look here and there to see if anybody had awoken and was listening.

When he heard the clink of bangles approaching, Ratan stopped talking.

Shyam's wife, Cheeni, appeared in the doorway carrying a tray of tea in tiny cups like they showed in British Tea Board advertisements.

'Have you taken leave of your senses? Who asked for tea at this unholy time? Don't just stand there, leave, hear me, leave!' Shyam snapped at her.

Cheeni's eyes flew to Ratan's face, smarting with tears. She turned to go, the tray of tea shaking in her hands. Shyam looked at Ratan, closed his eyes, and then got up. He caught up with Cheeni, put a hand on her shoulder, took the tray from her hands, and motioned her inside.

Ratan knew he was putting Shyam in a spot. He hated himself for doing it but he needed only a day or two to think over what he needed to do next. Somewhere at the back of his mind was also the bracing thought that he had every right to ask Shyam to do this for him. Shyam was his friend, after all, a friend whom he had helped quit a serious gambling addiction, some time back. Shyam would have lost all his forefather's farming land to Shafaqat Bhai if Ratan had not stepped in when he did. Bhai owned some of the largest gambling dens in the state and Shyam still owed him money. When Shyam was getting married, Ratan had asked Sara to request Bhai for more time to return the money and Bhai had reluctantly agreed.

After a while of pacing the floor, Shyam came to a decision. He asked Ratan to follow him out, leading him around the back of the house towards a small path that climbed up. That's where his father kept all the cattle. The buffaloes had been washed recently, no doubt, the scent of Lifebuoy soap lingered in the night breeze.

They passed the cowsheds and entered a small room that looked like it had been a barn of sorts at some time. Shyam did not speak a word to him all this while, stopping only to pick up an extra lantern on the way.

He put the lantern down by the window ledge, taking his time to light it. The room was bare except for a roll-up mattress, a lone broom, and a stick that stood leaning against a corner. An empty pack of Cavanders lay next to the bedding. Old newspapers lay forgotten in another corner. As Shyam prepared to go, Ratan stopped him.

'Shyam? A cigarette? Just one will do …'

Shyam shook his head, he had smoked the last one he had.

There was something else on Shyam's mind as he fidgeted with the latch on the door. 'Stay out of sight. Cheeni cannot see you again. I will think of what to tell her for now. Tomorrow, tongues will be wagging all over Simla. She is not as simple as she looks. If she breathes a word to my parents, her sister, anybody, even God can't save us.'

Three days had seemed a lot at the time. They had flown by like paper in the wind. Today was the third day of his stay.

He only saw Shyam when he came to leave some food and water for him. Shyam didn't have much news except that the police had been up at the Davenport House on both days. Mr Davenport had not emerged from his room except to talk to the police. Mark Easton, his ADC, was handling everything. What Shyam didn't say and didn't need to, was that the police were looking all over Simla for Ratan. It was only a matter of time before they came looking for him here.

Ratan needed to make a move. He was already going out of his mind, holed up here without a plan in sight. He had barely slept all night before the rat started making its presence felt. He could feel the bristly movement under the mattress again and could no longer remain inert. Ratan's eyes darted to the stick on the floor but he didn't move. He didn't wish the rat dead anymore. All the blank cold rage had left his body as suddenly as it had come over him.

There were footsteps outside and then there was a knock. Ratan opened the door to Shyam, who walked in and handed his friend a glass of fresh buffalo milk and a pack of Britannia biscuits. Then he went and sat on the window ledge. Shyam had something to say. For the first time in three days.

'Yesterday, when I was driving Sir Richard to the army headquarters, the police chief was in the car too. For once, they weren't talking about arresting Gandhi and the others, they were talking about you. About putting a price on your head and having posters put up all over Simla. They were also talking about a book they found close to Madam's body that night. Do you know anything about a book?'

'A book ...?' Ratan repeated. *Pages fluttering in the wind.* It wasn't just the wind picking up, that night. It was the fluttering of a book he had heard.

'Yes, a book. They say it has your name on it. They were talking about tracing the author of the book too. Somebody was going to Bombay to talk to them. The police chief said there was a link between the book and the murder.'

Lavanya's book. It had to be Lavanya's book that Sara carried with her constantly in her monogrammed leather purse. He had read her one story from the collection, a story called 'Sitara' and she had asked him if she could keep the book. Politely, like it was a request. Sara took, she never asked.

It had surprised him. They had driven out to Fagu, a little town on the outskirts of Simla where they could just lie on the grass, gaze at the purple-orange Himalayas and occasionally follow a shimmering bird with Sara's dainty but powerful opera glasses. Ratan had finished reading and the golden head on his lap had not moved. He thought she had fallen asleep but then she had spoken, quietly, like she was in deep thought.

'Ratan, may I keep this book?'

He had waited. Her voice sounded strange, like she was deeply moved, close to tears even. He had waited for her to say something more.

'These aren't ordinary stories, Ratan. They aren't only about Indian women, every woman all over the world is going through the same struggle in some way or the other. I feel awful, disturbed, like it's about me, how desperate I feel sometimes, I don't even know what about, but it's there in my heart somewhere, that flapping, like a bird trying to find its way out of a huge caged room, but there really is no opening it can see ...'

They were quiet then for a long time. Just breathing, audibly.

And then she had turned around and smiled up at him.

'I wish I could meet your friend. Tell me about her, what is she like?'

'Oh she is a pest and a wonderful writer and she can never know I said that, the wonderful writer part,' he had said, smiling, thinking about Lavanya.

When he first received Lavanya's book, he missed her so much, he didn't touch it for days. Then one night, he read them all, all the stories one after the other, carrying them inside his head for days. He felt an unusual sexual stirring in him too, like something that had been dormant for too long was stretching inside. He wanted to go out into the night and find himself a woman, any woman, every woman! Beautiful or ugly, fat or thin, married or a whore, it didn't matter. As long as she was willing. He would make love to her all night to make up for the way the world was.

He meant to write to Lavanya and compliment her, for a change. *Lava, for once,* he would say, *for once, you've outdone yourself. I don't want to kill you with kindness. I want to fill you with hope.* But he wasn't ready to write or talk to her just then. It would stir up too much. He wasn't ready. He had blundered his way around for the last five years. Getting in and out of trouble. He would write to her when he too had a story worth narrating.

That should be about now, Ratan thought wryly, and looked up to see Shyam's worried eyes on him.

'Shyam, I don't know what I should do next, I mean ...' he tried to find the right words to buy some more time but Shyam didn't let him finish.

'Ratan, for God's sake! You have to leave. Father returns from his pilgrimage today and I won't be able to hide you from him on his own farm. Cheeni knows I'm keeping you here, she won't dare ask me about you directly but once my parents are here, it will be another matter. She will vomit it all out and they will think the house has been … unblessed.'

Unblessed? There was nothing more to say. Ratan nodded.

'I will be gone today, I promise you', he wished his voice sounded more convincing to himself.

Shyam turned to go and Ratan had to ask him once and for all.

'Shyam, you don't think I did it, do you?'

'*Dost*, it does not matter what I think. It matters what *they* think. The one who wields the laathi owns the buffalo, yes or no?'

'You know I couldn't have stayed behind to prove my innocence. They wouldn't have believed me.'

Shyam looked at Ratan with his fish eyes and nodded like he understood. A resigned, reluctant nod of acceptance, not of Ratan's circumstances but rather the weakness of mankind, in general.

It was incomprehensible to Ratan. Why should an ex-gambler look so calm, so superior all of a sudden? That too, with him? Had Shyam forgotten how he had stayed in hiding for days, fearing Bhai's goons? Was it really so simple to forget your own frailties just so you could climb some invisible pedestal to judge others?

Before leaving, Shyam patted him on the shoulder, a brotherly pat. Ratan had this urge to take a good swing at him, make not-so-brotherly contact with his plump jaw. Bloody sanctimonious dog. *Anybody can run. The brave ones, who have done nothing wrong, don't run. They stay and fight.* He knew what was playing in Shyam's pretend-virtuous mind.

The kind of nonsense the entire country was fed by the so-called leaders. What brave people did and did not do. That's why the country had jails spilling over with brave people crying for freedom and unable to do anything about it.

Meanwhile, that figure in the trees was somewhere out there. Free. Nobody was looking for him, they were looking for Ratan.

He watched Shyam become a thin line through the crack in the barred window for as long as he could and then when he couldn't see him anymore, he turned around and picked up the stick.

He swung it around in the air. Swishing the air, then whipping it, again and again till he found a vague joy in the rhythm of his body swinging in a smooth motion, faster and faster, left to right, right to left.

The question that refused to go away

LAVANYA SAT ON A BENCH AT THE INDIAN IMPERIAL POLICE Force headquarters, hands clenching and unclenching inside the pockets of her kurta, waiting for Noor to arrive.

Once the inspector left, Lavanya rushed to Bombay Talkies in faraway Malad, only to find that Noor had left for an urgent location shoot and the director too was nowhere to be found. Or was it that he didn't want to be found?

Lavanya was well known at the Talkies. Not just because she had spent many hours with Noor inside make-up rooms, but also because her last meeting with another director had made her spectacularly notorious.

It had hardly been her fault.

She had finished her narration and was waiting for the director to tell her what he thought of the story. She remembered a feature on him in *Filmland* where the writer had described him as a 'talent with unique vision'. He was quiet, two fingers stroking his chin as if in deep thought, completely ignoring her. Meanwhile, an ornately carved pocket knife sitting atop a sheaf of scripts on his table had caught her attention. She picked it up for a closer look when the director appeared from behind the table, speaking softly or was he slurring, it was difficult to say. Why was she not an actress like her friend Noor? If she was willing, he could arrange for her to have a screen test, yes? He had a role in mind for her. She only had to say the word. There were roles for dark-skinned girls too, yes, yes, most definitely. It is a complex complexion, you see, and needs an artistic touch. It adds so much depth to the film, a sensuousness that other filmmakers did not know how to exploit. But he was not like the others, he assured her.

What was the role, she had asked, absentmindedly, caressing the serrated ridges of the knife.

'The role is complex. She is a woman of character, a Dalit woman. She is very beautiful, very sensuous, like you. Picture this scene. She is taking a bath by a waterfall, a cascading body of water, can you see it? When this Sahib driving by in a Rolls Royce sees her and is struck by her beauty. He stops and offers her a lot of money to come away with him but she refuses. So every day when she bathes by this same waterfall, he comes to watch. It's unrequited love, you see. It's full of pathos, very moving, the relationship between them will grow and grow. It will be something audiences have not seen. Lavanya, you could be a big star like your friend.

'If you wish, that is.'

Lavanya wasn't offended, she simply wanted to leave. She got up and asked if her script interested him because she wasn't interested in this complex complexion role. It was then that he had asked her to sit on his lap. A small smile played on his misshapen lips as his hand reached out to hold hers. He said they could write the movie together if she liked, later. That's when she had taken the beautiful, hand-carved pocket knife waiting in her hand and made her way to the swing door.

Looking back only when she was out, the door swinging behind her. She had slashed the air, barely struck him, but he sat crouched in a corner, weeping like a child.

It made her laugh now, thinking about it, even though she felt a deep fatigue. The Arthur Road jail was not a good place to sit by yourself and laugh. That too on a bench that seemed determined to push her out any moment.

All around her, people were being brought in and taken out in a constant parade of helplessness. Amrit Singh had asked her to wait for him on a bench that had filled up fast. She was trying her best to hold on to the edge of the seat as people kept sliding in. At first, she had been curious, trying to take in everything around her, look every prisoner in the eye, express some kind of solidarity. But everyone looked lost in their own world. Soon, only the sound of rainwater falling from a leak in the ceiling into a metal bucket held her attention. One at a time. Each drop taking its time to fall and then disappearing into the bucket, never to be seen again.

It was a while before Lavanya noticed Amrit Singh's looming presence next to her. An old woman beside her had nudged her, breaking her trance.

'Follow me, please. The Superintendent of Police will meet with you before the questioning.'

Lavanya was glad to get up. Once again, she hoped Noor was on her way. The old woman who had nudged her held out her hand, holding Lavanya's for a brief instant. She closed her eyes and then opened them again as if to say, everything will be all right.

Lavanya too did the same. Opening and closing her eyes at the old woman.

Amrit Singh was walking down a corridor that almost didn't seem a part of the same derelict building she had been in. It was empty, with mosaic flooring and ornately framed pictures of British royalty. Amrit Singh's footsteps echoed all through the imposing corridor.

She was shown into a room that seemed as big as the crowded hall she had been sitting in. Amrit Singh took a standing position as Lavanya found herself a little grateful to be sitting down on a thickly upholstered chair. To think that the hard wooden bench she had waited on was just a corridor away. The great British Indian chair manipulation. So many of her father's acquaintances had framed their *Kursi Nashin* certificates to display on the walls of their offices and homes. Such a privilege and honour to be considered worthy of a chair when meeting with a British officer, it was. She let herself sink in, lean back, sigh. Let the manipulation begin.

The orderliness of the dark mahogany table stretching out in front of her, held her attention. Papers in a neat pile in the corner. Fresh paper to write on in the deep centre held down by a transparent paperweight. Sharpened pencils and pens arranged according to height. Paper cutters in the other corner. Inkpots, sellotape and a magnifying glass. Everything meticulously arranged. The only thing that interfered with the neat symmetry was a craggy wooden picture frame with an unruly vine of roses carved around it. A sweet-looking buxom woman laughed from inside the frame holding a child who looked ready to leap from her plump arms. Lavanya was about to lift the frame and look at the woman more closely when she heard footsteps. Then somebody was clicking the door shut with a quick definite movement and walking over, past Amrit Singh to the ornate swivel chair, to sit down, facing her.

'Miss Shriram?'

Lavanya found herself looking at someone who definitely belonged at this table. Tall and straight-backed with a full head of hair pushed back slickly and surely. Nothing out of place. There was a slow smile playing on his face and he had eyes that made Lavanya think of tube lights. White phosphoric light that shone with such sharpness that it excluded all hint of warmth.

She must have nodded in response. His introduction was curt, precise, eager.

'Superintendent of Police, Donald Harper. I have been most curious to meet with you.'

'Oh. Why curious?' she heard herself ask.

'An unusual collection of stories you have there in that book we found next to the body, Miss Shriram. Very provocative. I wanted to see if the author matched the book.'

'... and does she?' she asked softly. He was a good-looking man, there was no denying that.

'I am, how should I say it, more than a trifle *disappointed*, Miss. You look like a fairly well-educated girl brought up in a respectable family, yes?'

Lavanya felt a flush burn her face. How little good looks mattered if you were easy to dislike.

'I'm sorry to have disappointed you,' Lavanya said.

If he caught the sarcasm in her voice, he did not show it.

'Oh don't be. Let me elaborate. I am disappointed because you are, no doubt, an attractive young woman with reasonable talent but how do I say this, you take a certain delight in being self-destructive and that's a pity, a real pity.'

Her clenched hands inside her pockets were sweaty. She made a mental note to ask Kamal ji, her *darzi*, to put in a satin lining on the inside of the pockets of the khadi kurtas. It was a wonder she had functioned this long without this one simple indulgence. Satin pockets would keep her hands cool. And nobody would be the wiser.

He swivelled in his chair, this way and that, then got up to pace about the room, stroking his chin as if in deep thought. It was a large room to pace about in. He stopped pacing and now, leaning on the chair, peered at her closely.

'Miss Shriram, why do you write dirty stories?'

Lavanya removed her hands from her pockets. She needed to see them, feel them. She put them one on top of the other and did not look up. The tube light eyes were upon her.

'Oh, would you like me to guess? Is that why you won't answer?'

After she finished writing Sitara's story, she remembered sneaking into Baba's sunken study in the middle of the night to celebrate with a peg of his finest whiskey. She knew in her heart, she had somehow stumbled upon words, sentences, thoughts, dreams, an idea of what it meant to finish something of meaning. Exultant, restless, her glass of whiskey in hand, she spun around the darkened room, her eyes wide open. Her father often escaped into his study to listen to his favourite opera records. Mostly late in the night, when her mother had fallen asleep. As she spun delirious, Lavanya could hear the full-throated voluptuously unhinged voices of the opera singers. Anguish, joy, love, betrayal—big feelings sung in big voices. The room, crammed with books, swam around her, the whiskey dangerously splashing against the rim of the glass. As she spun faster and faster, most of it spilled over on the heirloom carpet but the rest, she glugged down, trying not to notice its bitter taste. Finally spent, joyous, she had curled up in her father's favourite armchair and fallen asleep. The next morning, her mother had walked into her room to wake her up and the story, still warm, still crackling with some eerie energy, had found its first reader. She had woken to a stinging slap across her face. Then her mother asked her the same question she never tired of asking: *Why must you write dirty stories?*

Over the years she had tried, however unsuccessfully, to answer her mother.

'Because nobody else will!'

'Because you don't want me to!'

'If only you would read it, *really* read it, you would know.'

'Because everybody ignores women and their desires, including women themselves.'

'Because dirt is in your mind, Ma!'

'Because they write themselves!'

'Because it makes me happy.'

There had been hell to pay for all her answers. One day, there had also been a man who came to visit her when Baba was out of town. He came into her room, shut the door, and locked it. Asked her the same question. Then said he had been sent to cure her of her sickness. This was a religious man, revered by her mother.

Among other things, she had learned there was no correct answer to the question. It was a question that would not go away. She had made her peace with it.

'I know why you write these dirty stories, Miss.' There was a triumphant gleam in Harper's eyes.

Of course, he did. Everybody *knew.* Only she didn't know. She, who wrote them.

'I know about women like you. You like to provoke men to do things they would never do otherwise. You get a sense of power from it.'

So that's where Amrit Singh got his style of questioning. She shot a look at him from the corner of her eyes. He was staring right ahead of him, at the gently swaying trees outside the window, no expression on his face.

'I can see you now, reading your own stories and feeling the heat. It must be quite tiring,' Donald Harper continued.

Lavanya could no longer sit still. Her hands were shaking in her lap. She was also having some difficulty breathing and she needed to do something to distract herself.

'Is this part of the questioning? I was told it would happen only when my friend or my publisher ...' Lavanya turned around to look at Amrit Singh more sharply now. She wasn't following him anywhere again, that was for sure.

Donald Harper acted like she had not spoken. He leaned forward and said conspiratorially, 'There was an interesting note attached to the book. Do you mind elaborating on that? What was your evil plan, Miss?'

No, not that. Not that. Telling him a joke would be impossible, let alone an inside joke.

'Why do you appear flustered, Miss? If you can write about women and their desires so frankly then why should this line of conversation disturb you?'

Lavanya turned to face him.

'It disturbs me because it is entirely out of context. It has nothing to do with why I am here. You are simply using your position to intimidate me and that is pathetic.' You bastard, she wanted to add.

The slow, menacing smile was back. He was clearly pleased with her answer.

'Good. It does one well to remember who is powerful and who is weak in any given situation, Miss Shriram.' Donald Harper straightened his chair and sat down, leaning forward. 'You don't want to deplete your limited reserves of strength, do you? So here's what I'll advise you do. Do not make things more difficult than they already are. Your publisher will be here shortly. Together, come to an understanding and withdraw this book entirely from circulation. It should never be seen or heard of again.' He sighed, as if all this talking was exhausting. 'To provoke a crime is a crime too, do you understand? Go back to writing songs and dances for the film industry. Do not provoke, simply entertain, can you do that Miss Shriram?'

Lavanya wanted to say yes, she could do that. She wanted to nod emphatically, just so she could leave this insanely ordered room and breathe again. He had made her feel like a common writing whore. Her eyes were smarting in that dangerous way where she only had to blink and the tears would roll down. Yet she didn't look up.

When the man who had locked the door to her own room in her own home had ordered her to lie down on her bed so he could cure her, she had felt a similar panic. Knowing her mother was outside, lurking, praying, had made it worse. Then somehow, the thought of Baba, of what he would do when she told him what Ma had done, had steadied her.

As the thought of Noor steadied her. Her friend was, at this very minute, finding her way to her. A loving, dead father and a believing, living girlfriend were enough power for now.

'If you don't mind my asking, who is that lovely woman in the picture frame there?' she asked, leaning back in her upholstered chair as if they were having the most pleasant conversation that had relaxed her.

He looked at the frame with a jerk of his head, surprised by her question.

'Those are my wife and child.'

'She looks happy, don't you think?'

Before he narrowed his eyes to decide if he should answer her or snub her outright, Lavanya looked up and smiled. Her own small, menacing smile.

'Is this before she left you or after, Superintendent?'

It stung. She could see it stung from the way the tube lights flickered in his eyes. How had she known? A little instinct and a lot of luck. Luck was the straw that came to her only when she was on the verge of sinking.

She got up. Amrit Singh stood immobile, staring ahead. She moved her heavy chair, dislodged it completely from its position in the room. The perfect unnerving symmetry of the room broken, she made her way out. After a long moment, Amrit Singh followed, his footsteps tentative. Hers were lighter than when she had come in. Not a lot but enough to make her want to take the next step and the next.

A dirty story

When Noor burst in, in full costume and with all her makeup on, Lavanya was in another room, waiting for the questioning to begin. Back in the run down and leaky part of the police station.

Amrit Singh, who had not let her out of his sight since following her out, shifted from one foot to the other when he saw Noor. For a big man like him, that was enough to cause a minor rumble in the room. Gone was the remote faraway look in his eyes, they were swaying now. Like the trees outside Donald Harper's room, a while back, Lavanya thought to herself.

Noor had a presence, there was no denying that. Lavanya could see now what her drama teachers had seen on that first day, when Noor had announced herself simply by saying her name. It had the effect of a microphone tuned to full volume in an empty auditorium. If Lavanya set off curiosity, Noor ignited a passion in people they didn't know they possessed. It was a very physical reaction. A jerk of the head was what Lavanya had seen often, mouths opened too, a lot. In the darkened halls of movie theatres, where people were freer to be themselves, they hooted, whistled and sang as soon as she appeared on screen. Lavanya now enjoyed watching people react when Noor made her entry.

Noor flung herself at Lavanya. Her friend could be dramatic and the royal costume with full filmy makeup only helped. Lavanya hugged her friend, gesticulating with her eyes at the audience that was watching them.

For the last half an hour, the room had been filling up with policemen of every shape and size. As they walked in unarmed, without their laathis, they looked unrecognizable. They glanced Lavanya's way, then seeing Noor, stopped, as if struck. Then, pulling themselves together, they started moving towards the rows of chairs arranged to face her.

Noor gave them a sweeping look, managing to bat her lashes and look coy for a moment to acknowledge their admiration in the most humble way she knew. Then she pulled a chair close to Lavanya and whispered in her ear.

'Lavu, I am bleeding. I am bleeding inside a police station! Do you think they would jail me if they knew? Why are you here? What is going on? I had no time to remove this makeup, I rushed as soon as I got your message. How am I looking? It will take at least an hour to remove this cake from my face. Why don't you say anything? We need a man. I was going to get Mr Rai along, then I saw your face looking at me, absolutely forbidding me to get anyone but I'm telling you, we're surrounded. We need a man!'

In quick whispers, Lavanya told her how the inspector had landed at her doorstep that morning, wanting to know if she knew where Ratan was. She told Noor about her book, found not far from the dead lady in Simla, Ratan's disappearance, her note to Ratan inside the book, and how they had traced it all back to her in Bombay. Noor listened intently and then looked at the policemen sitting in their chairs like children in a classroom.

Lavanya had never been questioned by police before but she had heard of it. Nothing of what she had heard remotely resembled this scene that was unfolding in the room. There was even a photographer who had just walked in and was busy setting up.

Most pre-dinner conversations at home would be her father smoking his pipe, in his red and green robe, a glass of whiskey in hand, telling her and her brothers about the cases he had come across that day. They would listen eagerly, arms tightly folded across their stomachs. Their mother, passing by, busily preparing for dinner, would scoff, 'Like hungry jailbirds waiting for their next meal!' Baba would talk of every human struggle that was at the centre of each case like a precious thing to be examined very closely.

The man's honour was at stake so he lied to his brother. His greed got the better of him so he struck his own mother. His patriotism was greater than his love for life so he picked up the gun. He believed he was a maharaja in his last birth so he stole to pay for his habits. He felt betrayed by his wife so he killed her and her lover.

And on and on. Lavanya was always curious why there were no women criminals. Did Baba never come across them? Baba would smile indulgently and say women stayed out of trouble more than men. That worried her too. 'Trouble should belong equally to both, shouldn't it, Baba?' He would laugh and say he wasn't taking that to court anytime soon.

Then after he had finished discussing the cause and motive, he would explain how every case was incomplete without the police swooping in for the questioning. He had always made it sound like a one-to-one affair. That was when the convict usually broke down and confessed to what they had done if the police did their job well.

Lavanya was about to tell Noor about her meeting with Donald Harper when the man walked in.

Donald Harper looked pleased with the attendance in the room. He barely glanced at Lavanya but very genially acknowledged Noor with a little bow of his head. Then, wasting no time at all, like a surgeon about to begin a major operation, he held out his gloved hand with an air of absolute authority.

Amrit Singh placed the now-familiar cellophane packet in his outstretched palm.

With a precise movement, Donald Harper slipped the cellophane off the package to reveal the book and showed it to the policemen watching him grimly.

'Gentlemen, the lieutenant general's wife was found murdered on the grounds of Whiteflower Hall in Simla. This book here was found just a few steps away. We are here to find out if what is written inside has anything to do with the brutal murder. The chief suspect, a dear friend of the author here, is absconding. This book was sent to him by Miss Lavanya Shriram, sitting amongst us.'

Like a well-choreographed group, everybody in the room turned to look at Lavanya. The superintendent paused, then when their eyes were back on him, he continued.

'There was a note found addressed to the chief suspect and I will read it out:

Dear Rat,
Here is my evil plan?
Where is yours?'

He paused. There was utter silence in the room. The note had been duly noted. She could see the photographer plotting to get his hands on it. His story for the papers the next day would write itself.

'Today, she has been called here to read a few pages to help us gauge the contents of the book and the possible role it may have played in what transpired on the evening of 13 February 1936.'

He turned on his heel, opened the book midway, and walked over to Lavanya, who was watching him, transfixed. Her dislike for him was a secondary factor, first came her utter fascination. It was only when the book was sitting right under her nose that she realized what he wanted her to do. He wanted her to perform, too, for everybody in the room. Play her part. Read a titillating page or two full of descriptions of passion to an audience of glazed subedars and havaldars, confirming to all that this was indeed a vile book that could have only caused sexual violence leading to murder.

Lavanya looked down at the pages thrown open in front of her. It was the story that had started every other story. The story of Sitara.

The story began with young Sitara being summoned to the pyre of her husband by her in-laws and family. All of them are determined she should burn along with her aged, ailing husband whom she had nursed since the day she was married to him at fourteen.

Although she resists and locks herself in the bedroom, she knows it's only a matter of time before the angry villagers break down the door and drag her out. Sitara's thoughts go to her lover, an Angrez whom she had met under a tree-while waiting for a bus when it was raining. Seeing her soaked to the skin, standing and shivering, he had stopped and offered to drive her to where she needed to go. Something about the colour of his eyes had melted her so entirely that she had meekly followed him into the jeep. They had stopped at a haveli where he was working as a conservationist for the Raja of Binsar and there, as she was struggling to get into some dry clothes and fighting waves of fatigue, along with nausea and chills, she had rested on a magnificent blue four-poster bed and fallen asleep midway.

The Angrez waited for her to emerge and then decided to go into the makeshift bedroom to see if she was all right.

The page that was open in front of Lavanya began with a description of Sitara's midriff. The only part of her body that lay bare as she slept.

Lavanya looked at the page, then looked back at the superintendent. 'Why would I read a story from the middle, Officer … let me start at the beginning.'

She flipped the pages back until she was right at the beginning of the story.

If she was going to titillate this miserable gathering, she might as well do a good job of it.

Lavanya read. She read Sitara's story like Sitara would have wanted her to. Every agonizing detail of her plight before she was dragged to the pyre. Every torrid detail of her only solace, her memories of the times she and her Angrez made love, on the magnificent blue four-poster, each of which she had known like her own limbs in the few months she had had with him.

From the time Lavanya had flipped the pages back to get to the start of the story, Donald Harper's mouth had been set in a thin straight line. He had wanted to see her squirm as she read the erotic passage he had opened the story at. He had wanted to establish beyond doubt that here was another lewd demonstration of how words were carelessly written to provoke men to commit violence. Such as what might have led Ratan to outrage the modesty of his employer that evening on the grounds of Whiteflower Hall in Simla. Before he had killed her and fled.

But as Lavanya read, he could see something else on the faces of his men. They were following Sitara's story like she was someone they knew. Someone they may have grown up with. With each page that Lavanya turned, he saw them sitting still, gripped by the tale. And when she came to the descriptions of their lovemaking, he saw them stirred and moved. Each of them wished it was them who had rescued Sitara from under the tree on that wet day.

A taste of freedom

RATAN UNLATCHED THE DOOR OF THE SHED THAT HAD been his refuge for the last three days and waited in the shadows. In another second or maybe two, he had to bodily fling himself into the unknown by simply stepping out of that door. He started counting till fifty and at forty-nine, he was out of the door, taking in gulps of the fresh night, air stirred by the moonlit fields of ragi in full ripeness.

He had dreaded stepping out of the barn, barely slept fearing the real world outside. Now, as he looked at the swaying fields with the mountains rising against the starry night sky, he felt like he'd been let out of prison. A lot like he'd felt the night he had stepped out of his father's house, all those years ago.

Ratan looked up at the calm sky, no rain, no stormy clouds, just wisps of clouds floating by. The skies were conferring, it seemed, over what had just transpired in his world. All the howling winds had been called back to regroup and rethink their next move.

Holding the stick close to him, his faithful companion for the last few days, he tried to retrace the path Shyam had led him through, that first night. Through the cowsheds, down the water well, and now past the house where Shyam was probably tossing and turning, hoping Ratan had left by now. He cast a quick look at the house before curving around it to climb his way out onto the road that would take him to the bus stand. There was a lantern glowing dimly in the window at one end of the house; he slowed down. Was that a pair of binoculars looking his way right now? Shyam? Keeping watch to make sure he left? Then, as he stopped to watch, the binocular eyes turned and moved away from the window and he caught a glimpse of a face that was much smaller, more angular. Cheeni—it had to be her.

There was something up with her, he just couldn't put his finger on it. All through their wedding, only as far back as six months ago, as he came and went in and out of the many celebrations held at this very house, he had felt her eyes on him. He would be getting himself a drink or a plate of food and would look up to see her looking at him before hurriedly looking away. It wasn't an appreciative gaze, Ratan knew those quite well; no, hers was suspicious. Like she knew he was up to no good. Maybe she had a premonition that he was going to get Shyam into some kind of trouble, sooner or later. A woman's intuition kicking in early, perhaps. Anyway, he was getting the hell out, wasn't he?

Ratan could see the road in the distance and it cleared his mind in an instant. He had far greater things to worry about. The road out of the farm would put him out there, visible to the world. He couldn't step out looking like himself; he needed to disguise himself quickly, somehow. He darted back in the shadows towards the house. The grass around the house was drier and he was conscious of the sound his shoes made as he stepped through it. There was one window partially open towards the back. He crept around it and peered in for some clue about what he could take to cover himself up. He spotted a farmer's pagdi and some kurtas and dhotis hanging on a hook.

His stick coming in handy, he managed to pull out the pagdi first. He went for the thick woollen kurta next. It was several sizes larger than he wore and probably belonged to Shyam's father. Cream-coloured with brown buttons, it looked muddy and soiled, but it would do for now. He had almost got it close enough to the iron bars in the window but not close enough for him to pull it through the bars, when he heard footsteps. He let the kurta go and crouched under the window. Maybe Shyam's parents were back from the pilgrimage after all. He waited and listened hard. There was the slightest movement in the room above, there was no doubt about it. Whoever was there would see the kurta on the floor. Then it was quiet again. He let moments pass before he crept up slowly to peer in and look. The room was dark and empty. The kurta was no longer on the floor. It was folded along with the dhoti and a blanket, right next to the ledge near the window. Along with what looked like a rolled-up paper. Ratan straightened up, reached out for the bundle, and got it through the iron bars. He slipped on the heavy woollen kurta over his shirt, tied the dhoti, rolled up his pants and then unrolled the paper. The moonlight had been a travelling companion on many a night but tonight she was in her element. She shone with a soft translucence on a picture of himself standing smartly outside the Davenport House. There was a handsome reward mentioned above the picture. Anybody with any news of his whereabouts could contact Richard Davenport directly.

Almost on cue, the moon dimmed its light now, like it was urging him to get a move on and so he did. He rolled the poster and slipped it back inside through the iron bars of the window; he wanted Cheeni to know that he had seen the poster and understood just how precious he was to Mr Davenport. Why hadn't Shyam shown him this poster? He could see Shyam look at him beadily and say, 'What good would that do? You knowing how much Mr Davenport has put on your stupid head? Don't you already know you're the most sought after criminal in Simla?' Yes, yes, he had an idea. It's just that he hadn't stopped to think about how much his stupid head was worth. There was too much else to think about.

As he walked away from the house, he realized with a start that the first thing he had noticed about the picture was that he looked fine, really fine. He was almost pleased they had chosen a picture he would have chosen himself.

He must be losing hold of his mind. What other explanation could there be for his vanity to surface at a moment like this? Maybe losing his mind would be a good thing; for when they caught him and threw him in jail or executed him, he would have already turned into a babbling idiot. It wouldn't matter then. Nothing would matter then.

He remembered when the picture was taken. It was the day the famous photographer Samuel Bourne was visiting Simla to do a series on how the British lived in India. There were quite a few parties in his honour before he came to visit the Davenports. It was a big moment. All the staff had been gathered on the porch to stand encircling the Davenports, who sat primly on garden chairs, looking into the camera. There were thirty-three of them to look after the two of them. Later, as he stood around the Benz, waiting for Sara, reading *The Times*, Samuel had sauntered up to him and asked if he wouldn't mind too much if he took a couple more pictures of him with the Benz. Ratan was bored and it was something to do. He enjoyed posing for the clicking camera as Samuel kept up a pleasant prattle about how Ratan should seriously think about acting as a career, he had the looks to earn himself a movie career in Bombay. Had he ever been to Bombay?

Part of the reason why he had enjoyed posing for the photographs was that he knew Sara was watching from the porch. He knew she would be greatly amused by his exaggerated Hindi cinema poses. The one that had been used for the poster was taken in between the poses. He had just stopped to smile in her direction. She was too far away for anyone to know whom he was smiling at. It was their secret. Sir Samuel had clicked the enigmatic smile and it was the best picture of the lot. She had shown it to him a few weeks later when they had been shipped to the house.

She kept the pictures under lock and key in a drawer in her cupboard. Richard must be going through her things. He wondered if there was anything there that could incriminate him further but couldn't think of anything. He could no longer think about Sara without thinking of himself as a criminal. Someone who had to run and hide without having done anything to deserve it.

It was ironic how it had all turned out. In his mind, he was the one who was going to give Sara the slip, give her a bunch of lies, and disappear. She had beaten him to it. Without even saying a word. Who was the figure in the trees? Who would have wanted to kill her?

He was on the road now. The outskirts of Simla had been all dirt tracks until the British paved and metalled the roads, connecting them to every part of the country. Another hour and it would be dawn, when all the farmers would begin stirring. Soon, there would be enough bullock carts on this road and he could hitch a ride to the bus station. Once he was out of Simla, he would be safer than he was right now.

The plan in his head was so simple, a child could have thought of it. He would keep running and dodging the police until he reached Bombay. Once there, he would go home, tell his father the truth, and admit to being a useless, selfish, and utterly ungrateful son. Ratan gagged at the thought. It made him sick to think that all his heroics in the last five years were going to end with him at his father's feet, begging for forgiveness. He should kill himself now and be done with it. *That too will take a lot of courage, dear Son, something you've never had much of*, he could see his father saying with the customary raising of his eyebrow.

The idiot prince

THE NIGHTS KNEW RATAN WELL. ALL OF THEM MOONLIT and quiet, except for the ad hoc buzzing of the crickets and the occasional humming of the dragonflies. The night birds had their strange songs too, that often pierced through the night but if there was a sound that gave the nights a known rhythm, it had often been the unsteady beat of Ratan's heart.

From the time he left home, the nights had seen him fleeing many a scene. There was the time when he found himself looking into a double-barrelled gun, held by the raging principal of Auckland House in the first month he had arrived in Simla. Sir Briggs had followed his daughter to the room Ratan was sharing with his friend Bunty, who was the sports teacher at the school. Bunty was visiting his aunt in Naldehra that night and the girl had sneaked into his room to surprise Ratan. He had barely met her once when she had asked to share a few puffs of his cigarette near the common water cooler. Ratan was terrified to see her grinning at him in the dark of the room but even more terrified at what had followed. The gun in his face and his cold, shivering body, jumping and running out into the night in just his vest and underwear.

Then there was the night he had tried to defend the honour of a prostitute he had befriended at a bus stop in Kasauli. He had been robbed of his money in a crowded bus and Radha had paid for his ticket and offered him a place to stay for a few days. He had woken up in the middle of the night at the sound of pots and pans being flung about next door. He had broken the door down to see her defending herself with her utensils while a drunken client tried to get a swing at her. Ratan had overpowered the guy and thrashed him and would have continued to do so if he had not seen the client grab his gun from his khaki uniform hanging on a hook. The drunken police officer had fired many shots at Ratan and missed. Ratan had run out as Radha pelted the man with thaalis and katoris while he tried to aim at Ratan.

But there was one night that made every other pale in comparison.

On Bunty's recommendation, Ratan had started driving for the Raja of Suraiah, a small princely state in the foothills of Simla. It was no ordinary car he was to drive, but then the raja, Ratan would soon find out, was no ordinary man either. The car was a flaming red Rolls Royce Phantom and the raja had had it modified with spotlights, a mounted machine gun, and a Lantaka cannon for his favourite recreational sport, hunting. The raja had many queens but they had all given him daughters except for one, who had borne him a son. It was for his son's eighteenth birthday that the raja had organized the most lavish hunting expedition, inviting princes from neighbouring states as well as British government officials, whom he knew were more than fond of the sport. It was a coming-of-age party and his son, Vikram Singh, was to mark the occasion by killing a tiger.

Vikram Singh, a strapping eighteen-year-old, big and brawny, had the mind of a five-year-old. For him, killing a tiger was a game much like the one he played with his servants where he pretended to shoot them and they ran about the royal gardens, falling down and pretending to be dead.

On the night of the hunt, Ratan found himself driving the Rolls Royce with only the prince sitting next to him. The prince had been told exactly what to do. Or rather, Ratan had been told exactly what to do. At a predetermined spot next to a pond, an aged tiger would come to take his drink of water like he did every day. Ratan was to get on a big rock next to the pond with the prince and make sure the prince aimed at the tiger and got a good shot.

Ratan had been to many hunts with the raja and knew how things went. Everything was pomp and show. The villagers did most of the work, baiting the prey and sometimes risking their lives to trap them, so that the raja and his hunting party could shoot them. This particular hunt was perhaps, more show than the others because it had a lot riding on it. The raja wanted all his invitees to witness his only son kill a tiger and lay to rest any rumours of the prince being of unsound mind and therefore an unworthy heir to his empire.

The prince had been sedated so that he would be calm and easy to handle, and sat next to Ratan, looking out of the car vacantly. He was in full princely attire with headgear and a cape made of brocade, but all Ratan could see were the shoes the prince wore. Ankle-length green leather with dull gold buckles and tie-up laces, polished like someone's life depended on it. He couldn't take his eyes off them.

The Rolls was leading the hunting party and was being followed by half a dozen elephants with mahouts, horses and a pack of dogs. There were villagers on foot, officials, safely ensconced in protected palanquins on top of the elephants and royals riding their horses. The spotlights on top of the Rolls flamed the way ahead for the hunting party.

The spot where they were supposed to stop and wait for the tiger was about five hundred metres ahead when the raja announced a quick stop for refreshments. The prince looked at Ratan with a dead gleam in his eyes.

'I'm going to shoot the tiger between the eyes,' he made a sign with his fingers to indicate how.

'Why don't you get some rest, Prince. It will be a long night of celebrations afterwards,' Ratan said, rubbing his eyes.

'After I shoot this tiger and make Father happy, will you play "freedom fighter" with me?'

Ratan nodded absentmindedly. He needed to sleep. He hadn't slept well for days. Freedom fighter was a game he had made up for the prince because he was tired of playing one injured animal after another. He would play Bhagat Singh and they would re-enact the Jallianwala Bagh pre massacre scene but with him and the prince riding in on horses and shooting Colonel Dyer before he could shoot any of the protesters.

Yes, he nodded sleepily, yes they would play 'freedom fighter'. Now would the Prince please shut up and get this night over with.

He didn't know how but along with the prince, he too fell asleep and woke up to the sound of the trumpets announcing the hunt had resumed. Ratan groggily started the Rolls and began inching towards the pond and the rock. They reached the spot where they were supposed to get off and head for the rock.

Ratan rubbed his eyes and looked at the prince who appeared to be looking out of the window, his head turned over to the other side from him.

'Prince, you ready?'

There was no answer. Ratan touched his shoulder lightly, the prince didn't look back. Ratan jostled his shoulder more forcefully. There was no response from the prince. He was in deep sleep. Ratan reached back behind the partition in the car for a bottle of water when he saw the entire hunting party behind them, the raja atop his splendorous elephant waiting for him to get a move on with the prince. The tiger was to arrive in just a short while from now and they needed to be safe on the rock by then. Ratan emptied the bottle of water on the prince's head and waited for him to splutter and shake his head violently to end his subconscious trance but there was no response. It must be the sedative, either too strong or badly timed.

Ratan's eyes fell again on the shoes the prince was wearing. A thought started forming in his head. If he were to wear the prince's headgear, put on his cape and shoes, nobody would be able to tell it wasn't him. He could get out on the rock, shoot the doddering old tiger, and get back down and put the gear back on the prince. When he confided in the raja later, the raja would only praise him for thinking on the spot and keeping his prestige on such an important night.

Less than five minutes later, the prince still fast asleep in the car, Ratan was walking into the moonlit night, his new shoes glinting in the dark. Everything was well hidden behind bushes, the hunting party was further behind and only the Lantaka cannon on top of the Rolls peeking out towards the pond.

The rock was at least six feet high with a cluster of smaller rocks beneath it where the villagers usually accompanying the hunters would hide. The villagers had been told to stay with the hunting entourage this time as the raja had wanted it to look more heroic and also, the tiger was so aged, there was no need for all the paraphernalia. The more the villagers saw, the more they would talk is what the raja had said.

Ratan waited for the tiger. It was time. Thank god he had caught a few winks in the car or he may have fallen asleep on the rock, waiting. It was such a still night, he could hear the moon breathe above him. It was impossible to imagine the woods thronged with the hunting party just a few hundred metres away. As he crouched there, wondering how nice it would be to sleep six nights in a row, there was that unmistakable sound of lapping water. The tiger was at the pond. He trained his binoculars to get a better look, but he seemed to be hidden behind the shrubs. Then thankfully, the tiger came around the pond towards the rock and stopped to drink some more. Ratan looked again through the binoculars, spotting him clearly. It was an easy shot. Then something else caught his eye. The tiger's belly hung all the way down. Ratan's breath quickened. This was not an aged tiger, this was a tigress and she was pregnant. Very pregnant. He trained his gun but his hands were shaking. A few seconds later he knew he couldn't do it. The tigress continued lapping up the water contentedly. Any moment now she would be done and on her way. There was nothing to do but wait again. The raja would have to understand there was no way he or the prince could shoot a tigress and her unborn cubs. The villagers had given the raja the wrong tip-off.

The tigress was now making her way back the way she had come, about to disappear behind the thick shrubs and then into the forest, when Ratan heard a distinct sound some distance away. He trained his binoculars in the direction of the sound and saw the top of the Rolls. There was somebody on top of the car, in the carrier next to the cannon. A few blinks later, he was certain it was the prince. The prince was awake and had clambered on top of the car to see what was happening. The sound he'd heard must have been the prince getting out of the car and closing the door. This was not good. He looked to see where the tigress was and sure enough she was very still, listening carefully. The prince was now fiddling with the cannon which Ratan knew was faulty and not loaded. The clickety clack of the cannon levers pierced the night. The tigress started ambling towards the sound, he could see her every step was cautious and measured. She sensed danger. The prince was out there and exposed. One leap and the tigress would get him. He should never have left him alone in the car. Then the prince did something unimaginable. He stood up on the car behind the cannon and started beating his chest and howling. Low, deep howls that came from the pit of his stomach, or was it his soul?. The tigress stood for a long second as if pondering the sound deeply. Then the next instant her pace quickened, she prowled closer and closer, a few steps more and she would be right below the rock. He would have to shoot her. Or let the howling prince die.

The hunting party behind him must have been watching the entire scene, confused. The tigress was now in his range and hands shaking, he pulled the trigger. The gunshot pierced the night and drowned the howls of the prince. Ratan shut his eyes to absorb the impact, but a quickening movement below made him open them again and he knew he had missed. Relief and fear flooded him in quick succession. The tigress had forgotten about the prince and was now pacing around the rock to get to him, her teeth set in a snarl. Seeing that great heap of flesh heaving and breathing just below him, Ratan was immobilized. He could see the back of the rock, from where he'd clambered up. He needed to move now if he wanted to save himself but his legs were frozen. The pain in his calves was extraordinary. Then the tigress was climbing up. He could hear her on the rock below. The same steps he had taken just a while back. Summoning all his strength Ratan threw himself down the edge of the rock.

And then miraculously his legs started moving.

The tigress leaped down from the rock right behind him. Landing in a skid on the grass below. Ratan ran in the silvery light of the moon, the gold-studded shoes like eyes in the dark. The hunting party watching with their binoculars could never forget that moment. When the story did get around and if anyone asked who ran better, the tigress or Ratan, they would say without a moment's hesitation, it was Ratan. Ratan in his borrowed, bejewelled headgear and billowing brocade cape. The tigress ran at best, tentatively, like she couldn't decide who it was she was chasing. Man, beast, or a creature from her dreams.

Ratan wasn't sure what exactly happened next, at what point did the villagers storm in, brandishing laathis to divert the tigress, at what point in the chase did the tigress stop and reconsider her decision to chase him any further and disappear into the forest but he couldn't stop running, jumping and leaping over shrubs and rocks, falling and getting up and running again. At some point, he couldn't feel his legs anymore. It was like he was running on air. He ran till he left all the sound and fury behind him, the howls of the prince, the low grumbling and snarling of the tigress, the shouts of the villagers. And then he couldn't run anymore as he found himself leaping into a wide and dark ditch.

When his shoes hit the ground, he crumbled into a heap and lay quivering for endless moments as the night covered him with a thick quilt of utter darkness and he passed out.

The next day Ratan clambered out of the ditch dug by the villagers to trap animals and walked out of the forest towards Suraiah. By then it had become clear to him what the raja had intended. Everything had been thought out carefully, including the dose of medication given to the prince that night. The raja knew that if the prince slept, Ratan would shoot the tiger for him. He also knew the tiger was not aged but a pregnant tigress. Slow of movement, easily tired, but definitely not aged or easy prey. He may not have anticipated that Ratan would hesitate to shoot the tigress on account of her being pregnant or that his son would decide to get on top of the Rolls and start crying at the moon. Both of them had improvized on the raja's plan but it was Ratan whose life had been at stake, always. Though if he was the prince, half-witted or not, he would be very suspicious of his father's motives to send him out there alone with no one to protect him but Ratan. Maybe the raja had hoped the tigress would get them both if things went wrong.

He walked through Suraiah holding the dishevelled pagdi in his hand, still wearing the richly embroidered cape that was now muddy and torn, and the green and gold shoes that had lost every trace of polish when he heard the villagers calling out to him. Feeling used and foolish, he kept walking on, not once looking back to address any of them. He reached the palace to confront the raja but he had left that very morning on an important diplomatic visit to the neighbouring princely state, he was told.

Ratan cleaned up, packed his bags and left. He left the cape behind, the princely headgear, too, but the shoes he took.

Trouble is an old friend

SHYAM'S FARM WAS A HAZY BLUR AS DAWN BROKE WITH A slight tremor in the breeze, instantly chilling his neck under the woollen gamcha. Ratan reached the junction where all the buses came and went. It was icy cold and the wind had picked up speed. He was covered from head to foot, only his eyes were visible, and yet he felt exposed. He tried to tell himself how simple the next step really was. All he had to do was get on a bus and leave. Shyam had told him about the bus timings and there was one leaving soon. It would take him the farthest away from Simla, to a place called Tattapaani. From there, he would start making his way to the closest train station where there would be no police looking for him. He walked up to the bus stop and looked in the direction the bus was supposed to come from. The place was filling up slowly, it was a good place to sell anything, from vegetables to toys to street food to clothes and the hawkers were getting ready to set up shop. He decided to relieve himself before he got on the bus.

Five minutes later, he was walking back when he saw them all over the bus stand. Through the smoky cloud of dust raised by the arriving buses, he could hardly see the bus itself, but he could see the police all around it. They were outside and inside, frisking everybody who looked suspicious, stripping people of their turbans and their gamchas. Shoving some to one side where another policeman peered even more closely at them, holding the poster that Cheeni had been so kind to point him to, a few hours ago. The hawkers had started collecting their wares and were getting out of there fast. Then the cloud of dust settled and he could see his bus standing there, waiting. There were just one or two policemen and their scrutiny looked less enthusiastic now that they had finished checking the bus in front of them. There were more buses arriving and they wanted to check the next one. Should he take a chance and make a run for it? He could see many farmers getting on the bus without being checked. He took a few steps to break into a run, like he was late for the bus, then stopped. Trouble was an old friend and had a familiar smell. Ratan deliberated. Once caught, especially inside the bus, it would be impossible to make a getaway. He looked to see if there was another bus he could get on but the police were everywhere, they seemed to have increased in number too. They must have known. No, they must have been told. He had to get out of here fast. He took a few steps back and then a few more till he was behind a tree at the far side of the junction. He had to duck back in the field where he had gone to relieve himself, without being conspicuous. His not-so-brilliant plan had failed even before it could take off. Ratan didn't know what he wanted to do more, laugh or cry.

The only person who knew he was going to get on a bus today was Shyam. They had discussed the bus timings and together decided which bus Ratan should take and when—

no one else could have ratted him out. Maybe that was what Cheeni was trying to tell him. His friend was going to wait for him to leave the farm and then call the police. The reward money was too much to resist.

As he walked further away, he saw a bullock cart in the distance. There was nobody around. He walked as fast as he could, up to it. He had to act fast. The farmer must be dropping off the sacks of produce at the mandi, across the field. He clambered in and luckily for him, the bullocks were raring to go; they set off at a happy trot, and soon Ratan was on his way back into the city he had planned to get away from.

A dramatic interruption

THE INTERROGATION ROOM HAD TURNED DAMP AND cold. There was no trace of the sun filtering in from the torn bamboo blinds that covered the enormous windows. Lavanya hunched her shoulders to keep warm and was lost to the world and well into the story, when she felt a sharp jab on her arm. It was Noor. She ignored her. When she heard a minor disturbance and some hushed utterances, later, a voice boomed loud enough for her to stop reading and look up. The superintendent too turned around to face the voice. Amrit Singh was looming over two bespectacled men, glaring.

'If I may introduce myself, I'm Surya Kant, the publisher. This is my lawyer and he is here to tell you that no part of the book can be read aloud in a public gathering without my permission.'

So this was Surya Kant Chauhan of the *Voices* journal who had accepted her stories when all others had rejected them. She had never had occasion to meet him before this. He was her father's friend's son, who had inherited his father's publishing business and started a journal 'determined to raise its voice against the hypocrisies of an orthodox society' as stated in its mission statement. Surya Kant had accepted her first story 'Sitara' by post and sent her a cheque with a note on how he hoped she would write more as he would be happy to publish her when she did. Just the acceptance had sent her over the moon. She had given up on any publishing house or literary magazine accepting her stories after the slew of rejections.

'*Your* permission? Is that right?' Donald Harper, his left eyebrow raised, his mouth set in a mean curve looked at Surya Kant as if he was an errant fly that had somehow meandered into the wrong room at the wrong time.

Surya Kant nodded at the superintendent then looked at his lawyer, who seemed to be having trouble getting a single word out of his mouth. Then, with Surya Kant continuing to look at him intently, the lawyer started speaking.

He spoke so fast like he couldn't wait to be done with it. It was obvious he had been dragged here to do this and threatened with dire consequences if he didn't. The lawyer stated the exact rule in the law book that forbade readings of private publications in a public gathering unless pre-approved by the publisher, who was the sole owner of the rights to the printed book.

Once he had spoken, there was silence. Then with a decisive rustle of her zardozi costume, Noor broke the silence. She got up and hoisted Lavanya up too, whispering into her ear urgently.

'He is our man, do you hear? He is our man.'

Noor, the end of her lehenga in hand, walked over to Surya Kant and his lawyer.

'Janaab, I am Noor Ahmed and this is my friend Lavanya Shriram and we are so very glad to see you,' she glanced triumphantly at Donald Harper and then the rest of the policemen, who remained stunned by the proceedings, including this dramatic interruption.

Surya Kant nodded curtly in their direction and then addressed Donald Harper again. 'Sir, perhaps we could step aside and have a quick meeting, just the three of us, and decide the next course of action.'

It took a moment for Amrit Singh to realize he wasn't included in this little threesome. He looked at his superintendent for confirmation, who was still sizing up Surya Kant and his petrified lawyer. Surya Kant had spoken deferentially but it seemed like the words were carved in stone. Donald Harper looked at Amrit Singh, letting him know he was to keep watch here and then without a word or even a glance at Lavanya, picked up the open book covered in cellophane and marched out of the room into the corridor. Surya Kant and his lawyer followed as Amrit Singh reluctantly stepped aside.

All the policemen filed out of the room, their eyes cast down. They were careful not to meet Lavanya's eyes but Noor was another matter. They stole glances at her as they passed by and she obliged by acknowledging all of them with an exaggerated bow like she was a debutante at a ball and they were all would-be suitors.

'I was almost enjoying this ...' Lavanya said to no one in particular when the policemen had left.

Noor gave her a look that was half fed up and half indulgent, looking just like her mother, Jaddan Bai, for a flash of a second. Lavanya's eyes softened as she hugged her friend tight, grateful to have her here by her side. Noor hugged her back, then looked at her, made a clucking noise deep in her throat, and started patting Lavanya's hair, putting some strands into place, tucking the others behind her ears.

Noor's eyes were shining with the recent development. She wanted to know everything about Surya Kant.

'Lav, how is it you've never told me about *him*?'

'There's nothing to tell. Baba and his father were very close since school. He was a "problem child", Baba used to say, that's all.'

Noor liked the sound of that, Lavanya could tell. She remembered bits and scraps about Surya Kant from overheard conversations between Baba and his friend, Supratim Uncle.

Uncle had been grooming his only son to take over his publishing house for as long as she could remember. It was a family business and Surya had imbibed a deep, insightful knowledge of what good writing and good publishing needed to do to thrive. However, he never intended to follow in his father's footsteps. He would run away every chance he got to attend meetings called by the Jai Hind League since he was all of thirteen. He had to be dragged back by an anxious father who didn't want his only son to grow up to be a freedom fighter. Bhagat Singh had just been hanged and his death was held as an example by the British of what would happen if you went against them. His poor wife wept every night clinging to her pillow, worrying about Surya, Uncle said.

What didn't help was the fact that the Kant publishing house was fast gaining a reputation for publishing writers who wrote about the woes of the common man suffering under foreign rule. The books would be fresh off the press when Surya devoured them, swearing to join the fight to bring about change. His mother would try and calm him down but

Surya Kant was a young man, obsessed with his dream to see a free India.

Lavanya remembered how shocked Baba was when Supratim Uncle died of a sudden heart attack, leaving Surya to take over the reins at the publishing house. He couldn't run away to Jai Hind League meetings anymore. It wasn't the life he had envisioned for himself and soon, his disappointment at not being out there with the leaders of the struggle led him to become a recluse. He continued publishing young firebrand authors, started *Voices* and joined the Progressive Writers' Movement, though he never attended a single meeting. When Lavanya finished writing 'Sitara', Baba had said his dead friend's son was the only person with the foresight to publish her work.

She had never dreamed that she would meet her publisher for the first time in a police station.

Thirty-odd minutes later, Surya was led back into the room by Amrit Singh. There was no sign of the anxious lawyer who had accompanied him. He seemed to have made a speedy getaway. Surya waited till he could hear the policeman's retreating footsteps before pulling a chair to face them.

Lavanya, her shoulders still hunched as if guarding herself against any impending, literal or metaphorical, chills, sat on the wooden bench and looked up at her publisher expectantly. Had he been given the Donald Harper treatment or not? Strangely, he looked calm and was holding her gaze as curiously as she was holding his. It occurred to her that he was among the rarest of rare men who found it easy to ignore the fabulous Noor. It was almost like she didn't exist. She was sure Noor was not enjoying that.

'Miss Shriram, I'm going to dispense with the pleasantries,' he said, a finger adjusting the bridge of his spectacles. 'It is indeed a pleasure to meet you though I'm sure both of us would have liked to meet under more pleasant circumstances.' Lavanya waited for him to continue.

'Having said that, may I say it is about time our book got the attention it deserves? It is unfortunate that it was found at the scene of a crime, but I'm going to take advantage of that to make sure more people will be curious enough to read it. Not just *Voices* subscribers, the Progressives who are our loyal readers, but also the masses, anybody who can read, will be reading this book ...' He would have gone on if she hadn't cut him short.

'I'm sorry, what did you say? Didn't the superintendent just tell you that he wants you to take it out of circulation altogether?'

'Yes, and I refused.'

'What do you mean, you refused? He's not going to stop here, you know that. He is a powerful and vengeful man, he will go out of his way to link me to the murder. What then?'

'You, Lavanya, if I may, cannot be linked to the crime. It happened in Simla, your book, on the other hand will be linked, yes, but that may be a good thing for us. The more it gets linked, the more we stay in the news, the more people want to read us. There is just one thing ... actually maybe two ...'

He paused. She waited.

'You will have to go to Simla. They want you to visit the scene of the crime. According to them, you're inextricably linked to the murder on account of the fact that you're the writer of a publication found next to the body.'

'I will refuse. They can't make me. I know the ploy. They want to take me to Simla so that they can draw Ratan out of where he's hiding. They're hoping he'll seek me out and they'll catch him. I'm not stupid. I'm not going.'

'That's the other thing. I think you should go. Because you see, they're also going to take you, no, us, they are going take *us* to court and sue us on obscenity charges. Those are the consequences of not withdrawing the book from circulation. Right now, it's a threat but I know how this works. They will influence certain suitable individuals well-known in society, to do the needful. As your publisher, I think this too will be good publicity for the book. Even you going to Simla and visiting the scene of the crime will be good publicity. We need public support and media support, both of which I'm confident of getting. If you go, that is.'

Lavanya looked at Noor, who increased the pressure on her hand, squeezed it and nodded at her. Her eyes seemed to say that 'their man' was making sense.

Surya Kant now turned to Noor and addressed her more formally.

'Delighted to make your acquaintance, Miss Noor Ahmed,' he smiled. 'I don't get out much, but I have seen all your movies. It is an honour to meet you in person, in this ...' Surya Kant looked around at the bare room lined with benches '... in this exotic and utterly charming location.'

Noor giggled as she asked him which movies of hers he'd seen and he rattled off a few names; Lavanya watched him closely. Her publisher indeed.

Nothing remarkable to look at. The usual tall, thin, bespectacled, pinched face. The gaunt, underfed variety that belonged in a bank or a court, except for that full head of hair that kept flopping on his forehead.

He seemed to have emerged from his self-imposed isolation, determined to get every ounce of publicity he could for 'their' book. He didn't seem to care much for any inconvenience any of his plans would cause her. Though so far, she couldn't fault him on his part in the entire proceedings. He did seem like someone who couldn't be easily manipulated and she could use someone like that in this situation.

She cruelly cut into Noor's tinkling laugh that was warming up to Surya Kant's compliments.

'So, let me get this straight. Donald Harper threatened to have the book banned and you said, go ahead?' He turned to face her.

'Not exactly. People like Donald Harper like their victories, there's no sense in denying them that,' he said. 'He threatened, because that's what he knows how to do and I pretended to be horrified at what it would do to you, to me, to our reputation, our work ...' He paused as if reflecting on his words, 'I pleaded with him, too, pleasing him further. Then I hung my head and left, not once agreeing to take the book out of circulation.'

Lavanya had to admit, that was well-played.

'There is lots to be done, however. Let's leave at once before they find another reason to keep us here.' Surya Kant got up to leave and Noor rose with him. Lavanya took her time, giving the room one last look as she left. She had surprisingly not felt intimidated here. Once she was reading, she had even felt invincible.

Sitara was by her side. It was good to feel Sitara by her side after so long.

The bungalow in the forest

RATAN DREW THE BULLOCKS AS FAR UPHILL INTO THE forest as he could. The path was getting treacherous by the minute and he could see the bullocks were tired. They kept slipping on the small stones as they tore into the wild shrubs that covered the path entirely. A while later, he saw a small clearing and a hut with a patch of grass outside it.

Covered in bramble, he took the bullocks to the grass, got down, and slowly started walking away. He had taken one farmer's cattle and given them to another. As if that made it all right. Truth be told, he didn't give a damn. The universe owed him right now, at this very minute. Looking up at the clear blue sky, his mouth set, he muttered to no one but himself. He, Ratan, would take whatever he could from whoever he could and the universe could go settle matters and keep balance any which way it liked. He kept walking.

He knew he was in the vicinity of the bungalow that Sara had often brought him to. He had always driven there in the Benz but the motorable road was too risky and so the forest had been his best option. He would have to find the bungalow on foot now. The deodars, pines and firs towered over him, watching him trying to find his bearings.

After walking some distance, he saw the wild flowers in full bloom. Swaying in the breeze, they seemed to wave at him. He had often wondered about them to Sara. Bright purple with pink smudges on them, they were too good to be wild. Sara said they were born like that, they couldn't be grown in a cultivated way, in a pot or a garden. They were strewn all over the ground, and you had no choice but to walk over them to get anywhere. They were uncrushable, she had said, her eyes twinkling at him. Uncrushable. He had repeated the word to himself, loving the sound of it, or was it the meaning? They had stepped on them over and over again and looked back to see them spring back to sway gaily in the wind.

Now he did the same, stepping on them, listening for the stems bending over in the wild grass. He heard them squish and looked back to see them bob back up, waving. Something caught in his throat as he stood there, something unexplainable.

They had often walked up here, sat on the rocks on the edge of the mountain, and looked down at the twinkling valley below or the snow-capped peaks that looked like the heavenly abodes of real gods and goddesses. He had been close to happy then. Like he ruled over all that he could see from the top of that mountain.

The bungalow was at the edge of a mountain face, overlooking the valley. Built in a style that was the new craze for the English living in India, it was fronted by airy verandas to sip sundowners in, several 'cosy' rooms and halls to entertain in, and terraces to take the air in. It belonged to Sara's friends, Cathy and Roger Summers, who lived most of the year in England, rather than Simla. He'd never imagined coming here without her. It needed a good pair of shears, though. With all the dense overgrowth, it looked like an extension of the forest he had just emerged from. He lifted the shrub growing over a thick wooden sign on which was engraved 'Nevermore'. Unlike the stately names of other bungalows like 'Peterhoff', 'Chadwick House', 'Elysium', or 'Belvedere', the Summers had named theirs after a ballad, 'The Raven', by their favourite poet, Edgar Allan Poe.

He found the keys hidden under the floor mat in the veranda and cautiously opened the door. His heart was beating faster, it was almost like he would find her inside, sitting by the window, her feet up on the ottoman, reading Lavanya's book. Seeing him, she would wave him to her side and he would smile at her childish eagerness and flop down on the carpet beside her. She would begin reading softly, picking up pace and intensity, depending on the parts she wanted to dramatize, and he would play with her bare feet, hoping to distract her. Eventually, he would.

He stepped inside and gave the house a quick check, keeping his face covered. Nobody had been here for a long time. In the bedroom, there was a film of dust on the sheets that shone in the afternoon light. He pulled the sheets off the bed as the dust flew in his eyes, blinding him momentarily. He drew the curtains close and gave the sheets a final shake before dropping them down on the mattress. Then, wincing, he rose to remove every shred of clothing he had on, through which pieces of bramble stubbornly poked him. The next second, he had passed out from sheer exhaustion, lines from 'The Raven' echoing in his head, all jumbled up.

'And so faintly you came tapping, tapping at my chamber door …

And the only word there spoken was the whispered word, "Lenore?"

'… Ghastly grim and ancient Raven wandering from the Nightly shore—

Tell me what thy lordly name is on the Night's Plutonian shore!'

Quoth the Raven "Nevermore".'

When he got up, it was pitch dark. He let the first few waves of nausea and panic pass as he stared at the criss-crossing wooden beams looming over him. He could see them in motion, coming down at him at breakneck speed and he pried his eyes open to stop them midway.

He needed to eat. Wrapping himself in the still warm sheets he had slept in, he found the lights and started switching them on all the way down the staircase and into the kitchen. There wasn't a cupboard that wasn't stacked with dry food. He found tins of crackers, butter and cookies, and started stuffing them in his mouth without thinking. Then he sat down in a pool of light under the massive hanging lamps and forced himself to chew. Slowly, the dizziness passed and his eyes fell on a pack of John Players. He found a matchbox and smoked them all as he went through the house, looking through every room and every cupboard, picking up a dressing gown from one, shirts from the other, and finally, a pair of trousers that actually fit him.

The bathroom in the bedroom upstairs was his last cigarette stop and by the time he opened the door to its tiled whiteness, the first few rays of morning light were peeping in through the cracks in the thick forest green, outside the windows. He held the glistening cold metal of the tap for many steadying seconds before he turned it all the way to the other side. It burst forth with water pouring over the creamy white tub, scurrying the sediments of dirt further and further away. The promise of a bath after all these days of stewing in a cold sweat was making him dizzy again. He shrugged off the bedsheets, never taking his eyes off the water gushing forth in the tub.

A photo and a painting

LAVANYA WOKE UP AT 3 A.M. THAT NIGHT, DONALD Harper's threats ringing in her mind. *Do not provoke, only please, do you understand?* His hideous baritone echoed in a loop in her head as she turned this way and the other to escape it. Finally, she sat up, wide awake, staring into nothing for a long time.

They had proceeded from the police station to Surya Kant's office at the press in Colaba. She had spent the evening trying to find out all she could about Sara Davenport. Who was she? She had stared long at her picture in *The Tribune* that Surya Kant had pulled out for her. In it, Sara held a long, elegant cigarette holder in one hand and her face at an angle, blowing smoke, her mouth turned away. Her eyes were intent but her face told you she had finished laughing at something amusing. She had on a thin summer dress and her smooth alabaster skin shone like light to reflect in her glittering eyes. Something rustled, an old forgotten memory came whispering to the surface. Before it could pop, it dipped out of view. She knew this face but where could she have seen it? How could she know this face? Surya showed her many newspaper pieces about Sara's work in schools across India. She read one or two, glanced at the write-ups, taking some with her to read later. The face kept coming back. As incongruous with school work and education as it could get. Then it struck her as they were about to leave. An artist she had once met had painted a face that was a lot like Sara's photograph.

'Noor! Do you remember the exhibition we went to, where this flamboyant painter from Paris was showing her paintings? It was the talk of the town?'

'Uh hmm, yes, I think so. Amrita Sher-Gil, wasn't it?' Noor said, correctly detecting the excitement in Lavanya's face. 'You refused to leave till the gallery closed down, I remember now.'

'I saw Sara, a face like Sara's, the exact same face, in one of her paintings. I'm sure. It was one of my favourites. How is it possible?'

'It's quite possible, actually,' Surya Kant said. He had walked with them to see them out and Lavanya looked at him, intrigued, waiting for more.

'I am acquainted with Miss Sher-Gil's work, or should I say, I'm a huge admirer. I am also arranging for her to show her work this coming summer in Bombay, so we are in touch. What I'm saying is, these days, she lives and paints in Simla.' He let that sink in. So it *was* Sara she had seen in Amrita Sher-Gil's exhibition.

Lavanya remembered that day at the exhibition. She had found it difficult to tear her eyes away from Sara's painting. Noor had long since wandered away. It was the same face she had seen in the papers but rendered in a stunning canvas with the most beguiling colours. She had stood there, mesmerized and rooted at her spot when a voice behind her said, 'Do you like my muse?'

It was Amrita Sher-Gil standing by her side. She was wearing a sheer chiffon sari, her hair pulled into a small tight bun, a string of pearls clutching her neck. Looking like a modern-day apsara, Lavanya had thought. A little intimidated by the sight of the painter she had heard so much about, she nodded a yes.

'I didn't mean to interrupt,' she said, 'it's just that it's rare that people look at your paintings like they see them.' She had smiled then and Lavanya was put at ease at once.

'I like your work a lot. You paint women, I write about them,' Lavanya had told her.

'Ah, a writer. It makes sense. We understand each other a little better now. I have been so bored, watching people come and go, hardly stopping to look at what I've poured my heart into. Do you want to know something?' she dropped her voice to a conspiratorial whisper. 'She, who you've been looking at, looks even better in the *nude*.' Amrita raised her eyebrow and nodded at her as if to say it was the absolute truth.

Before Lavanya could say something, a group of people came and whisked Amrita away to meet potential buyers. The artist waved to her and said, 'I'm saving *those* for another exhibition, be sure to come!' Then she was gone.

Standing at the door of the press, Lavanya now knew that it was Sara who she had been transfixed by that day at the exhibition. Sara, who would turn up dead months later, with Lavanya's book of stories lying close by. Sara, who would connect her back to Ratan after all these years.

'It was Sara I saw at the exhibition and I remember being immediately drawn to her,' she said softly to Noor who was watching her, knowing she was having trouble working something out in her mind.

'There will be answers in Simla, Lavanya, I can feel it. It will be good if you go. Also if you like Miss Sher-Gil's work, I will write to her and she will be happy to meet you and show you around her studio,' Surya said.

'I haven't decided, let me think about it,' she lied.

Now at 3 a.m., there was another thought brewing.

She went to her writing desk in the far corner of her room and started cleaning the mess around it. Packets of half-finished food and invitation pamphlets to attend meetings with leaders like Gandhi and Nehru lay side by side, with all the hastily scrawled sheets where she had scribbled ideas for stories and screenplays. Ideas she had never finished. Half- awake and completely disoriented, she wondered if a country struggling to be free was an unfinished story too. If so, all it needed was one final act of courage, even if it was foolish courage.

An hour later, she sat down to write on a clean desk, her Scheaffer fountain pen poised over spotless white letter paper. She wondered how she could possibly introduce herself.

Dear Sir

I am Lavanya Shriram and I have come to know about the sad passing of your wife, Lady Sara Davenport.

I realize my book was found at the scene of the crime as I had sent it to Ratan, a childhood friend and neighbour.

I assure you my motives for writing the stories in the book were guileless.

I would like to come to Simla to help in any way possible to find Ratan and persuade him to surrender himself if he is guilty of the crime.

I would also like to write about Sara, the wonderful work she was doing in schools to promote education for girls all over the country, if you would allow it and if you consider me suitable.

Awaiting your reply and looking forward to making your acquaintance in person.

Sincerely
Lavanya Shriram

Lavanya folded the letter, found an envelope that did not have stains of leftover food, and glued it shut.

It had been a while since she had woken in the middle of the night to write, even a letter. Or wishing to write more than a letter, to write about a woman who was pulling her into her world more and more with each passing minute. A world she didn't belong in, not by any stretch of the imagination. Yet.

Lavanya didn't want to be used simply as bait to visit Simla, she wanted access to Sara's home, her life, and only Sir Richard Davenport could give her that. Somewhere at the back of her mind, she knew this was exactly what the superintendent did not want. This awareness only propelled her forward.

Simla was calling her in so many different voices, she had trouble separating them. First, there was Ratan's—a crusty, gruff, insistent voice. *Lava, I'll get out of this, don't come. Do you hear me, don't you dare!*

Which obviously meant she must. Why else was he asking her not to?

Sara's voice was more mysterious, but the single word it issued was clear and unambiguous. *Come. come. come.*

The painter too had a voice, it was gravelly and husky and whiffed of half-smoked cigars. *Darling, if you show me your nudes, I'll show you mine.*

Lavanya wondered if she was causing it all to happen, the events that were unfolding. She'd read somewhere—was it Dostoevsky?—that when you start thinking a lot about something like, say, death, it causes other things to happen, making you want to go deeper and deeper. Lavanya wondered if it was the death of her parents within six months of each other that had started her thinking about death. And somewhere in the recesses of her mind, a tale of crime. Then on the vast grounds of the Wildflower Hall in Simla, a book of stories had dropped down on dead leaves with a dead body next to it. *Her stories.* And one fine day, the inspector had found himself ringing her doorbell. Some determined lawyer could argue in court that it was she who had caused it all to happen.

For Lavanya, the next few days became a nasty whirl. The news team with the cameras at the police station had done their job. Soon there wasn't a paper that wasn't talking about the murder in Simla and the book found next to the scene of the crime. There was a profile on Ratan, who was the sole absconding suspect, and a write-up on Lavanya reading the incriminating story to a room packed with policemen where she'd left out the ending. Because the ending was unprintable, the newspapers concluded.

Questions were being asked about their friendship. How long had they known each other? Had they colluded together to commit this crime? Was it a crime of passion or cold-blooded revenge against an entire regime? Why had she sent him this book? What did her scribbled note to Ratan inside the book mean? Was it a secret code that only Ratan could decipher?

A self-professed scholar of languages had declared it was a coded message. He had researched it and it read as SHE IS THE ENEMY.

Her father used to say that Bombay was the only city teeming with people who had no interest in the ins and outs of your life. Somebody could get murdered next door and nobody would bat an eyelid. There were two exceptions though, Lavanya longed to tell her dead father. Bombay could ignore you as long as you were not a girl living alone and if they had not read about you in the daily paper.

Every newsreport came sprinkled with Donald Harper's quotes. *The Statesman*, *The Hindu*, *The Bombay Chronicle*—all carried long-winded statements on how the police were working hard to get to the bottom of the case. No effort was being spared to dig up all the evidence to pin the culprit down. They had tightened security on all fronts and it was only a matter of time before Ratan was put behind bars. And finally, Harper appealed to readers not to succumb to the 'evil plan' behind the book aggressively in circulation. By reading the offensive book, they would create more demand for the filth in it. A few upstanding individuals had appealed to the government to take legal steps to ban the book. The author and publisher were, unfortunately, not cooperating, he said.

Surya Kant did his best to milk the frenzy around the book. He printed enough copies of the book to meet the curiosity of all those who couldn't wait to read the famous ending. He called in favours from printers, publishers, calligraphers, illustrators and writers. If there is a patriotic bone in your body, he told them, sell this book. If there is love for the written word in your heart, sell this book. If there is hate for chains and things bent on tying you down, sell this book. Finally, he said, if you want business to pick up, you want to go home with some good news for a change, sell this book.

Lavanya was bemused to find copies of the book that had been lying in a dusty corner of Samarth Book Depot in Giraum Naka were now on display in the front window. Moreover, the Progressives, who had so far ignored her, were now inviting her to attend meetings. When her stories had first appeared in *Voices*, she had hoped some leading voices from the movement may pay heed, acknowledge her as a new, interesting voice, perhaps. No one had. Now that her book was linked to the killing, threatened with a ban in a court of law, both she and her writing were being hailed.

Lavanya locked up the house after the first day of madness, robbing her neighbours of a chance to show their concern with a shared cup of Lipton's tea. She packed a small bag and left for Noor's posh apartment, Krishna Mahal, on Marine Drive. She knew she would have to brave Aunty Jaddan Bai's endless questions but she also knew Noor would help her manage her mother. Jaddan Bai was a formidable name in the Bombay film industry and already, Krishna Mahal had become famous for her salons, where actors, producers and directors would gather to pay court to her, in the hope of working with Noor.

The only person she sought out to clarify matters with before she left, was Ratan's father. She let him know she had no idea of Ratan's whereabouts, that he had never reached out to her, nor sent her a single word of news about himself or what he was doing all these years. Ratan's father heard her out, a shrivelled man, looking much older than his years, his hands covering hers for a brief moment as he looked deep into her eyes.

'Where did I go wrong? All I wanted to do was protect *both* of them …'

She had not known what to say. He had sought to protect. His wife and his son had sought to be free. People and countries, there seemed to be very little difference.

They sat in silence for a long time. It was when she got up to leave that he called out to her softly, 'Lavanya … beta?'

She turned back.

'You're a good girl, Lavanya. Don't let anyone tell you otherwise.'

She had nodded, her lips trembling, overwhelmed for no reason. It was pathetic, her insatiable need to be told she was a good girl. Completely in conflict with her need to do everything that was considered unsuitable.

The summons knew where to reach her even though her house was locked and she had left no forwarding address.

She was alone at Noor's home. Noor had left with Jaddan Bai to discuss dates and payments for a forthcoming film. The servants too had fled, to gossip with the vegetable sellers and the shoeshine boys around the corner, glad to have a moment to themselves without her hawk-like eyes sweeping over everything they did. Lavanya was washing her hair, listening to Duke Ellington and his band perform 'It don't mean a thing' on the radio, when the doorbell rang. She let it ring. Whoever it was, would get the message and leave. The doorbell kept ringing. She finished washing her hair to the now stopping, now whirring of the doorbell, and went to answer the door.

Amrit Singh whipped out a brown paper package and handed it to her. They didn't need to exchange any words. There was a small note with the package, which she read first. It was on Superintendent Donald Harper's stationery.

Hello Miss Shriram. Hope this court summons finds you in the pinkest of health. If you'd be so good as to sign it. See you in Simla and then, in court. Eagerly, Donald Harper.

She crumpled the note and held out her hand as Amrit Singh, caught off guard, took it from her. Then not knowing what to do with it, slipped it into his pocket. She ripped open the crown-embossed 'COURT SUMMONS' with her heart beating and her hair dripping. Sinatra on the radio insisted, with a crash of the drums and a flourish of the trumpet, that it didn't mean a thing, if you aint got that swing. This summons seemed to have a decided swing.

The towel holding her hair in place had dropped and she didn't even know it. In less than a month, she was to appear in court in Simla to answer the charges of 'writing documents offensive to public morale and capable of inciting criminal acts in a civilized society'.

Instinctively, she looked behind her to see if her mother was watching. How could she not? This was the precise moment she had predicted all along. She should be peering over her shoulder with that 'I told you so' look. Well, it had. What a relief to get it over and done with, right Ma? She watched the words swimming in and out of focus. Her eyes stinging but dry, her wet hair dripping over the summons, smudging the Queen's order. It wasn't as terrifying as it looked, actually, she concluded.

Amrit Singh took the summons from her hands with a soft but sternly muttered, 'May I, Madam?' Brandishing a pen in his hand and keeping the papers at a safe distance from her hair, he gestured for her to sign her acceptance.

She did. He had another envelope for her which had her tickets for Simla. She nodded at him, she had noted the date, the time and she would be there. He nodded back at her. He left. Barely three meetings and they were already communicating like old friends with minimal gestures and nods.

She expected her brothers to seek her out, sooner or later. Surendra, her elder brother, was the first. He called Noor on her telephone connection at home, that evening. By the time Lavanya came on the line, he had worked himself up quite a bit.

What was this new mess she had got herself into? People at work were asking him all sorts of questions about her, he didn't know what to say. How did she think that made him look? Why hadn't she called him the minute she got to know about Ratan's involvement in the crime? Why didn't she come at once to Delhi and lock up the house in Bombay? She calmed him the best she could and assured him she would do just that, come to Delhi soon. By the time her younger brother Virendra called, she was spent. They got off on the wrong foot immediately.

'Lavi, the police? The police? All that nonsense you write! I knew there was something terribly wrong with that rat, Ratan, why on earth did you keep in touch with him?! Thank God Ma is gone or she would have had her second heart attack now …'

She didn't tell him about the court summons. What was the point?

'Viru, you little runt, have you called me to add to my troubles or maybe offer some brotherly support, you good-for-nothing!'

'What can *I* do? Can't even take leave for something like this, can I? What do I tell my boss, exactly? Sir, my sister is in trouble with the police for writing dirty stories, then sending them to a criminal who is on the run, I have to go and make sure she's okay … I mean, how does that sound to you?'

'It sounds like the most interesting thing your boss will have heard all day, if not all his life! Definitely more inspiring than having you for a subordinate, you useless …'

And so they had gone on for a while, calling each other names, familiar names and familiar insults, just worded differently, given the context.

'Seriously, do you want me to come, I could be there in two days …'

'Tomorrow, I will be on the train to Simla, so please don't bother.'

'Are you going alone? I forbid it …'

'Who are you, exactly? My "younger" brother, so stop acting like you rule over me. Anyway, I'm going to be accompanied by the police, so I will not need protection, dear brother, don't get your rakhis in a twist, just as yet.'

'I pity the police, I do, you're impossible …'

She had hung up then. He hadn't called back. It was all good.

That evening, they had a visitor. Noor had finished packing Lavanya's suitcase, insisting on fitting in some trinkets that Lavanya had assured her she would never wear. Jaddan Bai who had swished in earlier with a packet of meethi supari, handed it to Noor with a prim 'Baby, you'll see, Lavanya will thank me later for this.' When Deven kaka, Noor's aged help of many years, announced the presence of a certain Surya Kant Sahib in the living room, Noor had just shut the suitcase and was going to pour them a large peg of Green Crown Whisky smuggled surreptitiously from Jaddan Bai's room.

They found him sitting on the edge of the armchair as if he might want to leave at any moment. The initial niceties over and a tall, fortifying glass of sherbet in his hands, he still looked awkward. Lavanya didn't know what to say, she appealed to Noor with a glance. Noor flashed a dazzling smile and showed her dimples.

'I'm going to suggest to my directors that the film industry should shift to Simla too, in the summer, then it will be like Filmla in Simla ...'

It had the desired effect. He laughed and said it was a wonderful idea, indeed.

He started out being apologetic for the late hour but not overtly.

'It's late, yes, but I thought it was important to speak to you before you left for Simla.'

'You will be coming soon too, won't you, Surya Kant Sahib?' Lavanya asked.

'Please call me Surya. Yes, I will let you know when. Is there anything that is bothering you? Do you need any money?'

Lavanya hesitated. It was nice to be asked.

'I'm all right. Thank you,' she said.

'You're not to refuse. The book is selling handsomely. I just want you to know. If you need anything, you have simply to ask. When you get back, we will settle things better.'

She nodded. She caught Noor looking at him, openly admiring.

Surya handed her a card. It had the painting of a buxom naked woman napping under the initials 'AS' that rose like a tree. This was Amrita's calling card? She would have to call on her if things got dull in Simla.

'This is the artist Amrita Sher-Gil's address in Simla. I've sent her a telegram letting her know you will be arriving. You must look her up. You have my contact details too. Please do not hesitate to call if you need anything.' Lavanya nodded, she would. There was something else on his mind. She waited for him to find the words.

'Everybody calls me a recluse and they aren't wrong,' he said, taking a large sip of the sherbet. 'I have scarcely had reason to leave my home, my press, but that has changed now. This is important, this is purposeful, Lavanya. We have a right to our stories, whatever they may be. Why must we be told they are good or bad or dirty or clean? It's unthinkable that they are in our country, exploiting us, our resources, our minds, our lands, but we have to listen to them on what we choose to read and write? I'm going to do my best to not let that happen. As your publisher, I'm going to do everything I can to keep your words free, Lavanya. If we have to go to court to do that, let us.' But he hadn't quite finished. 'I also wanted to let you know that I've decided to act as the lawyer for our hearing. Unless, of course, you have any objections. I have studied law and may I say, studied it well enough. You should have no reason to complain.'

'I'm so glad. This is the best news I've had all day,' Lavanya said, smiling. Noor had held her hand all the while Surya had been speaking.

He left soon after. Noor tried to get him to stay but he had said what he had wanted to say.

If Lavanya was honest, she felt a sense of panic as he left. To be on her own from thereon, suddenly felt terrifying. She even considered not turning up at the station the next day, even disappearing from Bombay, going away to, say, her brother's home in Delhi. Not telling anybody, not even Noor. Then, as hurriedly as it had come, the wave of panic subsided. There was no way back, she simply had to keep moving.

Surya Kant's presence had been so comforting, it had paralyzed her. Made her feel like she wanted to lean on him, to take the weight off herself. Men had that quality, she had to admit. Good men had that quality, she corrected herself. It's just that there were too few of them. So leaning on herself, however troublesome, was a more reliable option.

A score settled

THE ENGLISH GENTLEMAN BABU HAD KILLED THE haggard farmer and hidden the body somewhere it could never be found. Ratan didn't recognize himself as he looked sideways in the gigantic ornate mirror in the Summers' dressing room. The European suit fit him well. The last touch was the hat. Ratan had taken one look at the dusty closet bursting with hats of all shapes and sizes and shut it, only to open it again a while later and choose one, unleashing a minor dust storm in the big airy room. He had just got used to being bathed and clean, and looked at the particles of dust like they didn't belong in his world. None of the grime that came with his recent past seemed to cling to him at this moment as he lingered, catching his scrubbed, clean reflection first from one angle, then another. He tried not looking in the mirror mid-centre but off it. Coming to it from the side, from the edge at times, looking back to catch a glimpse and nothing more. He couldn't bear to see himself in the centre of the mirror in these clothes. Vanity, his fondest flaw, was fast fading.

Intellectual vanity, no sign of it, his father was fond of saying every time he caught Ratan angling himself in the mirror.

Dear Papa,

That was another letter he had begun and not finished.

Dear Ma, too.

The time for letter writing was gone. For sitting at a desk, asking, telling, reassuring, promising, sending. He had to keep moving.

Ratan found the car in the garage, a 1920 Double Cabriolet by Barker, not long before he found the keys which were in a bedside drawer on the first floor. Once in the car, he could hear himself think better. The one thought that kept his eyes bloodshot was Shyam's betrayal. To think that all that time he was sheltering Ratan in that rat-infested shed, Shyam was planning to throw the noose around him. He must have been waiting for the award money to be announced. Once a petty gambler, always a petty gambler, Ratan should have known. He looked sideways at the cricket bat he had carried with him from the bungalow. What pleasure it would be to break it on Shyam's head.

Soon, he was moving slowly on the winding road leading down to the Ridge and the Davenport House. Shyam should be on his way there now to pick up Sir Richard and bring him to work.

Luckily, the Davenport House was in the most secluded part of the row of bungalows where the British army officers lived. Wedged in a corner, with vast grounds on either side, he could easily hide the car in the forest area behind it. From inside the car, he could see all the cars going into the compound. He waited.

After a while, the Benz he had driven every day until just a few days ago, came riding up the hill. Ratan got out of the car to get a better look. He had blocked the road at the turn just before the wrought iron gate to the residence, with a massive shrub. Ratan clambered over quickly to get to the side of the road just in time to see Shyam getting out of the Benz.

Except, it wasn't Shyam. It was Davenport's ADC, Marc Easton. Where was Shyam? Davenport was so particular about who drove him, it had to be Shyam, just like for Sara, it had to be Ratan.

He saw Marc look around concerned, then peer at the shrub with two elegant fingers stroking his chin, before dragging it to the side of the road. Marc, with his long, lean, angular looks had always appeared an artist in an army uniform to Ratan. Except when you caught the military glint in his eyes. Ratan watched as Marc dusted his hands meditatively, got back into the Benz, and slowly drove in.

Ratan remained crouching, long after the Benz disappeared from view. Where was Shyam? If Shyam was sick, he would be at the farm but going there again would be idiotic. By now, the police would only have stepped up their vigilance in the area. He got back in the car and looked at the cricket bat. Shyam owed him some answers. Tyres on dry grass exploding in his ears, he pulled out as softly as he could.

Cocking his hat at a slant, he glanced at the mirror. That's what an idiot looks like, he thought. Sara would tell him that all the time. Tousling his hair and playing with one lock from the middle of his forehead so that it curled up like a question mark right above his nose. She would do that and say, 'Now that's what an idiot looks like.'

She often said, he was so naive that she was certain it was bordering on stupidity. That he had been dropped at birth and that had done his mental faculties a lot of damage. He never minded. She liked teasing him. It was usually preceded by yet another spectacular instance of his attempts to help someone backfiring on him. He would tell her about it, pacing up and down, unable to make sense of what had happened and she'd break it down for him. What was not apparent to him was dead clear to her. And once she did, he had to agree he had been stupid. He should have seen it coming all along.

Why hadn't she warned him about helping Shyam?

What would Sara break down for him now? What wasn't he seeing, for God's sake?

He waited till it was dark and then left for Shyam's farm. His appetite for food and cigarettes had both come back with a vengeance. Nevermore was well stocked with both. He made himself a meaty broth and threw in tinned vegetables with cinnamon and cloves for that familiar aroma of the mutton curry made at home. He ate at the huge dining table and followed it up by smoking one cigarette after another, littering the stubs in the ornately carved gothic planters that lined the dining room.

He even managed to nap for an hour. The skies had turned dark earlier than usual, he could feel the clouds about to burst as he got back into the car covering his face as much as he could with the hat. By the time he neared the farm, it was pouring heavily. He was stopped only once on the way but because of the rain, the drenched policeman had barely looked at him in his Babu clothes and hat, and respectfully waved him on. Once there, he parked the car a little distance away from the farm under a massive oak tree and kept watch until he was certain there was no police lurking. Only the loud thrum of rain pattering on the tin roofs could be heard.

Carrying the cricket bat and covering himself with a huge polythene cover he had found in the back of the car, he moved as fast as he could. Walking along the path behind the trees, he was soon inside the covered area around the house. He looked in through the barred windows. Nothing, nobody, not a sound. Shyam and Cheeni would be at the back or in their first-floor quarters. He pushed the wooden door open and entered, removing the polythene as noiselessly as he could. There was no one at the back of the house either. Slowly, he climbed the rickety wooden stairs to the floor above.

The place was a mess. Shyam's charpai was lying toppled over. The trunks were open, their contents strewn all over like someone had kept tossing, unable to find what he had been looking for. They were mostly Cheeni's saris, blouses and petticoats.

What had happened here? Where were Shyam and Cheeni? Then he saw it, the deliberate, almost decorous trail of clothes. He let go of the cricket bat and started picking up the clothes. There were red stains underneath, blood stains. Someone had strewn the clothes over the bloodstains to cover them up. All the way from where the charpai lay, to the door. He followed the trail of bloody clothes, his head thundering and his legs wobbly, all at once. The trail continued on to the wooden stairs going down too. But it was so dark, he hadn't noticed coming up. He came down and back out, his eyes wild, looking in every direction. It had stopped raining and there was a great wind rustling the leaves on the trees all around. He glanced up and saw the closed barn door across and something started twitching in his head. A writhing, jagged nerve twisted and turned. He went as fast as he could across to the barn. He looked in through the small iron grilled window he knew so well. There was Shyam. His throat slit, lying in a pool of blood.

Shyam crouched and started crawling to get into the barn through the door around the corner. He crawled to the door, pushed it, and got inside. Sidestepping the pool of blood to get to Shyam. His trembling hand attempted to caress his friend's face who he thought had betrayed him. Whose head he had wanted to bash in with a cricket bat. Shyam's plump cheek was cold. It had been a while, how long, he couldn't tell. He smoothed his friend's hair, his tears coming down fast. Shyam looked calm, he had often seen him sleep like this, curled up in the Benz. Ratan slumped down next to Shyam. He couldn't feel his legs. They had gone numb, all the way from his feet up to his legs. Prickling with nothingness.

Two things happened at once that snapped Ratan out of his willing paralysis.

One, Ratan looked up through the window of the barn at the house and saw movement. Then he saw them all over the ground going up to the house. The police were here. This was a trap. They were going to catch him here with the body.

The second was the distinct sensation of Shyam clutching his shirt at the waist. A shiver went through him as he peered down to see Shyam's hands. They were by his side, not on his shirt. Clenched shut into a fist. Ratan tugged at Shyam's clenched fist, prying open the fingers one by one. It was a gold coloured button. He grabbed it, shoved it into his trousers, and crawled out of the barn, shutting the door behind him with his feet. Every movement hurt. The prickling sensation was going all the way to his head. As he willed himself out of the barn, still on his knees, Ratan found himself staring into a pair of worn-out, black-strapped shoes.

He looked up to see a policeman looking down at him, surprised, shocked even. The prickling vanished. Ratan scrambled to his feet, grabbing him as his mouth opened to alert the others. Covering his mouth with one hand and landing a blow with his knuckles, hard into his lower abdomen. The man doubled up and Ratan sat on him, pinning his arms down with his knees. He was sitting on a boy, barely of age. How did they recruit policemen these days?

He removed his gun and whispered into his ear with all the threat he could muster in his shaking voice. 'Open your mouth now and I swear I'll shoot you.'

He uncovered the policeman's mouth and shoved the gun into his mouth, looking into his scared eyes. This was probably his first field outing. He looked away before the boy could see he was equally scared. The rest of them were still in the main house. He should get out while he could. Ratan slowly removed the gun from the boy's mouth, keeping his eyes on the boy, and started walking away. The boy yelled out, the next second. A shrill, piercing unintelligible yell shattered the air. So he had seen the fright in Ratan's eyes. Ratan turned around, shaking, furious. The snivelling little bastard. He took the gun in his hand and hit the boy hard on the head with it, spilling blood and watching him reel as he collapsed in a heap.

He ran into the trees and up the hill behind the barn and past the dirt path strewn with buffalo shit and cow manure. Behind him, he could hear shouts, doors being banged, kicked open, shots being fired, thundering feet in heavy strapped shoes. A stealthy silent operation had turned into a loud raucous mission with the boy's yell. Ratan's hand ached from how hard he had hit the boy. He had made sure the boy wouldn't be yelling again for a while, if at all.

The car was where he had left it, hidden behind the huge deodars.

He got in, shut the door, and threw the gun at the back. His hands groped for the keys to start the car, but there were no keys in the ignition. He remembered leaving them in the car. He checked his pockets and fished out what Shyam had been holding in his fist. Shyam's killer had been wearing a shirt with gold-coloured buttons? With great difficulty, he shook his mind free from the glittering object in his hand. Should he leave the car here and make a run for it? Leaving the car here would mean leading the police right up to the Summers' Bungalow. He couldn't do that. He got out of the car and looked around. The ground started swimming, making him nauseous and he looked up at the sky. It was endlessly blue with a few feathery white clouds floating at their own pace. A flock of birds flew past, in perfect formation, completely unaware of the chaos below. Ratan wanted to bring the gun out and fire into the sky. To see them panic, screech, flap. The keys, where were the keys? Drawing quick, steadying breaths, he got back inside and looked at the ignition point. His gaze dropped down and there they were. A cluster of beautiful metal. Dizzy with relief, he grabbed them and turned on the ignition as the car lurched forward.

Once again, he was running away. Fleeing like a criminal, with blood on his hands. The anger inside him welled up, making him grip the steering wheel harder. Then the tears poured down. First Sara, now Shyam. They were closing in. He was on borrowed time.

A red carpet of letters

LAVANYA PUT HER SUITCASE UNDER THE SEAT AND LOOKED out of the train window at the crowded Victoria Terminus railway station. Amrit Singh had been annoyingly punctual in picking her up, insisting on carrying her suitcase despite her protests. She had kept her eye on him and her suitcase, all the while.

The train had started moving.

She was travelling first class for the first time. Her father had insisted on keeping the family unused to luxury. Even when he was flush with funds from a recent case. Her eyes took in the plush red carpet that lined the compartment and she sighed. She loved red carpets.

The shuttered door to her compartment slid to one side and two sparkling black shoes swam into focus. Her eyes travelled over an immaculate police uniform to rest on Donald Harper. He shut the door behind him and glowered at her.

Instinctively, she rose to her feet. She regretted it the next second.

'You look well, Miss Shriram … do sit down,' he said. 'We have a long journey ahead of us and we wouldn't want our resident author, no matter how *disreputable*, to fall prey to exhaustion, would we?'

'I am well, officer, and may I say, a lot younger than you. Why don't you sit down …' she refused to smile. Piss off, is what she really wanted to say.

He nodded, acknowledging the sarcasm with a slight raise of an eyebrow and sat down across from her. They looked at each other for a while, both expecting the missiles to come from the other party. Then he spoke up.

'You've written to Richard Davenport and expressed an interest to write about his dead wife, I hear. No, don't bother clarifying. I'm sure you mean well. Like your book of stories, mean *well*. Tell me, what makes you think he would want you of all people, to write about her?' he smirked. 'I want you to know that I'm going to do my best to dissuade him.'

'You must, Superintendent. Don't for a moment think I intended to clarify to you, of all people, why I would like to write about her,' Lavanya said, surprised by how calm she sounded.

'Also, your publisher tells me, you've refused to apologize for the filth you've written?'

She ignored the insult. 'If you're asking if I've accepted the court summons, the answer is yes, I have.'

'There's still time. The court will accept an apology even a day before the date of the trial.'

'I too will accept an apology a day before the trial, Superintendent.'

She started looking out of the window now. If he was going to share this compartment with her, she might as well shift into the corridor outside. So much for eyeing the red carpet on the floor.

'Right, then. I thought I'd spare you the trauma of what would follow if you persisted in keeping your stories in circulation. But it doesn't look like you're too worried about your reputation. Your dead parents will never know, but your brothers, I worry for them. Their government jobs are precious, aren't they?'

She looked at him sharply. The bastard. What was he trying to say?

'I don't like the tone of your voice, I don't like what you're trying to imply, maybe I should get down at the next station and make my own way back. I thought I was here to help with the investigation but it doesn't look like you need my help …'

'Both of us know you're going to do nothing of that sort. It is in both our interests to track down Ratan. For you, it's a lot more personal than it is for me. Your name is linked to the crime, you will want to clear your name … so suit yourself, get down if you must … but before I go, here's something you might want to look at.'

He got up and opened the compartment door, sliding it only partially. Amrit Singh's huge hand did the rest. He came in with a parcel in his hand. It was substantive. On getting the nod from his boss, he took a knife from his pocket, and tore open the parcel. A stack of letters and postcards spilled out. Amrit Singh cupped them back into the parcel and handed them over to Lavanya.

'The power of your writing … here's proof,' Donald Harper said. 'What you didn't see the other day at the station because you left the story incomplete. Your publisher has made sure the country is not thus deprived. The full story is now out there in circulation in most newspapers and magazines, too. And your readers are writing to you … so here you go. Your publisher may never show you these love letters so we have taken the liberty to bring them to you. This is just a small sample of the mail you've been getting. I hope you enjoy reading them.'

They both left her staring at the pile of letters in her lap and a copy of the paper where Sitara's story had been coming out in instalments in an exclusive agreement with Surya's publishing house.

She picked up a postcard. There was none of the Dear Lavanya that letters usually begin with. She read the few lines that thrashed into her line of vision in capital letters. 'SHAME ON YOU AND YOUR FAMILY! WHICH WOMAN THINKS SUCH FILTH? WERE YOU BORN IN THE GUTTER? THEN GO BACK THERE …'

She picked up another and then another, her eyes smarting at the sting from the words. The words jumped out. '*Randi …*' 'Whore …' 'trash …' 'Die …' 'Murderer …'

As the train hurtled on at top speed, she slipped down onto the red carpet, the parcel of letters still in her lap. They spread around her like a crumpled hand fan. She had spared her parents, at least. All the hiding she would have had to do. Stuffing all these letters under her bed and sleeping on them, night after night, letting the hate seep into her bones.

Sitara's story (cont.)

Indian Times, 15 February 1936.

THE STORY BY LAVANYA SHRIRAM EVERYONE IS WAITING TO FINISH.

SITARA CROUCHED IN A CORNER OF THE ROOM LOOKING AT the door that was shuddering. The hammering on the door had not stopped since she had locked herself in. She knew it was just a matter of time before the door gave way, despite the bed she had pulled in front of it to block the door. She knew she couldn't sit there anymore, waiting for it to happen. She may have grown deaf to the shouted pleas from behind the door, the veiled threats, the sudden wails convulsed by grief, but she knew better. The louder the wails and the beating of the chest, the louder was the intent to see her engulfed by the flames. Till that happened, there would be no peace for her, for them. This was her extended family, an entire village. People who had cared for her when she was ill and consoled her when she was homesick, for she had been but an adolescent when she had come to the village. They had been mothers and fathers, brothers and sisters, and now all they wanted was for her to do her duty by setting herself aflame. Then they would all hang their heads and march home in unison, get into their warm beds and sleep, tired and spent. Her ashes still smeared on their hands.

Sitara stood up and walked over to where her trunk lay open on the cot. She pulled out her blood-red wedding lehenga and spread it out. She had described it so often to her Angrez. How beautiful she had felt wearing it at fourteen. How smooth her legs had felt caressing the silk of the fabric as she stood for hours waiting to garland an aged man who would not meet her eyes. They had talked about how she could bring it with her next time. How he would untie the low-cut choli at the back and remove it slowly as he slipped his other hand under her billowing lehenga, in between her silken thighs. They would re-enact her wedding night, the way it should have been.

That meeting had never taken place. Now here she was, slipping it on. Tying the threads of the lehenga tight. Tying the back of her choli the best she could. She took her time with her shringaar. Smearing the lipstick over her mouth, darkening the kajal under her eyes, painting on her forehead a bindi with red fragrant powder. The last thing she did was tie her thick long hair into a coiled bun at the back of her head.

Then she walked over and opened the door. She stood there, letting them run their eyes over her. Satisfy themselves of the suitability of her attire and her grooming. How they fussed over her then. The women covered her head with her odhni, lovingly touched her face, made promises they knew they could not keep. The men ushered her forward, clearing the way, looking grief-stricken one moment, barking orders the next. All the preparations for the pyre had begun. The entire village scurried back and forth, all around her. She walked on. Kisses were raining down her face, fingers leaping to caress her, teary goodbyes. She didn't register a single face.

Her Angrez was leading her on, his was the only face she saw. Inches away from her, she could smell him, the fragrance of his skin as it rubbed against hers. She inhaled deeply.

On the pyre, the wooden sticks rubbed against each other as if finding their positions to lay down for the night. Perched on them, Sitara felt their heat even before the flaming torch had touched the wood. With the first lick of the flame, her toes uncurled themselves and her back arched itself upright. Her hand reached out to untie her hair, then her choli. She moved it down her left breast. Her nipples were erect and alive to her touch. The flames were picking up slowly. She was clearly visible to her grief-stricken, bloodthirsty audience. There was a collective gasp as they stared at her lifting her breast and licking at it, sucking it noisily. Then as her other hand lifted up her lehenga and slid up between her thighs, they looked at each other in horror.

Holding their sticks in place, the two pyre-keepers inched closer. To prevent her from running away when the flames got too hot. Sometimes the sticks wouldn't be enough. They had to catch them in mid-flight, by their singed hair, to bring them back to the pyre. Other times, they tied the women or chained them to iron weights at the bottom of the pyre if they kept trying to run away. Sitara posed no such challenge. She sat there like a yogini. Her hair spread out, one hand touching her nipple, the other hand under the waist of her lehenga. Her eyes and mouth were set in deep rapture.

Gopi, the elder pyre-keeper was the first to drop his stick. The few who could tear their eyes away from Sitara, watched him walk away in a daze. The younger pyre-keeper watched him leave, his mouth open to call out to him but no sound came. Soon, one by one, everyone dropped their eyes. Some waited to walk away with the others. Some left alone. Nobody spoke about what they saw. They would only find the words days later. And when the words came, they were barely audible. Hushed and low, cowered and ashamed, disbelieving and shaken.

Sitara on her flaming throne sat, swaying to the beat of her glass bangles that moved in an unbroken harmony. She let herself feel her Angrez deep inside her. Holding on till he had consumed her and then her hips bucked and she opened her mouth to let out a scream. Not a tiny one but one that would reverberate in the forests of her village forever.

The end.

Bhai and a plan

RATAN SPED UP THE ROAD AWAY FROM THE FARM, WITH one word bouncing off the walls of his mind. Why?

First Sara, now Shyam. Why would anyone kill them and make it look like he had done it? Why? He was certain Shyam had died because of him, if he hadn't involved him, he'd still be alive. Cheeni? Where was she? Why was Sara killed? He forced himself to think back, anything Sara might have said that implied she was in danger…that laughing face, those teasing eyes, had there been an untold fear behind them?

Her hands locking her desk. A picture flashed across his mind. She had been so particular about locking her desk in her study and keeping the key hidden. He would never have given it a second thought, just noticing those hands fluttering at the desk as they were about to leave. Then once, she had got in the car and suddenly remembered she hadn't locked her desk. He had already driven out of the gate when her hand had flown to her mouth and she had stifled a mild gasp, asking him to stop at once. Ratan had offered to lock it for her as they drove back to the porch. She had ignored his request and run back, her hands lifting up her skirt petticoats to hurry up the steps in the garden. That had got him mildly curious. She had, of course, brushed his questions aside and deftly changed the subject.

Her hands locking her desk.

His hands were firm on the wheels, his breathing even and for the first time since that cold wet night when he had found Sara on the grounds of the Wildflower Hall, he felt calm. Nothing like people you've known and loved dying around you to give you a sense of perspective, he thought drily. He was done with the scurrying around, the hiding, the wondering what he had done to deserve this happening to him. He had to *know*. What exactly was going on? Maybe start with getting back into the Davenport House, somehow, getting to that desk. He glanced back at the gun he had taken from the police boy's holster. It was smeared with the boy's blood. It must be loaded. The last time he had held a gun was when he was working for Shafaqat Bhai. He knew there was no putting off that visit to Bhai anymore.

Half an hour later, he stopped inside the thickly populated gully of a marketplace he had visited often when he worked for Bhai. Bhai owned all the gambling halls in Simla. He should have come to Bhai a long time back, but he had always known involving Bhai meant giving up all control of the consequences.

Bhai operated out of a sprawling flat on top of the local cinema house. A pitch-dark and steep flight of steps later, he came up onto a sunlit terrace. He took a sharp left, then a right into a dimly lit corridor, entering the suite that was Bhai's office. He removed the hat shadowing half his face as he looked at the two men who were approaching him, their hands on their guns. Ratan smiled and the men stopped in their tracks.

'Ratan, saaley!' Deven said as he covered the distance between them with quick strides, engulfing him in a quick embrace. Deven and Ali were Bhai's main men. Bhai didn't do a thing without taking them along with him. When Ratan started working with Bhai, Deven and Ali were like his first bosses, training him and teaching him the ropes of the business.

Bhai had gone to have lunch with his family. No calamity or crisis had ever been big enough for Bhai to miss lunch with his wife and daughter. He was expected any time now.

After he had arrived at Simla from Suraiah, he had boarded for a short while with a young doctor, who had found himself in a legal dispute over a case gone wrong. He had helped him out, advising him on how to present his testimony in court. The doctor, impressed with Ratan's knowledge of law and his ability to speak both Hindi and English, had sent him to his brother, an accountant who worked for Bhai. The accountant had convinced Bhai that Ratan would be an asset to his business.

It had started at an exciting pace. Ratan had dressed nattily and met with all of Bhai's clients, charming them, luring them to play more, stay more, drink more.

He had looked the other way too, when they couldn't pay more. Or less. Sometimes catching the spilled blood on his clothes before he could turn away.

The money Bhai made, he gave most of it away. Ratan shared cigarettes often enough with the accountant, so he knew. The organizations were called by many names but mostly they were all the same. Groups fighting for independence and self-rule with all the resources they could get. Bhai supported as many as he could, with a vengeance far more cold-blooded than what he used to rule his gambling empire. So many Europeans used his dens but none were the wiser about his real motives.

It would have continued to go well for Ratan if he had had his eyes on the darkening sky. If he had noticed that Bhai's daughter, Saba, had developed feelings for him.

One day, he had gone as usual to deliver an important message to Bhai at his home in the evening. He had found her alone. She was a rosy-cheeked girl with an infectious laugh and the most humorous way of narrating the most ordinary happenings that had everyone giggling at every gathering. Ratan had taken an instant liking to her but had been very careful to stay the 'humble employee', knowing the trouble he could get into.

'Sit for a moment, won't you? I want to read you my poems …' she had said.

This had so reminded him of Lavanya that he couldn't help but smile and sit down for a bit. He had also hoped Bhai would be back soon and he could deliver his message.

The session of poetry ended with Ratan coming to the quick conclusion that all the lovelorn verses weren't just for his listening pleasure, they were *for* him. Now that he had heard what she had kept hidden in her heart, what was he going to do about it?

Muttering many 'beautiful'-sounding compliments, he had sprung to his feet, remembering an urgent appointment. At once, her face had crumpled and her eyes teared up. Where was the girl with the infectious laugh and the giggly eyes? She had grabbed his hand and launched herself at his chest with such force that he lost his balance and held on to her.

It had not gone according to plan. Maybe he held on to her for a second longer than he intended to. He didn't know what exactly he did or didn't do, but he knew she thought he was in love with her but too scared of her father to do anything about it. She thrust the crumpled poetry sheets into his coat pockets and hid her face in her hands as he left.

The next day, he noticed a distinct change in Bhai's behaviour towards him. It was subtle but there was a sinister coldness that he could not shrug away.

It was in that frame of mind that he had met the Davenports. They had come to Bhai's card parlour, the one exclusively for his English clients, and Ratan had played the good host. Richard had grown tired soon and left, Sara had stayed on to play some more, and Ratan had gallantly offered to drop her home in Bhai's Packard. They had not spoken a word more than was necessary. Yet he knew that she knew he was more than enamoured by her. All of her. It was a rough beauty, the kind that had an edge you wanted to touch, to feel. From her throaty laugh to her commanding presence, she was a woman who could take over any space she inhabited.

Sara came by the next day, offering to double whatever Bhai was paying him if he came to work for her. He was to be her personal assistant, which included driving her exclusively. She assured him she would speak to Bhai about it herself. She knew he wouldn't refuse her.

By then he had had enough of the dark, dimly lit dens where the chandeliers swayed to the beat of the money being counted endlessly; seen enough of those who walked in with eyes that were glazed and hopeless. He was curious about the white-pillared, curved corridors of bungalows and clubs where people laughed, no, tinkled, without a worry in their heads.

Bhai had refused to meet him when he went to say goodbye.

The sound of heavy steps stopped Ratan's reverie and he saw Deven and Ali snap to attention. A door slammed. Birds twittering in the courtyard trees flew away, flapping their wings.

Bhai walked into his den, wearing a thick scarf around his neck like it was a coiled snake. It was his signature look. There was something sinister and coiled about Bhai too, something his enemies feared and his own people revered. Ratan had never been able to make up his mind if he feared Bhai or looked up to him.

Bhai took one look at Ratan and sighed dramatically, waving his hands in the air as if to say only Allah could predict what would happen next. Ratan knew Bhai well enough to know that this was a sign he was alive with excitement. Bhai was a small man with a big moustache. He played with it like women played with their hair. When he was excited, he played with it incessantly. He patted the ends into place as he sat down on the gaddis that lined his chair. Then took the end bristles of his luxurious moustache in his wiry fingers and tugged at them this way and that. He was getting ready to address him and Ratan knew he had to wait for the first words.

'Finally, you come to me, haan? First you defect, go work with the enemy, then you seek me out. But you're wasting your time. I can't help you now. No one can help you now,' Bhai said.

Deven and Ali left the room.

'Bhai, I know I should have come earlier but I didn't want to involve you till it became absolutely necessary … Sara was murdered and I found her …'

'I know all about that. Do you think I don't know? I've been sitting here wondering, when will Ratan show up and say "Bhai, help me!" But no, you only wanted to get away from me. What do you want from me now? You should never have left me for *her*. For *them*. She was playing with you. Women are gamblers by nature and she knew you were a player.'

'Bhai, it's not just Sara … Shyam is dead too.' Ratan's voice broke. He could see Shyam in the barn, sprawled, fish eyes and plump cheeks, asleep to the world, forever.

Bhai knew Shyam, a regular defaulter at his dens. All his father's fields and farm would have belonged to Bhai if Ratan had not stepped in and pleaded with Bhai to give him a breather, assuring him Shyam would give his money back soon. Sara too had sent word to Bhai, saying she would stand surety for Shyam. Some of the money had been returned. The rest, it was now clear, Bhai would have to forget about. Bhai did not like forgetting.

Ratan told Bhai how he had come by Shyam's body in the barn and how the next second he had heard the police storm in.

'Bhai, somebody is trying to frame me. I saw this figure running past the car and into the woods behind Wildflower Hall. Maybe one, maybe two? The police … they're involved somehow. How did they know I was going to be at the bus stand that morning? They seem to know *everything*. They even knew I was going to go back to Shyam's farm. They laid the trap and I walked into it! But Bhai, I have a gun now, a police gun, but that's not what I need. I need *information.* I need to stay ahead of them. I need to find out who is behind this and why … why me, Bhai?' He knew he was blabbering and he didn't care.

'Ratan, you're in shock and you're not thinking straight. It's a miracle you're still a free man. No, don't tell me the sordid details, I don't want to know more than I know already. You need to get out of Simla and I can help you do that, the rest is way over your head. And mine too, maybe.'

'I'm not going anywhere till I find out who is behind this. If you won't help me, I'll do it on my own,' Ratan said, surprised his voice was no longer shaking.

Bhai played with his moustache as he contemplated Ratan's decision. If he was exasperated, he didn't show it. Then he seemed to think of something that had been on his mind and after briefly rummaging under his desk, he pulled out a newspaper cutting and slid it across to Ratan.

'I presume, you know her …?'

God. She looked nothing like the Lavanya he remembered, yet there she was, unmistakably her. Looking at the camera like it wasn't there or rather like it was some minor obstruction in her path that would pass and she would soon be on her way again.

The *Simla Times* headline read 'Controversial author to visit scene of crime'.

'Lavanya … this isn't good news, Bhai. She shouldn't be coming here,' Ratan said, shaking his head.

'Good news? You're expecting good news in the times we live in?' Bhai laughed. 'Good news, my dearest, is on the run like you are. Like you, it is being kicked around like a common thug, a common *refugee*,' Bhai said with a snarl. 'You know the real reason she's being brought here, don't you?'

'To draw me out ...' Ratan said.

'So will you attempt to establish contact with her ...?'

'No, of course I won't,' he forced himself to say.

'I think you should ...'

Ratan looked at Bhai. His eyes were shining. For the first time since they had begun talking, Bhai, although excited by Ratan's predicament, had not seemed at all hopeful. Now, he did. Ratan could see why.

There was no better way to draw the killer out.

There wasn't a more dangerous way either. For Lavanya, especially.

Bhai could smell both. Danger and success. Ratan hoped he had done the right thing by coming to him.

'Now tell me about this book of stories your friend has penned. The one found beside Sara that night. With your name on it.'

In your room

LAVANYA GOT OFF THE TRAIN AND TOOK IN GULPS OF THE sprightly Simla breeze to steady herself. The last leg of the journey had been hours of winding through hills and stations, darting through a hundred or more tunnels with passengers letting out bloodcurdling screams in the dark just to hear themselves.

Even though the small little station was swarming with people, coolies and monkeys, there was that unmistakable mountain air that had found its way into the train, as if wanting to be the first to greet the newly arrived at the hill station. The breeze tasted of something toasty. Like the melting flavours of freshly roasted pine nuts on a sizzling tava.

Weary and dusty but momentarily soothed, Lavanya could see why the British wanted to claim Simla for their own.

Donald Harper had kept to himself after their initial meeting and Lavanya was thankful for that. She could see him now walking towards her with Amrit Singh in tow. All shiny shoes and slicked-back hair, Donald Harper cut through the mountain breeze with the grimace she had never seen him without. She braced herself and without realizing it, ran her hands through her hair in an attempt to look a fraction as slick as him.

'Miss Shriram, well done. I have received word that Sir Richard would like to meet you today evening for an early dinner. You will be taken to your lodgings by Inspector Amrit Singh. We will visit the scene of the crime tomorrow. Inspector Singh will take you through our findings so far. I have nothing more to say to you, Miss Shriram.'

Having delivered his message like he was testing bullets at a firing range, Donald Harper nodded dismissively at her and turned to walk away. His men began to brief him urgently as they walked together.

So Donald Harper had not been listened to. Lavanya wanted to do a little foxtrot. She kept a straight face, eyes wide, watching his receding back.

Lavanya was still looking in his direction when she saw him stop sharply in his tracks, his face darkening as he shot back questions to his men who struggled to reply. Now he turned and looked at her, glaring. What had she done now?

Two men with cameras came bounding out of nowhere and started taking pictures of her. Like flies, they were in her face. There was no permission-taking, no being nice. The next second, Amrit Singh was herding them off and the photographers, knowing they had got what they wanted, dutifully walked off.

As Amrit Singh led her out of the station, Lavanya wondered how the newspapers knew she was in Simla. Who was briefing them?

Just then, a coolie, looking the other way and carrying a massive suitcase, collided with her, causing her to lose her balance and drop the shawl she was holding in her hand. The next second, he was apologizing profusely and picking up her shawl, folding it neatly and handing it back to her, constantly bowing and keeping his eyes down.

Feeling jostled and suddenly aware of the swelling crowds in such a small space, including the constant clatter of monkeys on the roofs of the station, Lavanya stopped, anxious and cold. As she took the shawl from him to quickly wrap around herself, she felt her hands brushing against crisp paper tucked inside the folds. The coolie had slipped her something along with the shawl. Now panic-stricken, she turned to see the coolie briskly walking away and caught him looking back at her for a fraction of a second before he disappeared in the crowd.

She gripped the shawl tightly in her hands, making sure the folds were pressing the paper firmly in place. She couldn't wear it now, she realized. Amrit Singh was waiting impatiently for her just a little ahead, she kept her head down and walked towards him.

They reached the police jeep and Amrit Singh offered to hold her shawl so she could climb up inside.

'It's cold ... I think I'll need my shawl,' Lavanya said quickly.

Lavanya transferred the paper to her other hand, crumpling it into a ball as she wore her shawl over her sweater. She shivered a little and got into the back of the jeep. The inspector got in the front.

Once they were on their way, she uncurled her fist. She was alone in the back of the jeep. Amrit Singh was catching up with his subordinate as they drove through the throng of people outside the station.

She held the crumpled paper as low as she could under the seat and slowly smoothened it out.

The writing was familiar. Her stomach did an uncomfortable tumble as she recognized Ratan's hand. There were three words written on the note. *In your room.*

Amrit Singh walked before her as he led her into a sprawling guesthouse bungalow called Birchwood on the Ridge near the Mall Road. A nod at the receptionist and they went up the winding, carpeted stairs as her mind buzzed at the prospect of seeing Ratan.

She took in the gorgeous rococo interiors, the richness of the wooden banister under her fingers. There was wallpapered fabric on the walls, a profusion of roses and geraniums in vases all around, and the huge baroque chandeliers glittered as the glass caught the sunlight, and yet she was aware of how precarious her situation truly was.

The inspector opened the door to her room, went inside, and gestured to his men to check the place. *In your room*, the note had said.

It was an opulent room by any standard—a four-poster bed, silk tapestries and centuries-old oil paintings in heavy wooden frames. The carpets and rugs were thick and finely threaded. She would enjoy walking barefoot here.

The policemen were looking everywhere, under the bed, inside cupboards, in the washroom, behind curtains and she was right behind them, her heart in her mouth. Was he hiding here? Would he be so stupid?

Then they were all gone. Amrit Singh stood at the door, she could see he was going to say something significant.

'Just a piece of advice, Madam.' Lavanya cringed at the word 'advice' and waited.

'Your childhood friend is no longer the same person you once knew. He is dangerous. He is a killer. If he tries to contact you, please let us know. Somebody will be outside this bungalow at all times. Only for your safety. Please be mindful.'

She could see them stationed outside. There was no conceivable way for Ratan to establish contact with her here.

Two hours later, Lavanya woke up to two distinct sounds. One was the low deep growl in her tummy. She was amazed at the realization that she was hungry. She didn't remember the last time she had acknowledged her stomach with such reverence.

The second sound was coming from under the carpet on the side of the bed. It was a persistent knock knock knock knock.

She leapt out of bed and began pulling the carpet off. Except, the carpet was heavy and she had to finally slide it off to reveal the wood-panelled floor below. The knocking was louder now.

She stared hard at the wooden floor. What was she supposed to do? She bent down and knocked back on the floor where she thought the knocks were coming from. She saw the tiny latch then. A patchily painted brown latch to cleverly camouflage with the wood. She slowly shifted the latch to unlock it, as it flew back on her face at once.

'Ow!'

'I'm sorry, I'm sorry, you okay? Lava ...?'

Ratan's head emerged from under the floor. That familiar mop of hair with an unfamiliar beard on a face that had aged.

He looked so different from the boy she remembered growing up with. The eyes were the same, though. Always glinting with a kind of yearning. For trouble, for adventure, for connection; there was so much Ratan yearned for, it made her dizzy.

It was so good to see him. She felt her eyes smart at how good it felt and even though he was still half under the floor, she scrambled forward to hug him, managing to cradle his head instead.

He hugged her back, putting his arms around her awkwardly, and they stayed like that, breathing audibly for several moments, before her stomach growled again.

She heard a low chuckle as she finally let go of him.

'It's really good to see you too.'

'Rat … I don't believe it, I'm hungry. I haven't eaten for years, I think.'

'Of all the things you can't believe, is it really this we must talk about?' Ratan's eyes, dead serious a moment back, were crinkling.

'I can't concentrate, I'm sorry, of course, I can't believe any of this too … are you going to stay under here or … it's not safe …'

'Lava, listen to me. I need your help to make sense of this situation. We'll talk more later but right now, I need you to get me into the Davenport House. I have a hunch that what I'm looking for is there … Sara, she had this drawer in her study she kept locked. There's something there she didn't want me to see. I need to find the key and open it …'

She nodded. Then not knowing what to say, she nodded again.

'Wait, you don't think I did it, do you?' he asked, peering at her.

Before she could shake her head, there was a sharp knock on her door.

'I better go. We'll talk again. Find Sara's study. There's a small door there that opens into the garden. Unlatch it for me ...'

'How did you know I was going there because I wasn't, until ...'

The knocks were sharper now.

'Go! Just do as I say ... I have to get in tonight ... I don't have much time.'

'Do you realize it's not just about you? They are going to ban the book ... they think it was Sitara's story that provoked you to attack ...'

'Provoked me? Lava ...?' he looked at her. She realized what she had unwittingly blurted out.

He didn't wait for her to explain, he simply took a step down and let the wooden panel slide shut over him.

Lavanya had just managed to open and shut her mouth when the door crashed open.

The carpet was still askew and the brown-colored latch that was invisible a few moments before looked only too conspicuous now. She rose from the floor just as Amrit Singh burst in, his eyes wildly scanning the room.

'What is going on? How dare my door be broken down like this? Leave now!'

Luckily, she was on the other side of the bed where the floor wasn't visible. All angry flashing eyes, shaken body language, arm flung out with a finger pointed squarely at the door. Just as quickly as Amrit Singh had entered, with a panic-stricken maid in tow, he hurriedly retreated. The maid too retreated, taking the tea trolley out with her.

'Stop! Leave the tea behind, please!' She managed to keep her voice angry and stern.

The maid nervously but quickly rolled in the trolley and without so much as glancing at her, exited, closing the door behind her softly.

Lavanya skipped across the bed and in two or maybe three big strides, managed to get to the tea tray. Outside, she could hear Amrit Singh telling the maid off for creating unnecessary alarm.

There was tea inside a beautiful blue and white porcelain kettle but Lavanya had eyes only for the sandwiches, scones and cakes. Bless the British for their lavish tea customs; Indians had no concept of what a tea tray should look like. If only Noor could see her now. In less than five minutes, she had managed to devour all the sandwiches, all the scones, and most of the little cakes and if she stopped, it was only when she remembered that she had more or less promised Ratan that she would visit the Davenport home and somehow allow him access inside.

The most wanted man in Simla. Isn't that what Amrit Singh had called him?

Lavanya sipped on the long leaf tea from a delicate gold rimmed cup and stared long and hard at where she had last seen Ratan's head emerge from.

If she wasn't a co-conspirator before, she would certainly be one now.

You have been warned

LAVANYA STOOD STARING AT HER OPEN SUITCASE. Something was very, very wrong but she couldn't make head or tail of it. So she simply stood there as if by the very act of looking hard and long at the unfamiliar contents of her suitcase, an answer would emerge. She owned only cotton khadi kurtas and salwars and a couple of chunnis in mulmul. In sombre unadventurous colours, mostly shades of white, grey, black and brown. She was particular about who stitched them, how the cut had to be minimal, non-fussy, and all kurtas had to come with pockets.

The clothes in front of her were not hers. She picked up a long, brocade slinky gown with thin straps and held it against herself in the mirror. The colour was a shade of rose from the South of France she had once seen in a magazine in Jaddan Bai's room at Krishna Mahal.

There seemed to have been a terrible mix-up at the railway station. Had the same kohl-eyed man who slipped her a note from Ratan also switched her suitcase with this one, full of posh, glitzy clothes? She had heard about dacoits disguised as coolies roaming stations to pounce at baggage and whisk it away before the passenger was fully aware.

Later, much later, after she had found her lace underthings folded under the silks and brocades did a face swim into her vision. It was Noor. It had to be Noor.

Noor had been busy the few days Lavanya had stayed with her. She had tried to draw Lavanya out of the haze of self-pity she had enveloped herself in, endlessly contemplating the court case, Ratan's state of mind, Donald Harper's insinuations, how her neighbours had looked at her as she locked up the house. Then, fed up, Noor had left to attend to 'important work' even though she had promised Lavanya she had freed up her calendar just to be with her. Not that Lavanya had protested her absence, content to lie on her side of the bed, staring into space, in the same foetal position all-day long.

Now that she knew it was Noor, the contents of the suitcase were no longer surprising. All the cotton and khadi had been replaced with Noor's love for silk and brocade. In shades of black, ivory, blush and powder blue. Thank god for black, the rest of the colours she had not worn since she was old enough to choose her own clothes. Noor's fancy darzi had cut the garments like she was about to attend an opera with the Queen of England. Something Noor would like to do, no doubt. She wanted to shake her hard. She sat down, contemplating the next few days wearing these ridiculously plush clothes. A while later, with a crumpled face, fearing the knocks on the door again, she chose a grey-black silk kameez with tapered ankle-length pants and a turquoise, feathered cape to go with it. She looked at herself in the mirror. Like a mermaid had decided to attend a ball. She opened her vanity case and sure enough, there was a plethora of eye shadows, powders and foundations to choose from. It took her several minutes to find her old, worn-out black kajal. On a whim, feeling as unlike herself as possible, she dabbed on red lipstick—there were no other shades for her to choose from. There was another little box for trinkets and Lavanya avoided it. Her purse, she left behind. It was too big for these clothes.

She made a mental note to send Noor a crisply worded telegram stating exactly what she thought of her and her manipulative ways.

When she emerged from the guesthouse and tentatively walked across the lawn in her new clothes and old faithful brogues, she was, once again, struck by the breeze that greeted her. She had never felt anything this good, this pure, this hunger-inducing. Donald Harper was impatiently holding the car door open. If he thought she looked oddly different, there wasn't a muscle twitch to express it. They rode in silence, and before she had time to compose a set of questions for the evening ahead, they were driving into a huge tree-lined estate with manicured lawns on either side and a circular porch, where, flanked by servants, was a dapper, long-lashed Englishman waiting for them.

She clambered out, inwardly rolling her eyes at the way the silk rustled self-importantly against her skin. Donald Harper did the bare introductions, his mouth set in a thin line. 'This is Miss Lavanya Shriram and this is Marc Easton, Sir Davenport's chief aide.'

'Welcome. I am well-acquainted with Miss Shriram. She is rather famous, isn't she?' Marc Easton's elegant hand held hers in a firm but comfortable handshake.

Donald Harper declined to comment and kept his polite, disinterested expression on as they walked inside.

'Superintendent, how's the investigation going then? Hope to catch up with you on that front. Sir Davenport will be joining us in just a little while. It's been a difficult time as you know, and with the new development …'

Marc Easton ushered them into a grand foyer leading to a living room that was spacious, well-lit and warm. The servants stayed close at hand. They were sizing her up frankly, top to bottom. It was for them then that Noor had whipped up such a sartorial storm. She would seem alien and exotic to them, no doubt. Silkily dressed, red-mouthed, English-speaking and invited to an important British man's home for supper. She tried to engage silently with each of them, letting them know that she was one of them. Indian, not British. They did not make eye contact, except for a young girl with heavy bags under her kohl-lined eyes. She was constantly looking at Lavanya and then quickly looking away. Lavanya's low-heeled brogues rang out on the polished floors of the impressive hall lined with chandeliers.

Looking around the living room, taking in the art on the walls, the gorgeous carpet under her feet, the assortment of lamps and artifacts, Lavanya could feel Sara's touch everywhere.

'Eden, my wife, this is Miss Shriram. She is a writer, as we know, a famous one, too. She has very kindly offered to write about Sara and the wonderful work she had been doing.' Marc Easton was introducing her to a beautiful but nervous-looking lady with melting eyes and a waist that reminded you of a ring to wear on your finger. In a satin gown with a ruffled neck and long flowing sleeves, she looked very fashionable, if a bit shaken.

'Famous? Notorious, perhaps,' Lavanya offered. There was no point in adding that the reason she was even known was because of the murder.

'Yes, notorious is a far more exciting word, I do approve of your choice of words, Miss Shriram,' Marc Easton, amused, nodded at her, including his wife in the banter.

'It's a pleasure,' Eden smiled, a nervous tic playing near her mouth that twitched up and down as she held out her hand. Unlike her husband, her hands were cold and clammy. Her voice was soft and gracious, though.

'I do adore your dress, Miss Shriram, it is very fetching on you.'

'Thank you and please call me Lavanya.'

Donald Harper stood far away, not making any effort to join them. Marc Easton excused himself to go to him and soon, they seemed to be deep in conversation over something that seemed to involve the superintendent looking indignant, trying to explain himself.

Lavanya enjoyed the sight, trying to keep him in her line of vision as Eden led her to a sofa at the far edge of the room.

'Sara would have liked to meet you …' Eden said. Lavanya looked at her to understand better what she meant.

'She would read passages out to me … she said you wrote for every woman … not just your own …' Eden spoke haltingly.

'I would have liked to meet her too …' Lavanya meant it.

'So are you going to help find Ratan?' Eden asked.

'I don't know how I can do that … but I want to try …' Lavanya tried to keep her gaze away from Eden. She didn't want her to see any trace of guilt in her eyes. She saw Donald Harper walking very purposefully towards them. Marc Easton seemed to have drifted away.

'We should meet again soon … there's a lot I'd like to talk to you about …' Eden's hesitant invitation was cut short by Donald Harper's bristling presence. He was standing over her, his eyes blinding her with ill-disguised rage.

'Miss, if you know where your friend is hiding and don't tell us, I will personally put you behind bars, do you hear?'

'That's enough, Superintendent.'

A much older, very handsome, very distinguished-looking man spoke, as he walked towards them. This must be Sir Davenport, Lavanya thought, as she continued to shake inwardly at Donald Harper's outburst, a moment back.

'Miss Shriram is a guest here today and I will not have her disrespected at my home.'

'Sir Davenport, thank you for inviting me. I'm really sorry to hear about your loss.' Lavanya got up as Sir Davenport extended his hand to shake hers. She liked him immediately. Then she turned to Donald Harper.

'Superintendent, I've said this to you before. You do not intimidate me. If you speak to me like that again, here or anywhere else, I will not co-operate in this investigation that you obviously have no control over.'

'Miss Lavanya, do sit down. Let us all breathe a little. Can I offer you a glass of red?' Richard Davenport said.

'I'm having a particularly lovely 1920 French Bordeaux blend …' Marc Easton was back and his long-lashed eyes were now locking with Donald Harper intently.

The maid with the tired eyes magically surfaced with a wine decanter and glasses. Lavanya was thirstier than she had ever been. She wanted the entire decanter to herself.

'Yes, a glass of red should be quite apt,' Donald Harper was in no mood to be calmed down. He continued, 'Considering your friend Ratan Seth has been busy making the town redder. Marc, have you told our author here, we have had yet another murder and by morning, the red count could go up to *three*?'

'It is unfortunate and we are shocked and aggrieved …' Marc Easton began. The next second, Donald Harper took over.

'Oh bloody hell, shocked and aggrieved, indeed. Let me spare you the theatrics, Miss Shriram, even though you thrive on it. Sir Davenport's personal driver Shyam has been murdered at his own farm. Not just that, that low scum Ratan was found right next to the dead man, and tried to kill a policeman who is fighting for his life in the hospital as we speak. We should have his testimony soon enough. If he survives another day, that is,' Donald Harper said.

'And now if you'll excuse me, I've had a very tiring day and the next few days don't look easy either. Please enjoy your *red,* Miss Shriram. We shall meet tomorrow for a frank and uninterrupted session where I'll brief you on how you can help us. For isn't that why you're here, after all?'

His eyes held hers tauntingly.

Donald Harper nodded at Sir Davenport, Marc Easton, barely glanced at Eden, and with a precise turn of his heel, marched out.

Lavanya tried to absorb what she had just heard. Ratan was involved in two more murders. She was an accomplice already. She hadn't been before, but she was one now. She was withholding evidence even as she stood there, holding her glass shakily.

She took a large sip of the Bordeaux as the rest of them tried to keep the conversation going about Shyam and how devoted he had been to Richard, always. Lavanya took another large sip as she saw the maid from the corner of her eye, she looked like there was a war raging inside.

'I'd like to use the washroom, please,' Lavanya downed her glass and got up.

Marc Easton gestured to the maid to escort her.

'This way, Madam,' she said.

Lavanya followed her out, a little unsteadily. The wine was working fast. She wondered how she could lose the maid and find Sara's study. Ratan was somewhere in the vicinity, waiting to be let in. She shook her head in an attempt to think straight.

They were outside the living room now and walking towards a corridor of rooms on either side. It could be any one of these doors.

'I need some paper, please, I need to write a note for the superintendent urgently ...' Lavanya looked at the maid, feigning an anxious, urgent look.

The maid looked taken aback.

'Paper ...?'

'Yes, any paper should do, is there a study here ...?'

The maid walked over to a door and hesitatingly opened it and stood outside.

Lavanya went in, her heart beating. She tried to get her bearings, trying to find the door Ratan wanted her to leave open. She didn't have a clue. She walked over to the table, looking to see if the maid could see her. She couldn't. There were loose sheets of newspaper clippings on the table, held down by a glass paper weight. A glance at the headlines told her the clippings were about Sara's case. She pulled a drawer and it opened. There was a stack of opened envelopes and they were addressed to Richard Davenport. She was in the wrong study. She looked up and saw the knob turning. She ran back to the side of the washroom and was almost there when the door opened. It was the maid. She looked different. Not tired, not distraught, the eyes looked plain wary now. She closed the door behind her and stood looking at her without speaking.

'What is it?' Lavanya asked.

'This. Keep it safe. Nobody can know I gave it to you … nobody,' she said breathlessly, as she pulled out a small envelope from her petticoat and held it out for Lavanya.

Lavanya took it but the maid held on to it, forcing Lavanya to meet her gaze. Demanding an answer.

'Yes, yes, nobody can know. But what is inside, do you know?'

'No, I am not knowing anything … hide it!' the maid said as she looked behind her. Then she let go of the envelope and turned and left the room.

Lavanya stared at the door for a moment, composed herself, looked at the envelope, and decided this was not the time to open it.

She slipped it down her strappy, low-cut silk gown, till it wedged snugly in between her breasts, and adjusted the cape to cover it.

She walked out to see the maid waiting for her. She started walking fast towards the living room where everybody was. Lavanya hurried to keep pace.

Any of the rooms she passed could be Sara's study. Outside somewhere was Ratan, hiding, waiting. Lavanya sighed and continued walking.

Dinner was delicious, if a little quiet. She counted six courses. Each delectable, but her mind could taste only her own peril. There were many awkward silences that nobody tried to cover and the sound of the spoons and forks was more than audible. Lavanya, aware of the envelope with the strange letter sitting on her chest, concentrated on chewing softly. It was something that had been drilled into her head by her mother and something she had never adhered to, while she was alive.

The maid came and went, not once meeting Lavanya's eyes.

After dinner, as they were being served tea and coffee, back in the living room, Sir Davenport sat next to her and she took the first chance she got to clear her stand on why she was here.

'Sir Richard, about my book, it's not as the others are talking about it, I want you to know …'

'Miss Shriram, please. The newspapers report rubbish at times. My wife adored your stories. You don't have to explain yourself to me. She loved to write as well. She wrote in verse a lot. I would like to show you some of her verses, some time. In fact, would you like to visit her study, it was her favourite place in the house. I think she would have liked that very much.'

Would she like that? Lavanya had to put all her effort into composing her face to show only mild and an entirely polite interest in what he was suggesting. Inside, she was incredulous and quite disbelieving at the luck she had been served.

Ratan might get in after all. Maybe it was meant to happen.

Sara's study was in a different wing of the house. As they walked together, Marc Easton kept the conversation going. He told her about his passion, hunting. If ever she needed tales for her next book, she should talk to him. He would give her a book, he would. The last expedition almost cost him his life. But the danger was the best part. Unless you lived life on the edge, it simply wasn't much of an endeavour, was it? They took a deft turn from the corridor she had been eyeing. Only Ratan could have expected her to sleuth around at such an advanced level. To leave the little dinner gathering and gallivant around someone's home she had only just been introduced to. Someone who had done her the courtesy of inviting her into his home even as he grieved for his wife. Only Ratan.

It was an entirely different room to the one she had slipped into earlier. This one was light and airy. No heavy drapes, just Indian print mulmul curtains to partially keep the sun out. Sara and Richard seemed like two different people entirely. Even with all the lights on in the study, it had a cosy feel to it. In the corners were inviting armchairs and plush sofas that you could sink into and curl up on with a book and lose yourself to the world. And in one of those corners was the door that led to the garden outside. She could see the dimly lit porch outside. A little jolt went through her as she realized Ratan was, at this moment somewhere outside, waiting to be let in.

She walked over to the door, her mind racing. The most wanted criminal in Simla. The reason Donald Harper was a frustrated man today. The reason Richard Davenport looked broken as he fingered the bookshelves in his dead wife's study. While Marc Easton looked uncomfortable and his wife fidgeted with her dress for want of anything else to do.

Lavanya stood still for a minute as she accepted the fact that she didn't know. She didn't know if Ratan had anything to do with the murders. She had not seen or heard from him in five years. Donald Harper had said Ratan had fatally injured a policeman too, trying to flee the scene of the crime. That totalled up to three killings. Ratan was right to have seen the doubt in her eyes. Hadn't her father always said that every human being was capable of killing, given the right motivation? That life was just an elaborate arrangement of moments we strung together to keep ourselves from tipping over to the dark side? Had Ratan tipped over to the other side?

She realized she was barely listening to Richard Davenport as he picked one book after another, talking about what Sara liked to read.

'Is it all right if I open this door to let in some fresh air?' she asked.

She was finding it difficult to breathe evenly, all of a sudden.

'Are you feeling poorly?' Marc Easton looked concerned. She nodded.

He walked over at once and opened the door. The February air cut into the room, chilling it, stripping it of its cosy feel. She shivered as she held on to her cape. She shivered again as she realized she couldn't do it.

'I'm sorry, but it is rather chilling. The door's better off closed, I think.'

Marc Easton nodded politely and shut the door, bolting it carefully, she noticed.

Ratan wasn't getting in today.

'... lately, the only book she took with her wherever she went was yours, Miss Shriram.' Richard was oblivious to the door being opened or shut. It seemed like he was talking softly to himself.

'I wish I had taken the time to listen to her read it. It wasn't once that she asked me to sit down next to her while she read it aloud, it was more than once, I'll tell you that. I was too busy doing less important things, I'm afraid,' he finished, his words shaking.

Lavanya looked at Richard Davenport. She didn't deserve this praise. She wasn't even a writer. She dabbled in writing. She hadn't written a thing since. Nothing she had *finished*. That book of stories was a fluke. Just a way for her to meet Sitara. To tell *her* story … all her confidence was fast disappearing as she stood there, looking at Richard trying to hold back his tears.

There was a sharp but soft thud just then. One moment, Eden had been standing in her line of vision, twitching gently, then she vanished. She was lying in a heap on the carpet. Marc was over her at once. Richard Davenport had rung the bell and the next moment, the servants rushed in. Marc brushed them aside and carried Eden to the sofa as he gently said her name again and again, brushing the hair off her face.

'Eden, Eden?'

These Englishmen, Lavanya thought. Were they all so loving, so concerned? It was one thing to mourn a dead wife lovingly but Marc Easton's wife was alive and he looked so sweetly anguished at her state. One moment, hunting wild animals, the other, picking up his wife so tenderly in his arms—it was an attractive, if not a vitally important characteristic. Indian men were incapable of showing affection publicly. So sad for their women.

One of the servants sprinkled rose water on her face and she stirred. Looking embarrassed, at once. The twitch appeared, like an unsure dimple near her mouth.

'It's late, Richard. We'll leave now. Miss Shriram, can we drop you on our way?'

As they gathered their things and began walking to the porch, Richard took her aside for a moment.

'My dear Miss Shriram, I hope you'll assist in any way you can, with the investigation?'

'Won't you call me Lavanya, please?'

'Lavanya, I know this isn't easy. Ratan is an old friend, after all. Something seems to have snapped in him and it is a larger malady, no doubt. I'm afraid for him, he's a good lad, he was, I'm sure of that.'

Lavanya nodded, keeping her head down, gazing at her brogues.

'Also, I will send you Sara's writings so that you can get to know her better. She is … was incredible, really. I'm so glad you want to write about her. She was a fine woman, much ahead of her time.'

As Marc started the car, Lavanya looked back to see a lonely figure of a man watching them drive away.

The letter was still inside her tunic, breathing with her.

Secrets, one too many

RATAN SAT CROUCHED IN THE BUSHES, WAITING FOR Lavanya to let him in. He couldn't believe she had so easily disregarded his request. How was he to get in now?

Luckily, he had mapped out this path before. He knew how to get inside the residential compound without going through the gates. It was an inside path through the forest that surrounded the compound. He had used it on many occasions to meet Sara in her room without any of the guards and servants knowing.

Bhai had wasted no time. He had made sure Lavanya got Ratan's little note at the railway station. Much before that, he had, through his contact inside the police force, found out where they were planning on having Lavanya stay. Once Bhai had found out it was at Birchwood, he had done the really remarkable thing. Locating Kallu, a housekeeping contact inside, who led them to a secret passage through the basement rooms. Built during the First World War, these buildings were homes to a certain strain of British officials for whom it was imperative to leave and arrive unseen after long voyages.

It looked like the entire town owed Bhai. Or like him, hated the English enough to help him. Whichever way Ratan looked at it, so far, it was the best thing he had done, going to Bhai.

Meeting Lavanya after all these years had been exhilarating and confusing at the same time. She was nothing like the girl he remembered last, crouching behind his door, holding her head and making a face, before she started reading from her diary. Her pale skin had turned a smooth dusky complexion that made her eyes shimmer, glimmer, reflecting every emotion she was feeling. Her mouth had changed, filled out. And those breasts, he had been least prepared for them. All he could think about was the strange word 'developments'. So many 'developments' had taken place since they had met last.

She'd been scattered as usual but her eyes had never left his face, taking in the ravages of the past few days. He knew those eyes and all the mental notes they were constantly making. It was the easy familiarity in them that he had relied upon, always. That's why when she let it slip that he could have killed Sara, it had felt so much like betrayal.

Yet he had to admit, he had been dangerously close to taking that bratty underaged policeman's life the day he found Shyam dead in the shed.

He could have killed him. He could have. Or maybe he did. Ratan shuddered as he remembered how the boy had crumpled into a heap after that last blow. All his pent-up frustration had been used up in that one blow. It had come from some other place entirely, from somewhere deep inside where he was afraid to look. Poor kid. This is what it came down to. Being at the wrong place at the wrong time. They had both been trapped in that situation with no way out.

He was inside the compound now. The bungalow was all lit up. He had to get inside. The more he thought about it, the more he was convinced there was something in that locked drawer that would lead him to the killer.

So many other things had begun to connect now. He was beginning to see behind Sara's gay laughing face. There had been times she had let the mask slip. Her face flashed in his mind. He could see the unsure, flustered eyes just before her eyes found his and the familiar sauciness came on. The quivering of her mouth, as she did the most mundane of things like reading the day's news or stirring the sugar in her tea. He'd think of asking her just as she often asked him, 'a penny for your thoughts, or wait, a pound!' but then she'd look up and the moment would pass. She'd be grinning, ready to banter as always. So just like her strangeness around the drawer, it had piqued his curiosity for a few seconds at the most. Then he let it go. He was himself hiding so much. What did Sara really know about him?

She was allowed her secrets as long as he was allowed his. Except now he could see why that had been such a mistake. His entire life was in jeopardy because he had never really bothered to ask her if anything was wrong, if anything was bothering her, or more importantly, if *anybody* was bothering her … if only he had asked.

Ratan grit his teeth and wished Lavanya had not bailed on him at the last minute. The evening had gone on long enough. He had seen the lights go on in Sara's study and had finally unclenched his teeth. She was going to do it, any time now. A lifetime of reading all her stories, he had promised himself.

Ten minutes later, he knew she'd changed her mind. The door opened and then it closed. Even then he had kept himself hidden and hoped he was wrong. When, much later, Marc Easton's Buick left the porch with Lavanya in it, he went to the door and gave it a gentle shove, thinking that perhaps it just looked shut, but it was firmly bolted.

Well, he was getting in, one way or another. He would deal with Lavanya later.

Buy my silence

LAVANYA WAITED FOR THE CAR TO LEAVE. IT HAD BEEN AN awkward ride back with Marc and Eden. Marc drove quietly, constantly shooting concerned looks at Eden like she might pass out anytime in the car. Lavanya couldn't wait to get to her room and be alone with her thoughts. They were crowding her head in that uncomfortable jumbled way. What was in that envelope?

As the car faded into the distance and into the mist, she turned and ran into Birchwood as fast as she could. What if he was waiting for her already? If he wasn't, then she had to seal the wooden boards of the floor at once. She grabbed her keys from the reception and bounded up the stairs. The receptionist stared after her but she could not care less. Outside her door, she listened for a while for anything that might tell her he was already inside, waiting for her. Nothing. She quietly opened the door and shut it behind her. She threw the envelope on the bed in sheer relief and raced to the latch on the wooden boards. It looked like it would give way easily if he kept banging on it. What if she pulled the sofa over it?

She looked over the sofa at the far end of the room. It might be worth a shot.

Many minutes later, she lay exhausted in bed. She'd managed to remove almost all the furniture of the room to the place over the latch on the floor.

When her breathing seemed more normal, her eyes wandered over to the envelope she'd thrown on the bed. Still lying down, flat on her back, she let her arm reach out for it. It had been glued back but it wasn't a very sticky glue, thankfully. The single sheet of paper inside fluttered out.

She slowly sat up and read the letter twice.

1.8.35

I know what's going on. Your wife does not.
The government does not.
Your army does not.
Yet.
You can buy my silence of course.
If you choose to ignore this, it will be my last letter.
First, your wife finds out.
Then the government, then the army, and then the rest of the country.
Do not test me any more than you already have.

Lavanya stared at the letter.

This, here, was what was called a bloody blackmail letter.

She went over the letter again, stopping at the words: *If you choose to ignore this, it will be my last letter*. Last letter? It seemed Richard was being blackmailed for some time now. Long before Sara was found murdered?

What did this person know that could be so incriminating?

Your wife does not know.

An affair? But why would the government be interested in that? In Simla, they said, every British officer had a woman he was sleeping with apart from his wife. Even the brothels, the very elite ones, thrived because there was constant revelry in the little hill town.

It would get Richard a bad reputation, people would talk in hushed tones about him, but other than that, they couldn't care less.

Also, even a blind person could see that Richard was madly in love with his wife.

Was it Ratan then? Blackmailing the man whose wife he was planning to kill? Maybe Sara had let on some state secret to him and this was his way of getting rich fast.

That didn't make sense. Knowing Ratan, he didn't give a damn about money. Not enough to blackmail and then kill. Also, if it was Ratan, this letter could nail him. But the police did not have this letter. Neither the superintendent nor the inspector had mentioned it to her once.

Why? Because Richard knew it wasn't Ratan. And he didn't want the police getting into what the blackmailer did know.

Then something struck her.

What if Sara had found out about the incriminating evidence, tried to wipe off every trace of it to protect her husband, and been killed in the process?

Her mind juggled with all the possibilities at once. If only she could discuss this with Noor. She shook her head, not on a telephone line. Somebody could be listening in. She imagined herself looking into Richard's heartbroken eyes, trying to explain how she had ended up with this letter in her hands, accepting it from his own staff, so eagerly, without a word of protest? How pleased Donald Harper would be. What could you expect from a girl who writes 'filth'? No, the telephone lines wouldn't do at all.

She needed to think. She needed something else, something to literally chew on, yes. The pouch of meethi supari—Lavanya hoped fervently Noor had left Jaddan Bai's ingenious contribution to her travel bag. Two minutes later, the little pouch of supari in her hands, her mouth working steadily on the hard soft supari, she settled back to contemplate the letter.

Did she wish she had refused the angry maid? No, she didn't. This was important. But something told her the maid knew more than she let on.

Ratan the rat. Look what he had made her do. How she wished she could talk to him right now. Show him the letter. Lay bare the 1.,2.,3. theories and think of 4.,5.,6. together.

Together. Isn't that why she was in Simla—to help him? Then why was she suddenly so disbelieving of him? The goras were getting to her. She was thinking like them, already.

She looked at the huddle of furniture over the wooden boards with the latch. The sofa, the table with the lamp, an armchair, a footstool, the coffee table, all in one spot, very solemn and entirely ridiculous.

Here she was, all alone, in a place she knew nobody but Ratan. Yet he was the one person she found easiest to doubt?

The most wanted man in Simla? Those eyes didn't belong to someone who could kill. They belonged to her friend.

In a flash, she was off the bed.

Minutes later, she was exhausted again. All the furniture was back where it had come from. She looked down at the latch, took a deep breath, lifted and opened it. It didn't budge. It jingled and jangled, just enough to know it was a door to something below but it didn't lift. It must be bolted from the other side.

She went back to bed and lay down. She had to wait now. He would come. Those eyes would be full of accusations and she had to have her wits about her. Ten minutes later, she was asleep.

Sitara jangled her bangles at her.

They were a bridal red and sparkled in the sun. She lay on the blue four-poster bed in the restored part of the Nawab's haveli. It was noon and she wore only the light that fell on her from the windows above.

Beside her lay her Angrez, asleep. His arm draped over her bare midriff.

Sitara jangled her bangles 'Aren't they beautiful?'

Lavanya nodded, they were. 'Did your Angrez give them to you?' she asked.

Sitara looked surprised. 'No, why would he? These are my wedding bangles. They were lying in my trunk and I couldn't bear to look at them for so many years. I've finally taken them out. Half of them are on the floor, can't you see?' Lavanya looked down and saw the broken red bangles glittering on the floor. Even broken, they looked beautiful.

'He broke them the way every wedding bangle should be broken, Lavanya. You should have heard them breaking. It was like a thousand apsaras on swings, laughing, just glad to be alive.'

Lavanya nodded again. She could hear the apsaras.

If she ever married, she'd want her bangles to be broken like that too. She on her back, her man deep within her, and her red bangles jingling and jangling, Then he would go deeper. And she would be on the edge of the moon, her nails digging into him, and he would go deeper still and then they would both rise together in the last throes of passion, and their bodies would stay arched in rapture. Joined, deeply joined, clenched teeth, groins, muscles, skin, throbbing flesh and then when they couldn't take it anymore, they'd fall down in a heap and the bangles would break. The bangles, rolling over the mattress and on the floor in a merry jingle jangle. Over the sound of them exhaling.

'Isn't it sad that love is a crime, Lavanya?' Sitara asked, her eyes welling.

This time Sitara didn't even wait for her to nod, she closed her wet eyes and slept. Breathing evenly, her arm with bloody gashes from the broken glass bangles resting over her Angrez.

with a *chan chan* of her anklets. She was about to pass the hose to him when she asked, 'Who are you? How come I haven't seen you …?'

'I'm Ali, Sir Davenport's new driver. I haven't seen you before either. I would never forget such a pretty face, who are *you*?'

'I'm Rani, I joined yesterday only. I'm helping the cook and learning new dishes and also …' She gave him the hose and as he stepped closer to take it from her, let his hands brush hers. Flustered, she stepped away, leaving her sentence unfinished.

'What else are you learning, Rani?' he asked.

She shook her head. She was leaving now. He washed his hands and said the first thing that came to his mind, 'Wait a bit, will you? I'd like to come and say *pranaam* to Raghu Kaka.'

She said nothing but her feet hesitated, she was going to wait. That was a good sign. He took his time washing his hands. He could feel her eyes on him, taking him in, top to bottom. He ran the back of his wet hand over his mouth and then through his hair without looking at her.

'So, do I look all right to you? Like someone you would want to meet again …?'

Ratan looked up just in time to see her looking flushed. She knew he'd caught her looking at him. He smiled impishly again as he sprinkled some water from the hose at her, catching her off guard.

'It's okay. I'm used to girls looking at me,' he said.

A harmless flirtation like clouds occasionally caressing the moon. It meant little but there was some pleasure in it, for both.

He put the hose down, rubbed his hands dry on the back of his pants. He then took a step towards her. He let himself falter so that he would slip on the slushiness of the mud. Sure enough, she had stepped forward to catch his arm and steady him. Immediately, he pulled her close. His damp hands were on her bare waist now. His face was looking down at hers, inches away from her mouth.

'You slip a lot, don't you?' she said, her voice a whisper.

'I do …' he nodded and bit his lip apologetically, keeping his eyes all the time on her.

She was still now, he could feel her breath coming at him, a little strangled. There was nothing else to do. He let his mouth caress hers. The cloud and the moon. She didn't move but she leaned into him. The moon and the cloud. He licked her lip gently. She stepped back into the tree and he leaned into her now. As they kissed, he let his hands caress her waist again. The keys were just below, tucked into her sari at the hips. Which were pressing into his. He let himself respond, pressing back into her and the kiss grew deeper. She was responding now, moaning in his mouth, her hands on his shirt, gripping tighter and tighter. He let his hand hover around her waist, the smoothness of her belly, circling her belly button as he continued to kiss her. He stole a look at her, her eyes were closed. He let his hand dip below the waist of her sari. Finding her petticoat string, he gave it a gentle tug. It loosened but not completely. At the same time, he pulled her tighter and deepened his kiss. He had heard the soft jangle of keys falling on the muddy ground. She was pulling at the ends of his hair, her nails digging into his neck. She had heard nothing. He removed his other hand from her waist and squeezed her breast, under her blouse. She uttered a strangled sound. Something in between a curse and sob. He pinched her nipples lightly. She shuddered and her whole body relaxed, continuing to shake. He looked up at the sky. The cloud had covered the moon. It was darker now. Ratan wished he felt less of a turd as she leaned into him, clinging. He didn't know what to do next. He held her. The keys were right under his eye.

There was a shout from the servant quarters. He couldn't make out what was being yelled but it seemed urgent. Rani stirred and then in a flash, she had extricated herself from him. She didn't look at him as she quickly fixed her pleats, tightening the string. He kept leaning against the tree.

'I have to go … you coming?' she didn't look at him.

He kept his voice soft, 'Later. You go. I'll come by to see Raghu Kaka later … and you, of course.'

He could see her blushing in the dim light of the cloudy moon. He felt worse.

'Don't,' she hesitated, 'I'm married …'

Hell. hell. Hell. He managed to look crushed as he nodded.

'I won't … I'll talk with Raghu Kaka some other time … it's nothing important …'

She wanted to say something, then thought the better of it. She nodded back and turned to go, her steps quickening till she was sprinting across the clearing.

Ratan kept his eye on her as he slid down and reached for the keys glinting in the grass. He was spent. Feigning desire was more exhausting than desire itself. But strangers didn't judge you and that was sometimes all the good there was in the world. He forced himself to get up. He had a job to do. Other than seducing married women against trees under a permissive moon.

Ratan let himself in through the kitchen door, his shoes in his hands.

He walked down the corridor he knew too well. There were rooms on either side and on the farthest end was Davenport's room. Just next to his room was Sara's study.

From the crack under the door, he could see a lamp on in Sir Davenport's room. He had to move fast. He knew it was just a matter of time before Rani realized the keys were no longer dangling from her hips. She'd be back at the tree to search for them.

He latched Davenport's room from the outside and softly pushed open Sara's study door. There was his old friend, the moon again. Throwing him just enough light from the windows to spot the study table. He quickly went to the drawer and pulled. It opened with an audible creak. That was strange. Sara always kept the drawer locked. The keys were in the drawer below in a small yellow handcrafted box. He knew. He had watched her lock it many times and drop it there. Now the keys were dangling from the lock. Somebody had recently been through the drawer.

There were two packets in there. He opened one and a small pocket diary fell out. It had many jottings of Hindi and Urdu words that Sara was learning. Every now and then, she would grow fond of a certain phrase or word and quickly jot it down to memorize later. Then use it cleverly when her audience was least expecting it. It had worked like a charm with him, he remembered.

Her most recent favourite two words were 'sirf ittefaq' roughly translating as 'only coincidence'. One night, not too long ago, she had knocked at his door, it had been raining incessantly and he had been sound asleep. He opened the door to see her dressed in pants and a buttoned-up shirt with all her hair tucked into a hat. Groggy, a little annoyed at how little thought she gave to how dangerous this could get for him, he had asked her what in heaven's name was she doing. She had earnestly looked at him, then shrugged and said, 'Sirf ittefaq …' He couldn't help but smile and pull her in, hoping nobody had seen her.

Ratan opened the other packet quickly and let the contents fall out. Black-and-white photographs. First, he thought they were just pictures of her, but his heart froze when he realized it wasn't so. He was also there in every picture. He was there in parts, mostly as a blur, but it was unmistakably him. Here they were in the club suite. The rooms that were always reserved for Sara. Where he would sneak in or out. In the last picture, the photographer had managed to catch him tucking his shirt into his pants as he looked at Sara, who sat right in front of him on the bed in her slip, reading something.

Who had taken these pictures? Why were they here in the drawer? It couldn't have been these photographs Sara was protecting. It couldn't be. Somebody had put them there. These pictures in the hands of the police and there would be no doubt at all, he had killed her. He heard a sound. He grabbed both packets and thrust them inside his jacket. It was a soft groan. Like someone had just turned in their sleep and settled back down. The sound had come from *inside* the study. Ratan dropped down and slid under the table.

His calf muscles had frozen. His hands were shaking. At the same time, he heard a car driving in. It stopped. Somebody got out. He had to leave immediately. He peered outside the table and crawled out, he couldn't see anybody.

He was almost at the door now when he heard the footsteps outside. Had Richard stepped out and was coming back in?

Then he heard the low groan again and looked behind from where the sound came to see a figure lying on the sofa. It was Richard sleeping on the sofa in Sara's study! He was so close that if he were to open his eyes, he would see Ratan on his knees barely a few steps away.

Paralyzed for endless seconds, Ratan finally managed to get himself to move sideways and get behind the door just before it opened. Something glinted into his eye for a flash. A pair of shoes strode past him towards the sofa. Ratan crawled out the door and into the corridor outside. He kept crawling till he was midway down the corridor. He could hear muffled voices behind him. Whoever had come in was trying to wake Richard up. Ratan got on his numb feet and dragged himself to the kitchen door and let himself out into the cold night.

The moon was in hiding now. He dropped the key under the tree and limped back into the shrubby path he had hidden behind all evening, waiting for Lavanya to open the door. He hated her then, with every fibre of his being. He limped all the way into the woods where his car was hidden. Once he had pulled himself inside and shut the door, he began to breathe normally.

Ratan woke up with a start. There was a distinct movement under him somewhere. A hairy movement. A rat? He groped for his stick. He never slept without it close by. He couldn't find it. He spun around, feeling the movement again, shuddering. There was no rat. There was no stick, either. Yesterday he had driven himself back to Nevermore and passed out somewhere between the sofa and the bed on the first floor.

He sat up, pressing his temples as the previous night's narrow escape flashed through his head. His temples throbbed with pain as he forced himself to think about who could have been visiting Richard so late in the night. The flash of the shoes he had glimpsed as he had crawled out of there. He saw them clearly. They were military shoes. English military shoes. It must have been Marc Easton. He had left with Eden and then come back to check on Richard. The man was intensely protective of Richard. It was admirable, he had to admit. It was that old war cliché. Sara said they had both been in the same battalion during the war, striking a friendship that had lasted long after. Even their marriages to Sara and Eden had been on the spur of the moment and held just a few days apart.

Immediately, he remembered the photographs in the brown paper envelope. He had flung them in the car as he had driven out of there. He dragged himself to the washroom and dunked his head into the basin, turning the tap on.

Cold icy water poured onto his head, making his eyes burn. Why were the photos in Sara's unlocked drawer? Did the police also have a copy?

He crawled back into the car in the garage shed and at once, his eyes fell on the brown paper envelope on the seat. He looked at the photographs again. They were real. Anybody could tell they were having an affair. Sara, flushed and dreamy, her bare shoulders hugging a bedsheet. He, looking at her, eyes crinkling, bare-chested, putting on a shirt in bed. The others were different variations of the moment, a little before or a little later. Somebody had been lurking around the club suite, outside those huge windows that opened into the balcony. Somebody who knew about them. Ratan kicked himself for not being more careful. Which world had he been living in?

He tried to remember that club evening better. It wasn't that far back. Sara had lost a little colour by the time they were leaving the room. She had come away from the windows and he was right behind her, about to kiss her and she had looked pale but yielded nothing in terms of an explanation.

Was it even possible Richard knew all along? And if he did, would he not want his revenge on Ratan, would he not want to kill his wife for betraying his trust?

The more Ratan thought about it, the more sure he got. It was Davenport. He had found out about them, sent her to that party, cooked up an alibi for himself, made sure Ratan was going to be around, and killed her. Now all he needed was Ratan to be caught and put in prison, and he would have killed two in one stroke.

If he could get these photos to the police, would they believe him? Would they have the sense to see how it didn't make sense? If Ratan and Sara were already lovers, why would he want to molest her or rape her like they were reporting in the papers? He felt a glimmer of hope after days of bleakness.

A cold-blooded breakfast

Lavanya woke up to birdsong and no sign of Ratan. Had she slept through the tapping? Then she remembered she'd left the latch open. He wasn't coming. The birdsong no longer felt like the sweetest sound she had heard for days. It grated. Lavanya wanted it to stop. She got up, flung the quilt off, toes curling as they made contact with the freezing cold wooden floor under her bare feet, missing the carpet by inches. The blackmail letter was on the coffee table, staring at her. She took it and tucked it into the cupboard and closed the door.

She got ready as quickly as she could. She could hear small, intermittent knocks all the while she bathed. All in her mind because as she hurried out, there wasn't a sound to be heard. Ratan had given up on her after yesterday night.

She heard a knock at the door. The knocks grew steadier as she walked to the door.

It was Amrit Singh. As soon as she opened the door, his eyes were on the sofa inside. In Simla, he was an entirely different person. He wore his uniform a lot more lightly. Going home to a home-cooked meal had made him a lot softer, Lavanya thought. Simultaneously, she noted that her own appetite was still raging. She had never eaten breakfast in Bombay. Not since her parents died and her brothers moved away to different cities.

She sighed and moved aside. He made his way to the sofa and sat down heavily. Thank God she had put the letter away.

She saw him looking at her with a guarded look on his face.

'Hope you had a good evening at the Davenports'. You look poorly, though. Didn't you sleep well? We need you in top form for the next few days.'

'Inspector, please don't be so sweet, you'll spoil me. I know and you know that the superintendent is not as concerned about me as he is about catching Ratan. To do that, he wouldn't think twice about feeding me, a measly native, to the wolves.'

The maid was wheeling in a tray of tea and breakfast. The wolves wouldn't be disappointed; she would be in great form by the time they found her.

Amrit Singh shifted uncomfortably on the sofa. Lavanya realized the word 'native' had had its effect. Also, plain-speaking was a rarity in the world he was surrounded by. He cleared his throat audibly now. Why were Indians always clearing throats? It was a secret language almost, one that could throw light on many hidden thoughts if you learned to decipher its many nuances.

'Madam, if I may take you through the day planned for you …' Amrit Singh sipped his tea.

Her day had been planned meticulously. One appointment after the other with journalists from leading newspapers. Each of whom wanted to write the definitive story about her book and her life behind it. Then she was being taken to Wildflower Hall and the scene of the crime. Lunch would follow. The rest of the day would be at her disposal.

But first, she needed to know what the police knew about the case. Was blackmail even an angle they were investigating?

She helped herself to a plate of buttered toast and cold cuts, tucked her feet under her legs, and spoke in between mouthfuls.

'Inspector, before all of this takes over, can you brief me on the investigation so far? I want to sound a little informed when I speak to these clever people who will be asking me the trickiest of questions.'

Amrit Singh settled down on the sofa, adjusting this way and that and she knew he was going to level with her. The body was found at eleven in the night. The party was still in full sway. The earliest departing guest had seen Sara on the grounds and alerted the guards who had then alerted the police. Her clothes were ripped. It was clear she had tried to resist the attack. There were bruises all over her body. He cleared his throat. The book was found a few steps away from the body, next to the purse, face down. Open at the beginning of Sitara's story.

Lavanya stopped him there.

So the killer had killed her and then left her book open at the scene of the crime to give them a clue as to which story had inspired him to commit the murder. Wasn't that being too helpful?

Amrit Singh looked at her deadpan.

Killers are known to do strange things to challenge the police. Also, he was simply reporting the facts of the case. Should he continue or had she had enough?

'Please continue,' Lavanya managed a tight smile.

She had been stabbed multiple times. The wounds had been inflicted mostly in her abdomen. There was also a cut in her neck which had caused immediate death. Forensic reports confirmed the cut had come from a sharp instrument, not a knife, not an axe, something in between, just as sharp.

Definitely not breakfast conversation.

Lavanya's head spun. Such a cruel end. Ratan didn't have the stomach for this, she knew. He could barely take an injection. She had gone with him once to the local hospital when a friend's dog had bitten him without any provocation. He had taken her along to read to him while he waited in the hospital. He hated hospitals, he hated the sight of blood. When the nurse was going to put the needle in, he had looked at Lavanya sharply and asked, why had she stopped reading? What happened next in that stupid story, Lava? It was she who had been transfixed with the viscosity of the red spurt on his arm. No, Ratan would never. Correction. Ratan *could* never.

Lavanya bit into the soft bun oozing with chocolate.

The inspector was now telling her how Ratan had left no room for doubt that he was the killer—simply by running away. The police had nevertheless done their due diligence. Mrs Hotz and her staff had been most helpful. There were a total of fifty guests at the party. Each one had been spoken to and their whereabouts verified. They had tight alibis.

Mrs Hotz had herself accounted for most of them. Now the police had to do their job. Every day, there was a call from the governor's office. The pressure was increasing by the day.

Amrit Singh dropped his voice now.

If it was an ordinary murder, they might have gotten away with the time it was taking to catch the killer but this was a most extraordinary murder, you understand? A most extraordinary murder.

Lavanya understood, all right.

It was the murder of a high-ranking army officer's wife. An Englishwoman, at that. As far from a common native as she could be. It was the first time Amrit Singh had connected with her. Native to native.

Had the inspector and his team probed Ratan's end of the story? Spoken to his friends and neighbours? Or were natives and their friends presumed guilty without basic investigation?

Amrit Singh looked at her like he was surprised she didn't know the answer to that question already.

'Tell me, Inspector, what will it take for Ratan to be considered not guilty?'

'He will have to turn himself in, simple.'

'Besides that …'

'The evidence. Nobody can refute the evidence.'

The blackmail letter the maid had given her was evidence. Precious evidence.

It meant exposing the maid, though. And without the source identified, it was just another letter.

Ratan was right. The reason why Ratan had run was pure instinct. There was enough going on in the country to give the police reason to doubt every Indian. They needed an excuse to lock them up and keep them out of circulation.

This letter that seemed substantial right now could be torn apart on grounds of credibility if they didn't follow through with it.

Amrit Singh and Lavanya were both now looking out of the window, gazing at the flickering leaves, lost in their own thoughts.

Lavanya broke the silence, 'Inspector, has there been any point in your investigation where it looked like there could be another suspect besides Ratan?'

Amrit Singh tore his gaze from the green lawns glinting in the sunlight and turned to look at her, 'Now that you ask, yes, there was one …'

Lavanya looked at him urging him to continue. The scone could wait.

'At the party were four kings from our neighbouring states. One of them was accompanied by his son, the prince of Suraiah. In the course of our questioning, he said that he had seen Sir Davenport at the party having an argument with Sara in one of the balconies leading out to the garden.'

'What? That's impossible. Wasn't Richard visiting Mashobra that night?'

'He was. When we checked, his regiment captain confirmed his presence.'

Amrit Singh waited, shifted a little on the sofa, 'I continued to be suspicious. Because if we were to talk about the motive, it had to be Sir Richard, on account of being the husband who suspected his wife of having an affair with her driver.'

He was confiding in her. His entire demeanour had changed. For the first time.

'Then? Did you follow up on that or pursue that theory?' Lavanya asked.

'No, the superintendent rubbished it saying the prince was a certified imbecile. His testimony wouldn't stand in any court of law.'

'Is that true?'

'I'm afraid it is. We did our checks. The king keeps it a well-guarded secret but everybody knows. The prince is under sedation most of the time. In a court, it would take no time for that to come out'.

Interesting. Most interesting.

Amrit Singh started getting up. Lavanya saw that he was avoiding meeting her gaze.

She realized he had connected with her native to native, more than he was comfortable doing. She let him go. He was not going to go very far, she knew. Outside the door was as far as he could go. He was responsible for her.

'I'll wait outside. Your first interview will begin in less than an hour. The superintendent has said, no, requested, you tell the reporters everything you ahem, know.' He cleared his throat and lumbered towards the door.

'Take that single sofa, here, let me help you ...' Amrit Singh was clearly tempted. Lavanya started pushing the sofa towards the door. She had had enough practice last night moving the furniture around in her room.

She could tell Amrit Singh was surprised at her thoughtfulness.

Five minutes later, when she peeped from the eyehole in the door, he was spread all over the sofa, reading the paper.

Lavanya smiled to herself. We are going to be friends, Inspector, you wait and see.

By evening, she was worn out. The reporters had tried to find out in every which way how well she knew Ratan and what 'according to her' his motive could be. Did she think Sitara's story had provoked him? Sexually, then criminally? If not, why was it found in a suspicious circumstance on the grounds of the property, one reporter asked her with a not-so-subtle raise of his eyebrow. When she replied that she found nothing suspicious in the manner the book had been found, he did not look convinced. The reporter looked at her steadfast for a long moment, she held his gaze, giving away nothing. Not mirth, not contempt, nor superciliousness. He changed his line of questioning soon enough.

Unlike him, she had learned to play the deadpan game early in life. Men grew up, went out and their work taught them many skills women had to teach themselves. One of those lessons was never to let on too much, early on. How else could you stand up for yourself or retaliate in equal measure without letting them know what you were up to? If they knew they would either be offended and attack you or gag you at once. No fun, either way. Deadpan, you could say what you wanted and they wouldn't know for sure what exactly you meant. It worked like a charm, most of the time.

Only Noor would catch her out on her deadpan questions and answers. Warning her not to try her games with friends who knew her inside out. There was an ache deep inside her for Noor, to have her by her side, being dramatic and foolish and sweet. For Ratan too, the ache inside her, she was surprised to find, spread wide and deep.

The court summons had been an equally time-consuming question. Was she prepared? Would she apologize? No, she would not. What was she supposed to apologize for? Was it an option? They were relentless. It would stop the ban of the book, wouldn't it? If the freedom of expression was so important to her, then why keep the book out of circulation from its future readers? On and on the bewildering permutation and combination of questions went. She did her best to keep up but after a point, she was happy being repetitive and robotic.

Then the note she had written to Ratan had featured prominently in their questions. What did you mean when you wrote this? It was an inside joke. Friends have strange inside jokes that only they understand.

Would she mind explaining?

Okay. So every time he said something nice about something I wrote I would say dramatically as the English do, oh you are too kind sir, too kind, and clasp my hands looking grateful.

Then he would look at me menacingly and say, that's the evil plan, love, to kill you with kindness.

I would play along. But why kind sir, why?

So that I never have to say anything nice about what you've written ever again.

He would say this and laugh evilly and I would pretend to be shocked at this unkind revelation. So you see?

They didn't. They looked flummoxed, then suspicious at once.

Some gave up and moved to the next question. Some didn't.

So what was your evil plan, Miss?

To write stories that would make him swoon and, and make him want to, well, kill me with kindness.

She was making a mess of this, she knew. Inside jokes were impossible to explain, didn't they know?

Last and final question. If you were to die, would you donate your writings to the libraries of India? She couldn't believe this was a serious question. The reporter looked dead earnest and expectant of a sombre answer. 'You mean they'd accept the trash I write? Isn't that too presumptuous to hope? All my erotica in those hallowed halls? With the librarian going shhhh and the reader reading silently and sighing with desire at every word … I think I will! Thank you, I don't think it would have crossed my mind if you hadn't asked me that question.'

They left with grim faces. Nobody could have given them more material to write their reports than she had. The least they could do was look pleased but they denied her even that.

Oh Ratan, where are you?

She was frustrated and fatigued. Then like a fresh gust of wind, she remembered Surya Kant giving her an address. The painter, Amrita Sher-Gil!

She would look her up, yes, that's what she would do with her evening, stretching orange-pink-gold against the mountains.

Visiting the scene of the crime was like going sightseeing. All she saw were manicured lawns for as far as she could see.

They rode up the fabulous grounds of Wildflower Hall with the huge expanse of green, with Amrit Singh giving her a dispassionate account of what was found where. Body here. Book there.

There were no flashes of Ratan running or Sara stumbling and falling, wounded. There was no blood in the telling. She walked up and down, hoping to feel something, to perceive a forgotten connection, a clue, a question, but there was nothing. Except the old familiar urge to run.

She stood at the exact spot where Sara was found. Under a blossoming champa tree. Here lay the body. There lay the book. She imagined her book fluttering in the cold wind. Sitara, inside those pages. Sitara, watching Sara in her last moments. *In your blood I run. In your blood I run.*

Lavanya cast a look around the forest of trees looking down and away. They knew. They weren't telling. The wind whistled in and out of them, unable to shake the gloom that hung heavy in the air. They rode silently back. Lavanya rummaged in her mind for a single helpful observation. Was this cooperating with the investigation, this silence? What did the police want with her at this exact time? That Ratan would spring up from somewhere and they would rise to the opportunity and nab him? How deluded could Donald Harper get?

A mouthful of cake

BACK AT BIRCHWOOD, SHE ASKED FOR DIRECTIONS TO Amrita Sher-Gil's house. She wanted to walk. Her legs ached to walk. Amrit Singh spoke fast with instructions to two of his men, keeping his voice hushed to exclude her. He was telling them to stay out of the way but if they were to lose sight of Miss Shriram, he would come after them himself.

Half an hour later, slightly out of breath, the pine trees still whistling, the dampness of the evening setting in, she reached The Holme, a green, roofed house; the police chaperone had managed to stay successfully out of sight.

Nervous, unsure of herself, she knocked on the main door. It was a beautiful house with skirted windows and balconies all around its perimeter. It was a time of the evening when the birds were chirping endlessly, settling down on various branches of the trees that covered the property. There wasn't a sound from inside the house. Nobody answered the door. A policeman appeared ahead of her, 'there is a studio behind the house,' he whispered loudly and ducked out of sight again.

The studio was an outhouse almost completely covered by overgrowth. A blue door with a brass knocker, partly visible, stood out from amidst the mass of green. She rapped the knocker and waited. There was no response. All her senses were alive here. It wasn't just the wind tearing through the pines, there were other voices whispering in her ears, long-forgotten voices, familiar and unfamiliar. One voice stood out. Sitara had walked in with her, it seemed, out of the pages in the woods, up the road that led to this blue door. '*We think we have a lot of time on our hands, we do, then we look at our hands and they are empty. All gone.*' Lavanya pushed the door and it creaked open. She peered inside. All light had been blocked by thick curtains. She went in, leaving the door partially open to let in some light. The hall smelled of paint yes, but also something turpentine. '*There are things people do in the open, others they do in the dark. They may not want to but they do. Love is in the dark, isn't it? But cruelty, brutality? In the open, in the open ...*' She could smell pine cones too and cigarette smoke and yes, cake, the unmistakable smell of cake. The walls were lined with canvasses and sculptures, covered and uncovered. Ashtrays full of cigarette butts adorned every nook and corner. She went further into what looked like a room that was in full use. More ashtrays, many unwashed glasses dotted the only table in the room. There were more canvasses in various states of completion. On the wall across her was a canvas larger than any she had ever seen, covered by a white sheet. It was mounted on the wall and in front of it was a step ladder smeared with paint. At once she wondered if she was intruding, she had wandered far enough into a private studio and there was no sign of the painter. She turned on her heel to go back and then decided to take a quick peek at the huge canvas. She climbed the step ladder, removed the sheet partially, and before she could understand what she was looking at, there was a soft voice behind her. 'Ah, a curious visitor!' It was a voice so soft, and strangely gleeful, it sounded like another voice in her head. 'Would my curious visitor like some cake?' Lavanya almost fell off the ladder. Acute embarrassment being far more shocking than getting physically hurt. 'I apologize, nobody answered the door so I … but I shouldn't have …' She came down, eyeing the black-and-white mosaic flooring, composing her face to rid it of all curiosity. There was a shrill clatter that reverberated in the air as she looked in the direction the voice came from. She froze. The painter was lying in a heap on the floor, a cigarette still burning in her hand. A plate of pineapple cake lay scattered around her. Behind her was another room, covered in a thick fog of smoke.

She rushed to her, part of her in complete disbelief. She had been to an art exhibition once, where various artists lay in various heaps on the floor, hands tied, unmoving, staring at the ceiling. There were no canvasses on the walls of the exhibition. But it was art, to express the helplessness artists felt in their own country. It had been a huge success and glowingly reviewed in the newspapers.

Amrita Sher-Gil, wearing a purple and green silk robe, was foaming at the mouth. Her mouth was red, freshly painted. Saliva dribbled, little bubbles of white cake frosting too. She was trying to get up but she couldn't. If this was an artistic expression, Lavanya made an unwilling spectator. On unsteady feet, she ran to call the policeman lurking outside. He called out to two more of his men and all three of them came running in. They took one look at her and ran in different directions at once. One went inside to see if there was anybody else inside, the others ran out, ran in, and then kneeled down to see if she was breathing. They stubbed the cigarette, tried to revive her but she lay inert, no life in her. They looked at Lavanya, questioningly. Lavanya shook her head, she had no clue what had happened. As the police carried Amrita out of there, Lavanya stayed back, her mouth still open, her heart beating hard. She wanted to make sure she had seen what she had seen before Amrita had called out to her. She climbed up the stepladder again.

She threw the sheet off the huge mounted canvas. It was Sara. In the nude.

Sara, who lay spreadeagled on the bed, laughing. But that was not what had made Lavanya look again, in horror. Someone had ripped and slashed at the painting with a sharp object. *In between a knife and an axe.* She heard Amrit Singh calmly telling her of the weapon the forensics had described in their report. The gashes were deep and vicious. It looked like Sara had been killed all over again.

One of the policemen came back to get her. She was still on the stepladder when he spoke to her. They were going to take Madam Sher-Gil to the nearest hospital. There was nobody in the main house as well. She was to wait here till they sent another policeman to accompany her back to the guest house. She nodded, yes, yes, could they please hurry and get Miss Sher-Gil to the hospital?

Once they left, Lavanya tried to get a grip on herself. Her breathing was still ragged and if she tried to sit down, her legs ached. Finally, as the wind in the pine trees surrounding her started to pick up dangerously around her ears, as if to blare out a warning, she got up and started to run.

Feeling lucky

By the time Ratan reached Kaku's home, he had left for Birchwood. Disappointed, he returned to Nevermore and sat down to think about what he should do next. Five minutes later, he was fast asleep. He slept for most of the day. Got up to eat from the tinned cans, the usual nasty fare. Sardines, luncheon meat, kippers, and something particularly vile called a steak and kidney pudding. He went back to sleep, curled up, knees touching his chin. It was the only position that gave him any kind of comfort. That and the thought of seeing Lavanya again.

By evening, he decided to try visiting Birchwood himself. If he was lucky, he might spot Kaku and find a way to see Lavanya.

He took extra care with his disguise. No part of his face was visible once the hat and sunglasses were in place. He chose a cream-coloured shirt with dark blue trousers and a teal green waistcoat. His shoes, he refused to change. He often wondered if the prince missed his shoes. For his coat, he paused. There were many to choose from. Which one would he deign to be caught dead in? That was the question, always. Finally, he chose a beige, almost mud-coloured tartan-checked woollen coat. Just wearing the clothes they wore made him feel more invincible. Braver, even. It was a fact, not a myth. One that gave him no comfort.

Life was showing him that if you spent time wishing for a certain kind of life, you may very well get it. Even if in a form you didn't quite expect. On his way to the car, he picked up the binoculars sitting on the window sill. He got into the car, sinking into the luxurious leather upholstery, marvelling at yet another borrowed day of precarious freedom that lay before him. As precarious as the road he was climbing now, which clung desperately to the side of a steep hill. Ratan tried to breathe in the pine scent as deep as he could. It had a cleansing effect and distracted him from making a bad situation worse in his head.

He slowed down as he approached his favourite curve of the road. It was a strip with the gentlest bends and stretched out like a goddess in repose. At this time of the evening, the mist that rose from behind the tall deodars looked like it was fanning out to frame the road in a mystical halo. That's when he saw her.

A figure in a stylishly cut, silk and brocade tunic, running, her scarf flying. As he neared closer, he wondered if she was someone he knew. There was something familiar about her. He stopped and looked through the binoculars. Then he looked again. It was Lavanya! She looked wild-eyed and wild-haired, as if possessed. Was he imagining things? He was about to call out when he saw another vehicle parked on a level above, watching. He kept the car moving. Was this another trap? He waited till he was covered by a giant blue oak tree, then stopped and trained his binoculars on the waiting vehicle. It was a police jeep. Lavanya must have passed the jeep, so why had the police not stopped her? Only one man was sitting inside, looking in her direction. It was Superintendent Donald Harper. If he had stopped and gone to Lavanya just now like he still wanted to do, it would have been all over. What had happened to make Lavanya run like this?

Once Lavanya was out of sight, having fallen a number of times, then picked herself up and run again, the police jeep started moving towards her. Ratan too put the car in drive and stayed behind, making sure he was always well-hidden by the trees. Soon, he lost sight of them.

At the guesthouse, one hour later, there was no sign of Kaku, Bhai's contact.

He had arrived in time to see the police jeep leave. Donald Harper had come out in an angry stride. Which was encouraging. Yet what he had glimpsed of Lavanya; she must have been deeply shaken to have run like that. So the police were watching her but not protecting her, this much was clear. And he was the reason why. It had been a close shave today, yesterday, and tomorrow. He had no idea how long he could keep this up.

If he lived with danger like he was doing, going from one day to another, there was every chance he could become immune to the feeling. The illusion that whatever was lurking out there wouldn't get him, ever. The illusion that he could keep sidestepping imminent trouble for as long as he wished. In actuality, he would only be getting careless. It was just the way the world worked. He knew it all and yet he knew he was too far gone to employ reason with the world.

Minutes later, seeing the back door of the kitchen open as the khansama flitted in and out, he slipped in. He knew the way inside. He had watched Kaku carefully the last time. He grabbed one of many toasted flatbread rolls stuffed with flavoured minced beef fresh off the giant tava and slipped it into his coat pocket along with the greasy paper it had been lying on. For some incomprehensible reason, he felt lucky, all of a sudden.

The kindling

LAVANYA LAY CURLED UP ON HER BED FOR AS LONG AS SHE could. Donald Harper had been waiting for her, waving the day's newspaper in his hands. The questions came like a volley of gunshots. Why had she gone to see the lady painter? What did she tell her to cause such a severe reaction? Why couldn't she stay out of trouble? Between Ratan and her, how many people were they planning to get to the already spilling-over hospital in Simla? Had she read the papers? Did she know what they were saying about him? He could see her out of breath, doubled over, holding on to her waist as she stared at him, disbelieving, but he didn't stop till he had finished. Finally, she had walked past him without any acknowledgment. He didn't deserve any answers. This infuriated him more and he followed her inside. She was not to go anywhere till he could spare some policemen to go with her. She continued up the stairs, in silence.

When she first heard the knocks, she refused to move. Then finally, she opened the door to see an empty corridor. Not a single policeman dotted the corridor. The sun had dipped in her room and the orange glow of sunset cast a long shadow in the corridor. Her mouth felt dry and she could feel a dull ache in her heart. She closed the door and then carefully bolted it. She turned around and there he was. Standing exactly where she had imagined he would stand, all morning. He looked sheepish. Like he knew exactly what he wanted to say, but if he did say those exact words they would end up sounding foolish.

She stared at him. He wasn't a vision. He was real. Visions were real, come to think of it. More real than reality, which was made up of all sorts of imagined details. What she chose to do or not do seemed to be based on imagined details, more often than not. The reason why she had not opened the door for Ratan at the Davenport House. The reason why she had run from Amrita Sher-Gil's house, thinking Sara's gashed painting or the person who did that to Sara's painting was right behind her. The reason why she stood here imagining how nice it would be to stop shaking like a leaf by holding on to him.

Ratan's eyes were widening questioningly now. How long were they going to stand here like this? Or was she planning to bolt, open the door and make a run for it? He took a step. The next moment, she was flying into him. She came so fast, covering the distance between them in a whoosh, her shawl flying, the newspaper Donald Harper had handed her, still clutched tightly in her hands. Ratan held her, or was it she holding him? They stood like that for the longest time. He realized he was shaking too. She felt warm in his arms, just the right temperature to hold on a cold windy morning and fall asleep to. Standing, if need be.

'Where have you been?' she asked, finally. Her voice sounded like an old woman's. Thin and quivering, she hated the sound of it.

'Shut out in the cold? Waiting for an old friend to let me in?' he said.

'I'm sorry.'

'Strangely, I do think you are,' Ratan pulled back to get a good look at her. Lavanya, repentant, was a rare occurrence. She looked distraught.

'What were you doing running all the way from Kat Godam?' he said, resisting the urge to pat her hair down.

'You saw me?' Lavanya moved away from Ratan to sit at the edge of the bed. At once, she was cold again. Why would he watch her and not stop for her?

'There was a police jeep behind you. I didn't know what to do.'

Lavanya nodded. The superintendent had hoped to get lucky. No wonder he had been so livid.

'You're cold Lava … let's light that fire,' Ratan went to the fireplace and poked at the wood with the grater. He was looking for something that he couldn't find. Then he looked back at her. 'What's in that newspaper you were holding?'

'The superintendent said I should read all the news about you. A policeman you fatally wounded is in hospital. Also the friend you killed in his own farm who had given you shelter after you killed Sara and didn't know where to go. It's all here,' she gestured at the paper, now lying on the bed next to her.

Lavanya saw Ratan's face change colour—or was it the temperature? It had gone from a warm brown to a cold and pale yellow. She realized what she had said sounded accusatory. She didn't have the energy to take it all back and explain her intent. She was just repeating what the bastard Donald Harper had told her.

Ratan got up and picked up the newspaper. 'My apologies for depriving you of your morning news, Lavanya, but I need this right now.' He didn't want to be here anymore. He wished he had had the good sense to stay away. He didn't feel lucky anymore.

She had gone from the old familiar Lava to the cold familiar Lavanya in a matter of a few seconds. For a writer, she really had no flair with words when they were spoken aloud.

He had got the fire going, using the newspaper as kindling.

'Ratan, I didn't read the paper, I didn't need to. I believe you.'

'So tell me, why didn't you open the door for me last night?' Ratan sat down on an armchair and looked at her, his eyes like slits and his face closed.

He knew why. Of course, he did. There was no point denying it.

'Yesterday was overwhelming, that's why. Also, a maid gave me something, wait, let me show you.'

'Why are you here, Lavanya? Have you run out of stories?' he said, he wasn't going to let her go so easily.

She stopped cold. 'Is that what you think?' she asked.

'Well …?'

'How dare you? You, Rat, have implicated me! I had a policeman pay me a visit at my home, accuse me of writing offensive stories, drag me to the police station for questioning, force me to read from my book to an audience of policemen with journalists present, so they can report how it provoked a murder that YOU ran away from … and what was that you just asked me?' Lavanya was livid as she snatched the letter from among the clothes in the suitcase and went and thrust it in his hands.

It was Ratan's turn to not answer. He looked down at the letter in his hands. He read it, then read it again, slowly. He folded it and kept it in his pocket. He knew he was going to read it many more times.

'A maid gave this to you? Why? Lava, tell me everything, try and remember everything, do you understand, everything?'

'First, you tell me …'

'I'm sorry, I was angry at what you said …'

'I shouldn't have said that,' Lavanya flopped down on the carpet next to where Ratan was sitting, hugging her knees.

'There's too much to tell. I don't want to miss out on a thing. But right now, I want to be quiet. Please,' she said. He nodded, staring into the fire. The newspaper had burnt to a shimmering ash. The timber had caught the flames and changed colour from yellow to orange to mustard with flecks of gold. The room was warm again and he was ravenous. The letter he had read seemed to flash in the fire, each word smouldering with hidden meaning. Richard was being blackmailed. After which Sara ended up dead. It was the last letter sent by the blackmailer. Whoever had sent it knew something that could help him find out who killed Sara and Shyam. Somebody who knew the figure in the woods.

He remembered the flatbread in his pocket. Thankful, he took it out and was about to bite into it when he saw Lavanya look up. He got up and sat down next to her on the carpet. Outside, through the closed windows and the shaded curtain, he could hear the wind sigh and rustle among the trees. Lavanya took a big bite of the mince roll. Soon, he found himself wishing he had grabbed another one. He wasn't sure he was going to get any with the portions she was wolfing down. Between mouthfuls, she told him everything that had transpired since she saw him last.

The strange maid, the blackmail letter, Eden passing out, the journalists and their unending questions, the manicured lawns of Wildflower Hall where Sara was found, sorry, where he, Ratan had found Sara, and finally, her visit to Amrita Sher-Gil's house.

This is where she slowed down because the shock of it was still so fresh in her mind.

'Ratan, one minute she was chatty then she was quiet. I was so embarrassed, certain I was going to trip down those steps and make an even bigger fool of myself, that I didn't notice. When I looked up, she was no longer standing. She fell down so *noiselessly*. She had been eating cake. There was a lit cigarette in her hand. She was frothing at the mouth…'

'Sara and Amrita were friends,' Ratan said quietly. He was never part of her plans with Amrita. She drove herself there and back and was never forthcoming with any details of their time together.

Lavanya told him about the painting—Sara's face ripped and scratched, mercilessly. She saw Ratan's face harden.

'Tell me about the maid who gave you the letter again?' he didn't want to think about Sara's face like that.

'I think she saw me and thought, she's Indian and she's a woman, I can trust her. I think she knows more but she was too frightened, she looked brave but she was also scared, do you know what I mean …?'

They looked at each other. It was scary to be brave in the times they lived in. He knew what she meant.

'I have to try talking to her, you'll have to point her out to me, Lavanya, can you do it in the morning?'

There was a knock on the door. A gentle discreet knock.

Ratan was on his feet and out of sight at once.

It was the chambermaid looking most concerned.

'Miss? Your dinner?'

Lavanya nodded absentmindedly. The tray came in noiselessly and the maid left.

'I'm not hungry, I should have told her that,' Lavanya said, looking at the tray full of food.

'I'm so glad to hear you say that,' Ratan said as he helped himself to a plate. 'Don't even come near this tray.'

'Are you going to eat all that by yourself?' Lavanya inched closer.

'Watch me,' Ratan said. 'You should see what I eat every day. Prison might be an improvement, seriously. Now stay away and don't stop talking.'

Lavanya was about to protest but thought better of it. There was a lot on her mind.

As Ratan ate, Lavanya outlined all her theories on who could be blackmailing Richard Davenport. Behind them, the night descended like a fluttering bedsheet with stars on it. In another life he knew, he would have stepped out for a smoke, without a care in the world, listening to the lone dog bark.

'We have to find her. Tomorrow morning, be up early, leave like you're stepping out for a morning walk and I'll meet you not far from here.'

'Stay, don't go,' Lavanya heard herself say.

Ratan looked at Lavanya and remembered how she had held on to him earlier, then moved away, then inched closer. She was still shaken. But could he let her see how shaken he was? He had left his part of the story out, it was an old habit. He was better at listening than talking. Especially about himself.

'Aren't you going to tell me about Sara, Ratan?' As usual, she had read his mind.

'What do you want to know?' he asked.

'Was she the love of your life?' Lavanya kept her gaze on him.

'It wasn't like that. She had many lovers and so did I. But we loved each other, yes.'

'Did Richard know?'

The photographs. Somebody had taken those photographs. Was it the same person who had written the blackmail letters?

'Lava, I promise I'll tell you everything, maybe you'll make sense of it better than I can. But not now, I had better go now.'

Lavanya nodded. She could sense it in him. There was that old urge to run away again. They weren't too different, the two of them.

'What are you going to do?' Lavanya said, feigning a yawn.

'I have an evil plan I need to work on,' Ratan said, deadpan. 'See you in the morning?'

How he wished he actually had a plan. Even a stupid one, if not an evil one.

The fire spluttered and coughed before dying completely, once he left. But the room was warm enough to last her the night.

A musty almirah

THE NEXT MORNING, LAVANYA AND RATAN HID BEHIND the massive oaks that lined the Davenport house. The birds were singing their hearts out. Flitting from one tree to the other as the breeze ruffled their feathers. They watched the staff arrive, in silence. The sunlight filtered down from between the leaves in a golden swirl and fell on the flower garden that encircled the house. Some of the servants walked, some came on bicycles, often in pairs. Laughing and chatting, exchanging gossip. Then falling into a deathly silence as they came within sight of the main gate. It seemed ridiculous now to Ratan that it took so many people to take care of one or two people in a house. Ratan had never questioned this before. Looking at things from behind a tree gave one perspective, that was for sure.

She appeared at last, trailing behind the rest. Just when Lavanya was about to give up. She had just asked Ratan if there was another way in or was it possible she lived within the grounds of the house. He remembered his moonlit encounter with the girl under the tree. What if he were to see her again? Then Lavanya was gripping his hand tight. It was her. She walked alone. Like she was dragging herself every step of the way. Eyes blazing through the tall pines around her.

Ratan too recognized her at once. She was Cheeni's sister, Barfi. Shyam had arranged to have her work at the Davenports' right after his marriage to Cheeni. On Shyam's insistence, Ratan had spoken to Sara about her. They had never met, except for that first time when Shyam had brought her along with him, requesting Ratan to introduce her to Sara who was looking for a reliable day maid. He remembered a sweet-faced girl with wide curious eyes. A lot had happened since, no doubt.

He heard the guards change positions around the house, barking orders to the servants to send along tea and breakfast.

'That's Barfi. I think I know where she lives … I'll find her today evening …'

Lavanya was looking at him and shaking her head.

'Anything could happen between now and then …'

Before Ratan could stop her, she stepped out from behind the tree were they were hiding. Ducking as low as she could, he watched as she headed towards the path Barfi was walking on.

'No Lava, no, not now … it's too dangerous …' He might as well not have spoken.

Barfi continued to drag her feet. Lavanya called out to her in a tight whisper.

'Barfi!'

Barfi stopped at once, startled. Instinctively looking behind her only to find rows and rows of trees silently swaying to the breeze. Lavanya called again and saw Barfi swing her head around and spot her. She stared at Lavanya, breathing heavily, eyes questioning.

'Barfi, I want to thank you … for the letter. You did a brave and important thing that day by giving it to me …'

Barfi nodded, disarmed but not distracted. Her eyes kept scanning the trees beyond Lavanya for any sign of movement.

'What you wanting now?' she asked.

'I need you to tell me where you found this letter?'

'I found it on Sahib's desk.'

Barfi's eyes were getting darker and darker from the imagined danger she was sensing. Lavanya knew she had to probe more.

'Barfi, who put the letter on Sir Davenport's desk, do you know?'

Barfi shook her head. 'Nahin. I must go, I am being late …'

'Barfi, then I'll have to tell the police you gave me the letter. They will question you, do you want that?'

Barfi looked at her with stark naked hate. 'Oh my fate. I trusted you? Why? You are one of them, I can see now, say what you want, I will never betray my …' she spoke rapidly in Hindi, then stopped. She knew she had already said too much.

'Tell me, Barfi. Who will you never betray? I will keep your secret safe, I will never let you get into trouble …' Lavanya took a step towards Barfi.

Barfi tried to get past her but Lavanya stood resolute.

'You must tell me, you can't keep it a secret, I can help you …'

There was a clamour in the bushes and then Ratan appeared before them.

Barfi looked at him like he had materialized from the trees. Ratan nodded at her. 'Barfi. Do you remember me?'

To his utter surprise, Barfi stared at him, muttered 'Ratan bhaiyya ...' and burst into tears. Silently, the tears poured down her face. Ratan and Lavanya sat her down under the tree and let her cry for a while before Lavanya gave her the end of her silk dupatta to wipe her tears. She seemed to prefer her hands.

Barfi spoke rapidly now. Her words tumbling one on top of the other. Sara memsahib had promised her not to tell anyone. Sara memsahib meant the world to her. She had been kindest to her. She used to give her one of these letters every week and ask her to put it in the mail along with all the other letters. This was the last letter, she had said. Then she was killed. Then Shyam bhaiyya was killed. Then Cheeni, her sister, had come home in shock, having lost her voice. Cheeni didi had been unable to speak since Shyam had been killed.

Ratan's breath caught in his throat. He realized what had happened. Barfi had been carrying it all inside her for so long, all it needed was a familiar face from the past, a past that had been kind and sheltered and a far cry from the unrest she had known since. Now seeing Ratan, everything inside her had crumbled.

So it was Sara. Sara had been blackmailing Richard. Her own husband. The why was easy. She wanted to get away, go back to England, needed the papers and the money. But what did she have on Richard that was so explosive?

And Cheeni? She had gotten away the day Shyam was killed. Had she seen something? If she had lost her voice, would they ever know?

It seemed he too had lost his voice as he tried to find the words with which to comfort Barfi who kept looking up at him with her tear-stained face, waiting for him to tell her it was okay, things would be all right again.

Then he heard Lavanya speak.

'Barfi, you've got it all off your chest now, it's all going to be okay. You'll see it's all going to be okay. Now take a deep breath and go back to work. You have nothing to worry about.'

Barfi nodded at her, it was like Lavanya had spoken for Ratan. She got up, dusted her saree, took in gulps of air to steady herself, gave them one last look, and stepped out of the clearing between the bushes. Then she stepped back in and looked steadfast at Ratan. Her eyes no longer looked angry.

'Ratan bhaiyya, no matter what they be saying, Cheeni didi and I know you cannot be causing Sara memsaab any harm.'

'Or Shyam, Barfi, I would never hurt Shyam, he was my friend.'

Barfi nodded, wiped her eyes once more, and left.

Lavanya kept her eyes on Barfi making her way back on the open path. The guards continued to chat on their tea break as Saigal sang sorrowfully on the radio. Ratan looked at her peering from behind the tree and had a sudden urge to shake her. He remembered how he had called out to her, telling her it was dangerous and she had not listened. What if Barfi had reacted differently? Screamed for help to look innocent? The guards would have been upon them instantly. Lavanya turned around, looked at him, and stared.

'You've got Barfi's eyes now …' Lavanya said.

'Lavanya, what you just did was stupid, you know that, right?' Ratan hissed.

'Better stupid than sorry,' she muttered.

He refused to acknowledge the hint of a self-congratulatory grin in her eyes.

'You can't do what you like. If I remember correctly, it isn't a free country, yet.'

'I'm sorry,' she said demurely, eyes down.

'Let's get out of here …' he held out for as long as he could, '… stupid.' He grinned, giving her his hand.

They walked together for a while. Both of them mulled over what Barfi had just told them and then looked at each other and said the name together.

Sara.

She was the one behind the blackmail letters. Neither had seen that coming.

'We need proof. Barfi's words won't do. If it was Sara writing those letters, there must be proof. We can take that to Davenport and confront him.'

'Confront Richard? Are you mad? He's behind all this, going to him will be the end of me.'

'Okay. If we can find out what she was blackmailing him with, we won't need to confront him. We could just go to the police.'

'The police know how to mishandle evidence, Lava, which world do you live in? These are powerful people, one word from Davenport and I'm done for.'

'Ratan, I know it looks bad, very bad, but can we please focus on getting some answers? Think, think, she must have let on something.'

Ratan thought back to the last few days. He knew how much Sara wanted to leave India and go back to England. She wanted none of the guilt of ruling over the people she had grown to love. Politically, the heat in the last few years had only gone up, even in cool, breezy Simla, from a persistent simmer to a furious boil. She wanted to take sides, she *couldn't* take sides. She wanted to leave and she knew Richard would never let her leave. He loved his life in India with her by his side. Politically and publicly, a single married man in India held little meaning. Every time she brought up the subject of returning, he would refuse to discuss it. One of the few matters she had known him to be implacable about.

'You know what I like about you, Ratan? You need me as much as I need you,' she had told him once. He had shaken his head, he didn't understand.

'Don't you see? You don't want me to be your whole world. I am free with you. With him, all I can think of is unshackling myself, getting away. Far away.' They were at Nevermore, it was the farthest she could get from Richard. She would often go there to be alone. Luckily for her, the Summers were rarely in India and the keys to the bungalow were always with her.

Something struck him and he stopped walking. Had she written the letters at Nevermore? It was possible, it was impossibly possible.

He started running to the car, pulling Lavanya with him. He had a vision of Sara sitting on the escritoire facing the window, the huge white bougainvillea outside framing her. Those were her two favourite places. The armchair for reading and the table by the window for writing. Once, when he had crept in on her, wanting to surprise her, her fingers had been poised on paper. There had been creases of worry on her forehead. She had been completely oblivious to his presence. The first thing she had done was not look up at him with that impish eager smile she always had for him. The first thing she had done was cover the paper she had been writing on, with her arm and her scarf. Completely blocking it from view. He had teased her, he wanted a peek, he had said. She had laughed, asking for time. It wasn't ready, she would show it to him when it was. He had believed her.

He gripped Lavanya's hand.

Ratan now knew with a startling certainty, Sara was writing the very blackmail letters she would soon hand over to Barfi.

They drove in complete silence. He didn't say much to Lavanya, just that he was following a hunch. She kept looking at him, wondering if he was going to be forthcoming with any more details about where they were going. She wanted to know if she was being kidnapped and if she was, would he be kind enough to tell her beforehand? She knew she was rambling on but it felt good. He nodded absentmindedly but continued looking intently at the road.

Lavanya gave up and looked at the road instead. Slipping away from under her and stretching out in front. Looking up, the rolling countryside framed by snow-capped peaks and dense forests of pines, deodars and rhododendrons seemed to be spreading a carpet of colours she had never seen. With the hills unfolding before her, her mind opened out like one of those Japanese fans her father kept in his study. Drifting like the clouds above her. The painter was on her mind, all of a sudden. How was she? She could still smell the pineapple frosting on the cake in her studio.

Ratan rounded up a hill to reach a meadow carpeted with wild flowers. Velvety, lavender little things with white dots on them. He drove through them and she looked down, sad to see them crushed. As she looked, the little lavender heads bobbed right back up at her.

The car stopped and Ratan raced out without looking to see if she would follow. Lavanya stepped out in a trance, the journey up the hill had made her light-headed and now this little spot with the bungalow clinging to the edge of a mountain made her more dizzy.

Ratan walked past the living room and down the corridor that connected the rooms and past the kitchen garden, to the little library window with the Chippendale desk. He could feel his heart beating a little faster with every step. He kicked himself for not having done what he was about to do. He knelt beside the desk and inspected it. It was bare and clean. A little too clean maybe. He ran his hands over the fine grains of teak, then knocked on it. Once, twice. Then slipped his hand under the table, groping. There was a false drawer in there. He bent to look and sure enough, there was an opening small enough to hold a drawer. A small tug and the drawer slid out and a small key plopped into Ratan's hands. He emerged from under the table, looking for Lavanya.

He turned around to see her, flushed from finding her way around the bungalow. He had this sudden urge to kiss her as she knelt down beside him. His face was radiating an excitement she had not seen in a long time. He looked hopeful. She wanted to cup his face in her hands too. He waved the key at her. Then he was up on his feet, his eyes telling Lavanya to follow him.

He walked with long, fast strides, all the way back down the corridor to the landing in the living room. He looked up at the staircase going up to all the rooms on the first floor. All the almirahs were on the first floor. On his first day here, he had opened each and every one of them with the set of keys he'd found inside a jar in the foyer. Except two that were locked. Could this be the key to those? It was worth a try. He had felt lucky earlier today and so far, the day had given him more breaks than he had hoped for. One more and he would be more than grateful. He took the stairs two at a time with Lavanya behind him. He went from room to room, trying to find the locked almirahs but they all looked the same. He tried the key in each one and it didn't fit. Finally, when he was close to giving up, one of the doors gripped the key and held it. He turned the key and it opened. It was tunnel-dark inside. He should have brought along the torch. Lavanya ran to the windows and drew the heavy drapes apart to let the light in.

It was full of hangers with clothes grown musty with time. He groped along the edges inside. There was nothing under the hangers. He looked again, slowly this time, then again, nothing.

'Why would she hide the key and keep nothing in the almirah to find?' Ratan muttered aloud. His luck seemed to have run out. His throat dry, he stormed down the stairs with slumped shoulders.

Lavanya went to the almirah and peered inside. There were rows of mouldy suits and jackets, coats and overcoats, but nothing else. All in the darkest of colours. Rows of naphthalene scented memories covered in dust. Like her grandfather's almirahs in Ranikhet, where every summer, they went to spend their vacations. Most days were long and boring there and she waited for those rare occasions when Dadu would leave home forgetting to lock his almirah. Then she would open them, to sniff into his collection of ittar and eau de cologne bottles collected over the years. The little glass bottles in many shapes and sizes sat lined on one shelf. Every day after he had bathed, still in his bathrobe, she would watch him lifting them up one by one. Sniffing each one and sometimes, right away, knowing what he wanted. He never touched any of those coats. He had too many, it seemed. Soon, those dark corners deep inside Dadu's coats became her favourite hiding places. Everything from tiny scraps of paper with minutely written confessions to stolen coins from her mother's *gullak* went into the pockets. Lavanya stopped reminiscing and stared hard at the rows of coats hanging inside. Every woman was once a little girl with secrets. With pockets to put them in. And Sara, it had been well-established today, was full of secrets. She went to work. Dust flew, pockets hung upside down, kerchiefs and cigarettes, bills and notes fluttered in her hands and she threw them aside. Finally, in one dark green tweed coat with deep pockets, her hands found a packet. A heavy packet covered in brown paper. The shade of brown appropriated by the government for all official communication. Her heart beating a triumphant wild drum, she cried out for Ratan. He came bounding up the stairs to find her holding the packet like it was an offering of explosives and the sooner it was taken off her hands, the better.

Five minutes later, they were at the desk by the window, staring at the contents of the packet which lay open in front of them: two tickets, two passports and a fairly large bundle of cash. The tickets were for the *Duke of Grafton*, a ship that was set to sail from Bombay the following week. The two British India passports belonged to Sara Davenport and Eden Easton. The names on the tickets were the same.

Lavanya looked at Ratan checking inside the packet again and again, to see if there was anything else. It took her a while to piece together that he was looking for his own ticket, his own passport. But there was none. There it was again, his inability to face facts.

'She was going to leave without me ...' Ratan finally said the words aloud.

Lavanya nodded, with as much sympathy as she could manage.

'She knew I wasn't going to come ... and all the while I was planning to lie to her ...' he broke off, shaking his head.

Again, Lavanya nodded.

'It doesn't make sense. She had imagined a whole life for us in England ...'

'She changed her mind, Ratan. It's as simple as that,' she realized she shouldn't have said that last bit as soon as it left her mouth.

Ratan looked at her, disbelieving.

'This, all this, you think it's simple?'

'That's not what I meant, you know that.'

Her mind scrambled to veer the subject away from his present dilemma.

'But why *Eden*, Ratan? What do you make of her? Do you think she knows anything?'

'They go a long way back. Eden and Sara travelled together on the ship from England to India. They met on the ship when Eden fell quite ill and Sara basically nursed her back to health. As a result, Sara was always extremely protective of her. They were both husband-hunting so they stayed together once they reached Bombay, went everywhere together. "Fishing Fleeters" they were called. They met Richard and Marc almost immediately at a party in Bombay and got married a few days apart. It's only when they got here, to Simla, that Eden started having all sorts of ailments. She couldn't take to living in the mountains like Sara had.'

She had always seemed on edge to Ratan. Sara was always her gentlest with Eden, minding her words so that nothing would upset her but something or the other always did. Dinner parties would be hastily terminated as Eden would come running out in tears. Marc Easton always followed soon after, gently coaxing her to calm down but mostly driving her home.

Ratan had driven Eden home a few times too. Mostly in silence. All the sniffling stopped as soon as she was in the car and on her way home. As he drove, he would watch her from the rear-view mirror, wiping away tears, looking out of the window into the inky night, no trace of worry on her face. She never spoke to him directly except when it was absolutely necessary. Once, just once what had happened, had happened. It had made him wonder about her.

Lavanya saw Ratan get up and take a deep swig from a bottle of water. Some of the water dribbled down his chin and he wiped it off with the back of his hand. He looked flummoxed. She had to keep his mind working.

'If Sara was blackmailing Richard for the fare to go back home, why was she taking Eden along with her? What about Marc? Did he know?'

Ratan looked at Lavanya and shook his head. This was news to him as well. Sara had spoken endlessly of the two of them, Ratan and Sara, taking off together and how there would be no more looking over the shoulder. No more pretending. There was never any talk of anybody else on the journey.

Even though he had never planned to go, Ratan had been careful to show enough enthusiasm for all her plans. He had needed time to think things through. Sara could not have known he was never planning to leave India, of that he was certain. Yet here it was. Two tickets. One for Eden. One for Sara. She had known.

Lavanya could see why Ratan was so perplexed at all of this unfolding the way it had. Ratan had never been part of her plan. It had been Eden all along. For a moment, it seemed like Sara had framed him.

'I have to go now. Take me back,' Lavanya said softly. Ratan needed to have an internal monologue, she was in the way. She looked around at the bungalow and the sun streaming through the white bougainvillea window. How she wished she could stay.

They didn't speak as they hurried back to the car. There had been no time to tell Lavanya about the photographs he had found. If it was all borrowed time he had before the police found him, what was he doing with it?

'Can you come back, Lava? Tonight? It's not fair that you're in my mess without knowing how it came about …'

Lavanya looked at him as he drove. Come back? There was nothing she wanted more. Yet her heart was beating wildly at how dangerous it all was. She could almost see her door being broken down and Donald Harper charging through to find the room empty, pulling off the carpets to see the trapdoor hinge concealed in the wooden floorboards. She could see the yellow fury in those white tube-light eyes.

'I'll cook for you,' Ratan said, taking his eyes off the road to look at her briefly. There was that yearning in them again.

'You said the magic words,' she grinned at him.

If she tried she could

LAVANYA SNEAKED BACK IN WITHOUT INCIDENT. SHE EVEN managed to lie inert staring at the ceiling for an uninterrupted half hour before the first knock on her door.

She didn't move. So many new developments. How did they all come together? If Sara was writing the blackmail letters, giving them to the angry maid to slip inside Richard's mail, what had he done about it? Except give her the money. Which meant that whatever she had on him was nasty but could he just let the blackmailer escape? Had he found out that it was her? Was that why he was so broken? Killing someone you loved could do that to you, couldn't it? She turned over to the other side. The tickets were for Sara Davenport and Eden Easton. Who was the packet of money for? Sara? If the police were to question Eden would she accept or deny she was going to leave the country with Sara? Did she know about the tickets? Had she told Marc? It was worth finding out.

Amrit Singh was at the door. By now she knew his short, even, impatient knocks. He made his way to the sofa and sat down, shifted his great bulk on either side and found a balance that worked. He cleared his throat. He had something on his mind. It was Amrita Sher-Gil.

Yes? Did he want to say something accusatory like his boss?

'I'm sorry I wasn't there,' he said simply, looking everywhere except at her. She was glad to be spared his gaze because that simple statement brought a sting of tears to her eyes. She swallowed it in a blink.

'Tell me about her, Inspector. How is she? Can I visit her in the hospital?' she asked.

'Her parents drove down from Naldehra and took her back with them. They will be leaving for Lahore soon. The doctors say she was poisoned, that she reached the hospital just in time.'

The cake! It had to be the cake. She knew it in her bones.

'Did she say who had visited her that day? Before me …'

'We couldn't get her to say a thing. She couldn't understand why she was in the hospital to begin with. She had no memory of meeting you, either,' Amrit Singh was looking at her now. She could see how frustrated he was with the whole event.

'We are investigating all the people who had visited her that day. We will find out soon who tried to poison her. She is a well-known painter and is a favourite on party lists. Hosts like to have her come to their parties because she is also known for her colourful remarks about people that lead to a lot of mirth and amusement for the guests. Of course, not everybody is a fan, especially if she's said something about you to a party full of guests.'

That sounded like her. Did he know anything about her relationship with Sara? Were they close?

'Some say, too close,' Amrit Singh said, with hooded eyes.

Ah, interesting. *Too close.* That explains why Amrita would paint Sara so lovingly. *Too close.* But not as close as Sara was to Eden? For finally, the person going with Sara back to England was Eden. *Too close.* She could see Ratan still pacing the grey-and-white mosaic tiles on the sunlit veranda, deep in thought. He had been upstaged and he had not seen it coming.

'Do you have any plans for me today because there are a few things I would like to do, visit the town library to start with, and then a visit to Richard Davenport to discuss a write-up on Sara ...'

'Today, we would prefer you stay in ... I have strict instructions,' he gestured helplessly at the newspapers he had brought along with him. Not the papers again, Lavanya thought, as she recalled the series of interviews yesterday.

She spent the next hour reading one report after another where she was being portrayed as a writer of trash, a villain of words and a vamp of the freedom of speech. Except her plea to Ratan to give himself up, nothing else had been reported without distortion.

Readers and various groups were questioning the police as to why she was in Simla to begin with. Hadn't the hillside town seen enough unrest in the last few days? Was she here to hide their own incompetence at not being able to find Ratan?

'The superintendent has asked you to stay in for your own safety.'

'More like make his job easier than it already is?' Lavanya asked rhetorically.

Amrit Singh refused to meet her gaze. It was a mess and he knew it. As for Lavanya, the audacity of spending an evening with the very person that was giving Donald Harper sleepless nights made her feel infinitely better.

She nodded meekly at Amrit Singh and went to the table in the corner of the room and sat down, as if to write a letter. He was on his feet soon enough and walking to the door.

'I'll stay in. I won't need you today then. I'll see you tomorrow. Have a good day, Inspector.'

This sounded so unlike her that Amrit looked twice to see if she was perhaps joking. She kept her face straight.

After he left, Lavanya bolted the door. Finally, alone, flushed from all that she had read, she felt an old familiar urge rush up in her. *Bastards.* Lavanya picked up all the writing paper she could find. On the study table, inside the drawers, and in her suitcase. Noor had left her journal diaries alone. She took them all and flopped down on the bed. Soon, she had created an island of sorts. She, in the centre of the bed, surrounded by an ocean of blank pages. She couldn't write anywhere as well as she could where she slept. Something about where she lay and dreamed, sometimes stared at the ceiling. Thoughts flitting about like clouds, dark and translucent, stormy and lit, hovering. It was a space crackling with curious energy. And some days, if she was lucky and willing, the energy travelled. Coursing through her body, looking for a way out. Up her arms and down her fingers into those blank pages. Pen poised, she waited. Behind her, the sun shifted its gaze and the light went mellow through the ivory white curtains. She pressed pen to paper and her hand began to move.

This was how she had first met Sitara. She could sense her again. Sitting somewhere on a corner of the bed, amused, watching. She didn't look up. Hours passed and she didn't know it. Not until her stomach growled. The sound of a lunch tray wheeling through the corridor broke her trance completely. Reluctant to put her pen down, she wondered if she could forego lunch and continue moving the pen along. She was afraid to call what she was doing, writing. Then her stomach growled again and she put her pen down, promising to pick it up again. '*Emp-ty promi-ses*'. Was that Sitara taunting her in a sing-song voice? After lunch, her bed looked different. All the papers, the scattered mess, did not feel half as alluring as before. The sleep she had not thought about in the last two days came in a rush. She waved the papers aside and made enough space for her sleeping form to fit in. The sun from behind the curtains covered her in layers of golden shimmering sheets. The last thing she saw was Sitara lying down, too, and closing her eyes.

Ratan had explained to her in excruciating detail, how the floor trap door was to be lifted. The latches would shift easily as he had left them unlocked for her. Once she went inside the trap door, it was a simple enough path, a flashlight was all she needed and she'd be out in the garden soon enough.

She wore one of Noor's twilight-blue lace gowns to blend into the evening. It was sheer lace till her neckline and then a delicate gathered ruffle that dropped down with velvet ribbons as flyaway embellishments. Over it, she wore a ruffled cream capelet with rich floral embroidery. The flowers had the tiniest crystals embellished all over and glittered like stars on a clear night. She lightly dabbed the ittar Noor had slipped into her bag in a satin pouch. It smelled of jasmine and roses, with a dash of something woody, was it pine? As close to a date as she had felt in years, Lavanya fretted if she was overdressed for the evening. Would he notice and if he did, how embarrassing would that be? She considered changing into something more inconspicuous but Noor had not planned on invisibility, rather the opposite. She told herself it was nothing, just an evening with an old friend to discuss ordinary issues such as murder and dead lovers. Hopefully over some delectable food and beverage.

Lavanya pulled herself together, refusing to look at herself in the mirror anymore. Taking a deep breath, she pushed the carpet aside. She bent down to lift the trap door. She tried again, putting all her weight behind it. It refused to budge.

Lavaṇya paced up and down, wondering what to do. Ratan had told her the story behind the secret trapdoor. The Birchwood guest house was once a bungalow that belonged to a British lord, Jim Glynn, who had a not-so-secret mistress. He started smuggling her in to his room. This was in defiance of his wife's wishes, of course. She knew of the mistress but had one simple instruction. She should never set foot in her home. Unable to keep anything simple, and to spare his wife any further angst, Jim Glynn built the secret passage. The entry was from the kitchen to the suite above. Knowing his wife would never set foot in the kitchen, his secret was safe. There would be little chance of a collision between the two. His servants were sworn to secrecy and his mistress had a free run of the kitchen and up to his room. Later, when he passed on, his son found the secret passage. He started using it as his gambling den, having learned from his father that there are some secrets every man must have. It became a famous haunt for gamblers and that's how Shafaqat Bhai first heard of it. When Birchwood came up for sale, he did his best to buy it. Instead, the Glynns sold it to the government and they made it into a guesthouse for state guests. The passage was still a well-kept secret and only Bhai's men knew of it.

Lavanya wondered if slipping down into the kitchen to find his man, Kaku, would help. What were her choices?

Ratan was waiting for her just beyond the garden. Would he come to see why she hadn't turned up? He might think she had changed her mind or she wasn't alone.

She had to think fast.

The melting

HE SAW HER, AT LAST. HOBBLING TOWARDS HIM.

She was fixing her hair, smoothening her capelet, trying to smile in greeting but she still looked like she had been in a catfight.

He had seen her look worse after a brawl with her brothers, often. She would give it back to them tooth and nail, and then sit somewhere dark and quiet, writing her fury down.

At least she was here. He had endured the worst possible happenings in his mind just sitting here, waiting for her.

He wanted to crush her in the tightest hug possible. Till he saw the dark clouds flitting across her face. She was in a mood.

'Don't start telling me you were waiting for me! That door wouldn't open. I spent an hour trying. Then went to find Kaku in the kitchen but the police were all over it. Making tea, eating pakoras. So had to come back up and jump down a window, into a thorny bush!'

'Oh god, are you okay? Let me see,' he tried to reach out to steady her, but she went past him.

Lavanya limped over to the car and sat down at the edge of the seat. So much for looking her best.

'Can you be still for a second?'

Ratan lifted her leg and stretched it, looking for signs of injury. He knew, like him, she felt everything in her legs.

'Lie down … I'll drive … unless you want to go back?' Ratan asked. He kept his eyes on hers to see if he could see the thought even remotely lurking somewhere in the corner of her eyes.

'No point in breaking your leg and then turning back, is there?' she said.

Lavanya went and stretched out on the back seat, keeping her leg straight, the pain coursing through her legs. Like hell she was going back.

He leaned in to help her get as far back as possible without her head hitting the door. She could smell him. Something cinnamon. The cinnamon mixed with the jasmine and roses in a way that could excite, well, a perfumer, for sure. His face was inches above hers and for an instant, she felt like wrapping her bruised legs around him to hold him there. It was a startling thought and she was sure he could see what she was thinking. She shrank. At once, he pulled away.

She drew her breath in. That was close.

Ratan drove and conjectured aloud what could have possibly happened with the trapdoor. Either it had jammed or Kaku had panicked and checked it once after his shift was over. Found it unlocked and locked it.

She didn't say anything. He fell quiet too. She wanted him to apologize but he was going on a tangent. Though what exactly was he supposed to apologize for, she wasn't sure. It was a long list, she decided. He wished she would say it was all right, the jump wasn't that bad. Even though it looked bad.

In the silence, the trees waved in the evening breeze and the road rustled up page after page of empty sound. The sun was going to set and the birds were returning home. She rolled the window down and let the cold air in. Her cape rippled and bounced around her neck, keeping it warm; the rest of her was still tingling from the fall.

Then they were there. Nevermore looked like it had been waiting for them to arrive. She got up. She felt fine. Ratan opened the car door and waited. Lavanya put her feet down and stood, wincing immediately. She looked up at Ratan and made a face. He moved in closer as she put her arm around him and hoisted herself up. He put his arm around her too, to steady her. Her waist felt tiny in his hand. They walked like that for a bit and then without exactly thinking about it, he swooped her up in his arms.

She looked up at him, catching her breath. He was looking straight ahead, covering the distance between the garage and the bungalow in long, easy strides. She took her time to gaze at all the contours of his face. How they had changed in the last five years. All the angles were much harder, more jagged than she had ever known them.

He felt like a human mountain and yet, snug. She had never felt more *carried*. Mountain outside, river inside, that was him. He carried her across the living room. Stopping at switchboards to switch on lamps and chandeliers. He went up the stairs and stopped at a divan on the first floor, covered with cushions. He put her down, all the while looking elsewhere.

'I know what you need.' He was gone.

She looked around. She was in a large plush hall with big picture windows on all sides. She could hear water running somewhere inside. Her eyes skimmed the place, taking in the paintings, the drapes, the crystals. The mountains outside the picture windows, twinkling with lights from the distant villages. How long could Ratan hide here? How long before the police found out? She shuddered at the thought. Ratan was putting off the lights now. She saw him taking quick strides down the stairs and back up, carrying candle stands. Soon the place was dark, only lit with flickering candles.

She knew what he was doing. Lights in the mountains travelled far.

Ratan was sitting beside her now. Carrying an ivory-coloured ceramic basin in his hands. He looked at her legs lying rigid on the divan and lifted one, then the other. She winced. Her lace gown had tiny thorns poking out of everywhere. Her feet stuck out, all red nerves popping out.

'Lava, your feet look very, very angry …' he smiled.

'I should consult them before I leap off …' her voice trailed off. He was cradling her left foot, his fingers on her ankle.

'You'd think by now they would know, no?' he said, his eyes laughing. 'Watch, they're going to stop complaining …'

He propped her with pillows against the wall. One by one, he placed both feet in the ice cold basin. Lavanya shuddered involuntarily as her feet touched the ice-cold water. Then there was another involuntary sensation, one she wasn't ready for.

Ratan was massaging her feet in the water. Smoothening the popping red veins. Crooning to them to calm down. She felt a hot prick of something graze at the back of her neck and whip around like a tiny tornado. She wanted to tell him to stop. She wanted to tell him many things she hadn't even told herself since she had seen him last. If she opened her mouth now, all that would burst forth. So she didn't. Except that her mouth, unlike her feet, was always ahead of her.

'Ratan, why didn't you write back to me all these years?'

Ratan didn't hear her, at first. Richard Davenport was on his mind. There must be some way he could trap him at his own game, he was thinking.

The foot in his hands wiggled. Ratan came back with a start. He looked up to see Lavanya, eyes wide and questioning. The sheer wonder of her sitting in this blessed borrowed bungalow with him, her feet wiggling in his hands. Then the foot flew out of his hand, swooped into the water and water splashed all over his face. Like a bird drying itself in the rain.

'Ratan, why didn't you write back to me all these years …?' she asked again.

'I was going to, at an appropriate time,' Ratan said. He felt compelled to add, 'I didn't know what is appropriate for me isn't appropriate at all.'

He dried her feet and put them down. Giving her his hand to stand up.

'I waited to hear back from you. Did you even read the stories?' She tried to keep all expectation out of her voice. Her feet, planted on the ground felt new. Though she liked holding on to him.

'I read them not once, but many times. I read them to Sara too.'

'And …?'

'Lavanya Shriram, when will you stop fishing?' Ratan was looking at her in mock amazement.

'Once, tell me once, I'll never ask again, I promise,' Lavanya said. She continued to put one foot before the other, not looking at him.

'I had a tough time reading them, especially Sitara's story. My eyes kept welling up. I missed home so much, my room, my city, our lane, the tree outside my veranda, the one you would climb to jump in, Ghonchu, his wife, how she was like a mother after Ma left, my sad father, his sad ideas, his wasted life, I missed it all so much, I felt like I had lost something I would never get back. I missed home because I suddenly missed Ma. I had told myself I would never ever think of her. She had left me, I would let her go. But these stories brought her back. All the memories, the happy ones, before they got sad. I finally understood why Ma left, the oppression she lived with. That she broke free from. I didn't blame her anymore. You freed me, Lava,' Ratan was looking out at the twinkling valley, a lost boy in a lost town at a lost time.

Lavanya didn't know what to say. 'I shouldn't have asked, sorry.'

'No, you shouldn't have had to. I'm sorry.'

She sat down on the divan. Every word Ratan had just said, lingered in the air. She was holding on to them, like a child holds on to a kite that could slip out of her hands any moment to get entangled in a tree that she could never climb. She had waited so long to know if he had liked reading them. If he was going to 'kill her with kindness'. Or not.

'And that note, Lava, it made me smile on a day when I felt so alone,' Ratan said, as if reading her mind.

The kite was fluttering happily in her hands, roaming the blue skies.

'I've had a hard time explaining that to the police, to the reporters, I sound deranged and quite possibly criminal-minded, I'm sure,' Lavanya said, watching Ratan's eyes crinkle with laughter.

'I've needed an *evil plan* ever since …' his voice sounded distant now.

' Ratan, have I told you, I feel like I *knew* her. Will you talk to me about Sara …?' She tried to get him back to her.

'First, let's go get our drinks? You're not going to believe how well-stocked we are.'

She held on to his arm as he took her down a carpeted stairway to the cellar. Rows and rows of wine stacked along the walls, all neatly labelled, and an array of decanters and glasses shone within. Another wall held a rack of dark rum, gin, whisky and other liquids in colours she couldn't give a name to.

'Which one would you prefer?' Ratan pulled out a bottle of German wine and read out the label. She would not know which to pick, why was he asking her?

'Why don't we make our own drink?' as soon as she said it, she liked the idea even better.

Ratan wasn't warming up to it as fast as she was. That was fair, considering it was her idea. But he caught on soon enough. He placed the bottle of wine back on its rack, and looked back at her.

'Our own signature cocktail? That is, Lavanya, the second best idea you've had this evening.'

'Is it? What was the first?'

'The first was jumping out of that window in that very posh dress.'

They took turns to pick out the alcohol they wanted in their drink. Dark rum, definitely, whisky, perhaps, cointreau, orange liqueur, absinthe, sure. Arms laden, they went up to the veranda where the sky had turned an orange-purple and the mountains inky black. Ratan disappeared and then came back with sliced lemons. The lemons were fresh off the trees surrounding Nevermore and he had plucked a few to prepare for dinner.

They decided to take turns mixing the liquid in the crystal decanter. Taking deep sips to make sure it was going in the right direction. The table, when they were done, looked like the celebration was over before it had begun.

'Right, now spill …?' Lavanya flopped down on the big cushioned armchair that could take at least three more of her. He preferred to stand, walk and talk.

The next one hour, Ratan told her everything that had happened since he left Bombay. All the stops he had made before coming to Simla and running into Sara at Bhai's card parlour. Then he told her about how Sara became a friend and a lover and the reason why leaving Simla became difficult. When he made up his mind to leave, he saw how excited and determined Sara was to take him along with her to England. The night he was going to tell her he was leaving, she had died in his arms. She had broken his heart before he could break hers. And the two tickets they found earlier in the day proved she knew he was leaving. How? He had no clue.

She saw his eyes start wandering, despairing.

'Who do you think … is there anybody you think who could have …?' Lavanya asked.

'I don't know but that day you didn't leave the door open … I did get inside.'

Ratan told her about the pictures he had found in Sara's unlocked drawer. Sara and him, together, in the club suite. 'Sir Davenport knew about Sara and me, Lava. Yet he didn't do anything. Why?'

Lavanya thought about a doting husband's quiet rage. Knowing his wife had a lover, an employee, a native, going in and out of the home they lived in.

'Maybe he did confront her about you, but she didn't tell you?' Lavanya said.

'Or that he was planning on killing her all the while. That day at the party, he got his chance. He said he was going away to Mashobra but he didn't or he did and came back, did the deed, and went back ...'

Lavanya sat up. 'Do you know there was somebody at the party who said the exact same thing? The inspector said there was a guest at the party, an Indian prince, who said he saw Richard. It had come up when they were questioning all the invitees and this young Indian prince ...' she stopped.

'Go on. This young Indian prince ...?' Ratan was looking at her oddly.

'He said that he had seen Richard at the party arguing with Sara in a garden balcony. When the inspector told his superintendent about it, he dismissed it.'

'Why?' Ratan asked.

'Because the prince is of unsound mind. It's a well-known fact. What they call, a half-wit.'

'The prince of Suraiah was at the party?' Ratan couldn't believe his ears.

'How do you know? Yes, yes, it was the prince of Suraiah. I remember Amrit Singh mentioning the same name.'

'I was working there, for the king, for a short while. Never mind that. It's a long story. And I will tell you …' Ratan's mind was racing. '… but it's possible Lava, then, it's possible Richard killed her and framed me. Only I don't quite know how to prove it.'

Ratan held his head in his hands, almost willing it to stop churning.

Then he felt Lavanya slide down next to him.

'We'll think it out together, Ratan … that's why I'm here,' she said.

He turned to look at her, nodding. Then snapping himself out of it, he got up and held out his hand.

'Come, I've been slaving for you. You think better when you've eaten in the mountains, they say.'

He helped her up. She took the still half-full decanter with her.

A bunch of pink and white bougainvillea stood in a huge glass vase at the centre of the table, next to a brightly burning, large silver candle stand. Exquisite porcelain dishes with sparkling forks and knives beamed at her. Ratan loved the little touches. He loved the good life. He was a dreamer caught in a horribly real situation.

'Rat, you realize you're playing house-house here, no?'

'Beats playing prison-prison, doesn't it?' he grinned.

He sat her down at the head of the long table.

Oh the fragrance. Lamb curry and basmati rice. Lavanya remembered how when Ratan's mother left, it was the one thing his father made for him every Sunday. Ratan hated eating alone with him and would often call Lavanya and her brothers to join him at that huge table. They would go, say a cheery namaste to his father and proceed to polish the curry off. Eating with their hands as Ratan ate with a fork under his father's watchful eye, stealing envious looks at them every now and then as they licked their fingers. Watching him scowl at her, she would give her fingers a few extra licks.

Now here they were. Ratan, cooking for her in faraway Simla. As she sipped her drink, surrounded by ice-capped mountains, in absolute wilderness. Here they were. Ratan, on the run from the police after the brutal killing of a fascinating woman. Inches away from prison. As she sipped wine and ate with him, deceiving the police and the doting husband of the fascinating murdered woman. Perspective was so unnecessary at times. She banished the second scenario and focused on the first.

He poured her some more from the decanter. Refilling his own glass as well.

'Promise you won't watch me eat. I hate it when you do that. I know I eat like a cannibal. My father sort of encouraged it. He said they enjoyed their food more than anybody else. And eating like a lady was such a bore.'

'I love to see you eat. It's one of the reasons I cooked.'

She took a little curry with her spoon to taste. Then, heaped rice and lamb curry all over the gorgeous porcelain plate. She watched the white of the rice disappear under the rich brown of the curry. Then she sank her hand in and swooped her first bite. Lord in Heaven. All the nuns in the convent school she had gone to, serenaded her for thinking of the lord. As a child, she had always associated good food with the nuns. Every time she passed their living quarters, the aroma would waylay her. There would be the gong of a church, a choir in the background, and that aroma wafting through. She would imagine them cooking, stirring broths on large shiny pans. Singing opera in high-pitched voices as they stirred. Now, of course, she knew they had an army of good native cooks stirring the pot for them. Her own mother had been competent, at best. Never managing to stir anything up that needed any kind of serenading. Lavanya ate and licked her fingers. Somewhere in the middle, she looked up and saw Ratan watching. She scowled at him. He grinned.

Later, as she settled back on the divan, he too sat down with her, bringing their glasses with him with fresh ice cubes swimming in them. They could see the twinkling lights down in the valley.

'Thank you. I should go while I can still move …'

Ratan looked at Lavanya, trying hard not to touch her face. Only to remind himself she was here. Nothing was so bad when she was here. When had that happened? He would not cling to her. No more clinging. His hand stayed where it was, by his side. He nodded at her. Yes, he would take her back now, see to that damn trapdoor too.

He got up, his legs aching. He hated the thought of coming back here alone. He gave her his hand to test her legs. She took it, balancing herself as she steadied herself on her feet. He let go of her hand. Both of them hobbled a bit and then realized what they were doing and started to laugh. He caught her as she was about to fall, laughing, back on the divan. One moment he was laughing, looking at her in his arms and then he wasn't. He was smoothening her hair from her face, there was so much hair all over her face. Wondering why she was always so dishevelled. How he loved parting her hair from her eyes, such lovely eyes, so much laughter, and so much unrest, all mingled up. Could he separate the two? Unrest on the left, laughter on the right. Then she was touching his face, his cheeks, brushing something away again and again. He was crying. Oh God. Those were his tears on her hands. When was the last time he had cried? Her arms were around him now and both of them collapsed on the divan. It was the same one Sara always sat on, curled up with Lavanya's book. Why was everything so mixed up? His head found Lavanya's shoulder and buried itself in it as she held him.

He cried for Sara, who had waited for him that night and he was late, for his mother, who hadn't looked back once after she had left. For his father, whom he had loved to disappoint again and again. For Sara, whom he couldn't tell he was never going to go away with, to England. His mother, who he had never gone looking for. His father, who he wanted to go back to, but only when he couldn't disappoint him anymore. For Sara, whose kindness he had taken and never had the courage to return. For his mother, who wrote to him and cried her longing in letters, to which he never ever replied. For his father, alone and anxious, reading about his son, the criminal. For Sara, whom he wished he had cared enough about to ask what was troubling her. What she was keeping from him, because there was so much he was keeping from her.

From nowhere, another image leaped into his collage of loved and lost faces. The tigress from Suraiah. Heavy with her cub. Looking at him with infinite compassion. The hunted have only one choice to make. How long they choose to wait. How long before fear and trepidation turned them into something no longer worthy of the hunt.

His shoulders stopped heaving. The tears dried. The tigress turned and walked away.

He held out his hand to Lavanya.

'Let's go.'

'No, come here,' Lavanya said.

She took his hand and pulled him to her. They sank down on the divan. She unbuttoned his shirt, one button at a time. All the while looking at him, daring him to stop her. Planting slow small kisses along his chest, feeling the hair on his chest perk up at the touch of her lips. She looked up to see him watching her.

'Do you want me to stop?'

He nodded and mumbled a yes.

'I can't hear you ...' she said, intent on her path. Tracing his nipples now.

'I want you to stop ...' he said softly. Eyes pleading otherwise.

'Now?' She licked a nipple, circling it.

He groaned and reached out for her, pulling her mouth to his. His mouth on hers plunging deep, as if wanting to taste all of her at once. Jasmine and rose and cinnamon with cedar and teak and pine cones and the dust from the lemons still in his fingernails. She inhaled deep, reached out for his hands and let his fingers twist around the pearl buttons on the gown, on the side of her waist. Soon, his hands slipped inside, grazing, cupping, squeezing, roaming free, till she held her breath, waiting for them to take the plunge. They rose up, and found her breasts. Then just like that, his hands were no longer on her. They were over her. Removing her cape, stopping to see her skin through the sheer lace before finding a way to unfasten the gown. She removed his shirt. He led her to the big window where she could see the lights below, he had eyes only for her. The more he looked, the bolder she got. Letting her hands roam over her body as his eyes followed. Then his kisses were tracing the path of the moonlight on the curve of her waist. She didn't want him to stop but she didn't want the night to end either.

'Let's go out,' she bit his earlobe.

Covered in blankets, they stepped out into the inky night, and almost on cue, the valley went dark, all the lights in the valley below went out. Only the moon peeked from behind a cloud, with just enough silver to light the way.

'Let's go to the edge,' he whispered, his hands around her waist, roaming her bare hips, his mouth on hers, his tongue teasing hers. Was there an edge and wasn't she already on it, she wondered as they walked and she covered his hand with hers. Let them roam together. His hands in hers and hers in his and their fingers together, slipping in and out. Bare feet on grass, she felt the blades of grass poke her, sending shivers up her legs as she held onto him, their mouths never leaving each other. Finally, he stopped and turned to face her. Behind him was nothing. A sheer drop, that made her take a step back. But he pulled her towards him and deepened his kiss.

'I'm scared,' she broke away. The valley below was the colour of heartbreak.

'Me too,' he said into her mouth, biting her lip. She held his gaze as she stepped in front of him, looking down at the valley. If it was heartbreak from here on, she needed her fill. Still looking into the inky black, her body leaned back into him, feeling all of him against all of her and nothing below and beyond. She moved against him, finding a rhythm, melting, melting, till he found her molten spot and let her know it. Turning her around so that she could put her arms over him, and he could pull her up to him. Her legs wrapped around him, her neck arched, she found a way to kiss him as he slipped in, going deeper and deeper. She closed her eyes, as the wild flowers climbed up their feet, up their legs, and they let the blankets drop. When they dropped down on the grass, their bodies fell and rose back up just like the flowers they were crushing. Soon, the valley, shook to a fused single cry breaking the silence and soaring up to the skies.

'Can I tell you something?' Ratan said later. Lavanya nodded. Her mind had caused her heart to lose control over both in one night. Now in the weak light of the dawn, she felt an intense shyness and was conscious of everything, including his hands resting on her breasts. He was lying on his side, his body wrapping her, the blankets wrapping him and the valley below bathed in the early orange-yellow light. They had slept and woken, slept and woken. Now they were wide awake.

'When you read to me, I liked it. I know I asked you to shut up, I ran away, but actually, I was afraid.'

'Of?' she asked softly.

'Of the way you read. All those words going up and down in a rhythm of their own. Like you were playing the piano with them. It was music. Of a kind that would pull me closer and closer. So—'

'So you ran away?'

'That was the attempt, yes. Mostly drama. I liked the drama of running away.'

'I liked the drama of it too'. Lavanya murmured into his cheek. 'When you ran, I could chase you. That felt good.'

'It could be said you're still chasing me. Or what are you doing here, haan?'

'And you're still running. Not just from me and my stories but from yourself and the world, it could be said.'

'It's time I shut you up.'

'Why don't you?'

'Wait, I know what we should call our little cocktail. "The Simla Fugitive". In honour of all the running you've done.' Lavanya said.

'I really should shut you up, come here.'

Sitara had her arms wide open as Lavanya walked towards her. She looked so happy to see Lavanya. She walked through tall blades of grass, not caring how they bruised her arms and legs. She walked for what seemed like endless moments. Till she saw the sun blaze and cover Sitara completely. Lavanya blinked, putting her hand over her eyes to see Sitara better. But Sitara was a blaze of light. As Lavanya looked with dismay, blinking to see Sitara better, she saw Eden instead. She, not Sitara, beckoned her now. Lavanya couldn't move.

She sneaked back up easier than she had thought. The easily agitated receptionist wasn't at her seat.

Lavanya had ten minutes to get ready before Amrit Singh would be back on the sofa in her room. There was a reason why she had dreamed of Eden. It was like Sitara had lured her into the dream so that she could see Eden was waiting for her. Why would that be?

All she wanted to do was lie back and rewind to last night. But there wasn't any time. She could feel it in her bones, Ratan had very little time left to while away in Nevermore.

When Amrit Singh came, she insisted he have breakfast with her. The maid brought up another plate and put it down before him with measured politeness bordering on defiance. The police were making little progress in solving the case that had so ruined the reputation of their little spirited hillside town. Amrit Singh ignored her and looked at Lavanya with rapt attention.

'My court hearing is around the corner. Before that, I've promised Richard I will do a series of write-ups on Sara, her work with children in schools, her poetry, theatre … Eden can help, she and Sara were very close, from what I hear. I want to visit her today, Inspector.' Amrit Singh was quick to nod in agreement.

He was glad to be on his feet and seen doing something purposeful. He went to the window and barked orders in Punjabi to his men to ready the jeep. Then he sat back and buttered a scone at leisure. Lavanya wondered how she could get time alone with Eden to tell her she knew about the tickets.

The Eastons lived closer to the Mall Road, and on the way from Birchwood to there, Lavanya relived her time with Ratan. She wanted to memorize every little detail. She wanted to disappear inside her memories, somehow be with him again. Every sound that was uttered in the streets, strains of songs from the radios of street hawkers, the clip-clop of the trotting horse-driven carriages, the shrill bells of the rickshaws, the hissing of corn on the iron tavaas in makeshift stalls, all became a symphony to aid her slow-motion reminiscences.

They arrived too soon at the Eastons' bungalow lined with fountains and trees.

Two servants answered the door, ushering them in. Their muffled steps rang through the corridor that opened onto a sprawling sunlit garden veranda with a table and two wicker chairs. The servants bowed in an exaggerated fashion.

Sir had left for his office and Madam was resting, please. She would be down soon, please. They were to wait, please.

A third servant scampered in with another chair. A fourth started pulling down the bamboo blinds to shut out the sunlight. One by one, the blinds came down, darkening the veranda and bringing in a chill, Lavanya dreaded. She asked the servant, set about his task, to stop. Let the sunlight be. The servant stopped, looking aghast.

'Eeyan memsaab does not like light, she will be here any time now, please.' With pleading eyes, he let down the last blind with a whoosh. There they were, on a bright sunny day, sitting in a veranda cloaked in darkness. The light, in defiance, continued to peep in through the cracks in the bamboo. Lavanya watched as a shaft of sunlight fell on her arm and lit it up.

They brought in glasses and a pitcher full of lemonade and set it down next to a vase of fresh daisies. The life they lead, Lavanya thought and sighed. Eden took her time to arrive and when she did, Lavanya could see why. She had taken the trouble to look grand if a bit glazed. She was wearing a taffeta skirt that trailed behind her and an elaborate ruffled blouse with wide shoulders, that was much in fashion.

Almost sleepwalking into the veranda, she held a glass of lemonade, darker than theirs, that she put down with great care. She sank into the cushions and raised a delicate hand to shield herself from the stray light piercing the blinds. In the light and shadow play, she appeared translucent, like she was slowly disappearing. The nervous tic was working gently on the left side of her jaw. She nodded at Amrit Singh, who was trying his best to look like he was invisible. Then took her time focusing on Lavanya.

'Ah, Lavanya,' was all she managed to say.

Lavanya smiled her warmest smile. She meant it. If anybody was fragile at this moment, it seemed to be Eden. What they needed here was a chaise lounge, what they called a fainting couch. Somewhere Eden could collapse in, instead of sit.

An ayah barefooted in and placed a tray with a glass of water and a small jar of white pills next to it.

'Saab said not to be forgetting to take your medicines, memsaab.'

Eden came out of her trance, looked at the ayah like she had never seen her before, then dismissed her with an aggravated wave of her hand. The ayah was out of there in a flash.

'They're *everywhere*,' Eden whispered to Lavanya like she was warning her.

Lavanya took a deep breath. She watched as Eden took a long sip from her glass and looked at a point somewhere between her and Amrit Singh.

'It's good to see you, Eden. Hope you don't mind me stopping by. You've been on my mind since the other evening. How are you feeling now?'

Eden pondered the question deeply, a long silent moment passed.

'Oh better, yes, better, it's sweet of you, *to drop in*,' Eden turned to look at her and smiled. The nervous tic disappeared when she smiled.

Lavanya decided to launch into her piece without further ado.

'Eden, as you know Sir Richard Davenport wants me to write about Sara and I'm trying to find out more and more about her. I've heard you were very close, old friends … would you be so kind as to share anything about her to help me along?'

Lavanya looked at Amrit Singh to include him in the conversation. Amrit Singh shifted, looking uncomfortable. He regretted agreeing so eagerly to bring Lavanya to see this frail lady, this was no time to be grilling her with questions on Lady Sara.

Eden's gaze dropped as soon as she mentioned Sara. She looked away, shook her head, then downed her glass in one go. Realizing her glass was empty, she looked around at once.

The ayah came in holding another glass, which she gave to her. Making sure not to look her in the eye, yet holding on to the glass till she was sure she had it. Then she left.

Lavanya was wondering if she would have to repeat her question when Eden spoke.

'Sara was my friend, yes. She's the crummy reason why I'm here, *here*.' Eden's eyes wandered all around the veranda like it was the last place she had imagined she would be.

'Sara was all I had in this miserable, godforsaken place, actually. It was always the two of us. Now it's just me. And all these servants.'

Eden put her head back and closed her eyes. Lavanya waited. After a while, it seemed like Eden was napping.

Lavanya looked at Amrit Singh, who, not knowing what to do, cleared his throat.

Eden opened her eyes and looked at Lavanya.

'Eden, I can imagine how that must feel. I'm sorry for your loss. I should come back some other time. Thank you for the lemonade and …' Eden didn't let her finish.

'Your friend Rat-an, he should be the one telling you about Sara. *They* were close. I knew he was trouble for Sara the moment I saw him. She thought everybody loved her, Sara did. Isn't that hilarious? But let me tell you one thing …' Eden took another long sip from her glass. '… nobody, nobody loved her more than me, no, not even Richard, especially not Richard.'

Eden was crying now. Tears flowing fast. Her face seemed to be melting.

Amrit Singh looked at Lavanya and got up. There was no point staying, he gestured with his eyes. She nodded at him and kept sitting. He started walking, nodding respectfully at Eden to excuse him, please. Then registering she didn't even know he existed, he continued walking heavily towards the door. Lavanya waited, making certain the inspector was out of earshot, before leaning closer to Eden. Eden was now crying into a napkin, looking the other way.

'You loved her best, Eden. Is that why it was only the two of you sailing back home?' she asked, her voice low.

Eden's tear-streaked face turned her way, eyes uncomprehending.

'What did you say?'

'Eden, I know you were going away, the two of you. You and Sara.'

Eden was looking at Lavanya like she was seeing her for the first time. The tears seemed to have stopped mid-cheek.

Lavanya rose to go, clasping her purse and putting her glass down, when Eden's hand held on to her arm. It was a vicious grip. Lavanya stood still.

'What do you know about the tickets?' Eden said in a tight whisper.

Amrit Singh had stepped back into the veranda to see what was keeping Lavanya.

'I'll tell you if you'll tell me,' Lavanya looked frankly into Eden's wide, wary eyes. 'The ship leaves in three days, Eden, you don't have much time.'

'Marc doesn't know, Marc *can't* know. Do you understand?' Eden had stepped close to Lavanya and was now breathing into her face. Alcohol fumes, that's what was in that glass of lemonade, Solan No.- 1, was it? Eden's grip had travelled up to her arm. 'What do you want to know?' she asked.

'First, call out to the inspector and ask him to wait outside. Find a good reason.' Lavanya freed her arm and started walking towards Amrit Singh.

She could see him ahead, looking towards them. Eden got to her feet too. She lurched after Lavanya and caught her arm again. As Lavanya turned around, Eden buried her face in Lavanya's chest and started sobbing her heart out.

Lavanya wasn't prepared for Eden's frail, petite body heaving in her arms. As she raised a clumsy hand to soothe Eden, she saw Amrit Singh, from the corner of her eyes, lumber away. He would let the women have a quiet moment to themselves. It was an altogether tragic affair, his body language said.

Lavanya stood there and let Eden cry. Something told her it wasn't only grief finding vent but hope too. Eden now saw hope where she thought there was none.

The servants surrounded them in no time. Eyes pleading and fearful at the same time. They looked like they wanted to take turns to console Eden memsahib. Unmindful of them, Eden cried on for a while more. Then looked up, her kaajal smudged but eyes clear.

'Come …' she held Lavanya by her hand and led her towards a flight of stairs. On the way, she gave tremulous but curt instructions to one of her servants not to disturb them.

'Hari, no one, hear me? No one.'

He seemed to be her most attentive help. He was the one who knew the exact angle he should let the blinds down. So that Eeyan memsahib doesn't get too much sunlight in her eyes. Lavanya saw him acknowledge her command with a quiet nod. Yes, it was clear. Eeyan memsahib was taking her guest to her private chambers. The inspector was to wait *outside*.

All the servants now nodded along with him, faces beaming. Memsahib was talking to them, looking at one of them in the eye and talking to them. It would suffice. It was a good, remarkable day and would be the cause of much chatter in the servant quarters.

Eden's private chambers had a musty odour the veranda did not have. No sunlight had streamed in through the windows here for a long time. The curtains stood as if on guard, heavy and silent.

Eden sat her down close on a deeply buttoned dark sofa with perfectly symmetrical sunbursts on them. Her eyes were questioning but not accusing.

'Where did you find the tickets, Lavanya? I looked everywhere for them, everywhere. In Sara's study, in her bedroom, her bedside table, the day you came to supper, I had been to each room looking for that packet … tell me, won't you?'

When Lavanya didn't answer, Eden moved closer to her, breathing fast. Lavanya detected a top note of eau de cologne along with Solan No. 1 fanning her face now. Doctors claimed it was a healing water, just inhaling it would rid you of a headache; some strange devotees were putting it in their soups too. Eden's eyes had gone wide, almost frantic, all of a sudden.

'Good lord, Lavanya, did Ratan find them?' Eden asked in a feeble half-whisper. 'I've been going out of my mind, wondering, hoping, somehow, I'll find the ticket and get out before I die here. Sara promised me, you know, *promised me* it would all turn out, right. Then, *she* gets killed! And nobody, nobody knows that in two days we were going to get out! *Except* for Ratan. And the police can't find him, Marc can't find him. It makes Marc so mad to think of Ratan out there and not locked up. Did you, did you find him, Lavanya?'

'Eden, listen to me. Please listen. I'll tell you everything you want to know about the tickets, but first tell me about Sara. Do you know what she was up to? What happened that night? I need to know.'

'All I know is that Sara said she was going to get us out of here. Get us back home. She said we had done our time here. Even if Richard and Marc didn't want to go, we would go. She was going to get the tickets and enough money for us to live. She saw that I was losing my mind here. I never had a constitution as strong as Sara's, even on our journey here,

I almost died. Sara looked after me and nursed me back to health somehow and we made it. I hate it here. There's nothing to do and Marc, Marc wishes … I was more like Sara.' Her voice broke. 'Be strong like Sara, don't be needy, look at Sara. Sara reads, Sara writes, Sara works with schools, see what *you* can do'. Eden said. Lavanya had to admit she mimicked her husband well, even in a broken voice.

'I know he can't stand to see my bored face every day but that's all I have, Lavanya, this bored face. I can't change it. Not like Sara could.'

Lavanya was growing impatient. There was no mention of blackmail so far. Had Sara not told Eden what she was going to do? Lavanya decided to interrupt Eden's life story. Which she would have liked to hear on any other day but not today. This was too depressing a room to cradle life stories and give them the comforting ear they needed. And those curtains. She wanted to take an axe and hack at them for looking like they owned the air she was breathing in that room.

'How was Sara going to get the money? Richard? Would he give it to Sara?'

'That's just it. We didn't have any money of our own. We've never had any money. Sara thought marrying Richard and Marc would make us independent women. We could live as we chose, visit England, bring our family here, but no, no, no. They like us like this. Dependent. Also, they like it here too much to go back. Richard would keep promising Sara to send her but make some excuse or the other not to. Then Sara found out something, she wouldn't tell me what, but something she said that could free us. She said I was not up to hearing what she had found out. She kept repeating, ever,

ever, that word ever. We wouldn't need Richard and Marc, *ever*, she said.'

Great, just great. Eden didn't know what Sara knew. Was it the intoxication that kept her so dazed? She had been so coherent and so sober at the Davenport house. Lavanya was fast losing whatever sympathy she had scraped together for Eden. She tried again.

'That night, Eden, did you see anything strange? Do you think Ratan killed her?' Lavanya asked, pinning Eden in her gaze, forcing her to concentrate. Eden looked away then looked back at Lavanya, sure then unsure.

'I'm thinking, I'm thinking. Maybe, Ratan found out Sara was leaving without him, that's all I can think of. Otherwise, it doesn't make sense. He wasn't even supposed to be there to pick her up that night.'

'What do you mean?' Lavanya said.

'I was there when she told Ratan she didn't need him that night. We were at the club. It surprised me, because Richard was going to be in Mashobra and they would never miss a night like that. So I remember.'

Finally, Eden had told her something useful.

'What else do you remember about that night, Eden?'

'We were on a high. Me more than Sara. She was miserable because she would be leaving Ratan behind. But Sara knew he didn't want to go, so she didn't let herself get too sad about it. That was Sara, always, always looking at the brighter side. She didn't talk much about him to me. She knew I couldn't stand it. He was the reason why Sara was strong, I resented that. Also, he didn't belong back home, so I never encouraged it. I have felt trapped here for so long, how could I have wished that utter misery on someone else? Sara saw that, finally. It broke her heart but she felt, what was the word she used, *free*. She said, Eden, I'm sad as sad as can be, but I do feel free too.' Eden's smudged eyes were misting over again.

'That night, we were going to have a good time. We were going to look pretty, sing, dance and celebrate our last few nights in Simla. She came with us in our car but once we got there, I never saw her. Perhaps only once on the dance floor with Marc, then at the bar counter with an Indian raja, then poof! I remember going to look for her in the middle but I couldn't see her anywhere and, and …'

Eden broke off. Unsure whether to proceed.

'And what …?'

'Marc says I see things, I hallucinate, so it doesn't matter.'

'It matters to me, tell me, please Eden.'

'I went near the back garden to look for Sara, all the smokers would go there, and I saw *Richard* rushing out. Yes, *Richard*. But Marc says it's impossible. How could I have seen him when no one else did and when he wasn't even there.'

Lavanya froze. 'Did you call out, say something to him?'

'No, I couldn't. He stepped in from the shadows into the balcony and turned into one of the corridors and left. He didn't see me … so it's quite possible that I imagined him. I do that sometimes when …'

'Think, Eden, was it only you or was someone else there too?'

Eden's eyes brightened a shade. She nodded. 'The prince. Yes, the prince too was there, hiding almost, from the party, I thought. In one of the dark corners of the garden balcony. I saw him first. Then I saw Richard and forgot all about him.'

'Then you didn't imagine it, Eden. Don't you see, you didn't imagine it,' Lavanya said, her heart beating fast.

'Have you told the police, Eden, what you've just told me?'

'No. Marc said not to announce to the world that I too am a half-wit like the prince …' Eden said, her eyes glistening again.

'Eden, the ticket is with me, all the money you'll ever need is also with me. Including Sara's share. It's not mine, it's yours. But you'll have to tell the police …'

'I can't, don't you see? Marc won't let me. Richard is his dearest, dearest friend … he will never let him come to any harm …'

'Then I'll have to give the tickets and the money to the police. You can explain to Marc and Richard how the two of you were planning to take off for good …'

'Show me the ticket, Lavanya, I want to see it, to feel it …'

'First, you must agree …'

Lavanya couldn't finish her sentence because the door flung open and Marc was in the room. Holding Eden's glass and a tray with the pills the ayah had given her at the veranda.

'Darling, I am very, very upset with you. Miss Lavanya, what a delightful surprise to see you here … whatever were you going to agree to, Eden?'

Eden's hand withered in Lavanya's. Yet she looked up and put on a bright smile but she sat so close, Lavanya could see her lips were trembling.

'I would so like Eden to agree to show me around Simla. I am cooped up in my room all day and I don't want to go by myself or with the police. Tomorrow? Please say yes, Eden.'

Lavanya squeezed her hand letting her know she needed an answer from her, now. Eden wriggled her hand out of Lavanya's at once. It fluttered and went to her face as Marc came and sat next to her.

'First, my wife needs her medication, don't you, darling? Look at you, you're wilting. Ayah told me you have not touched your pills. I had to leave everything and come ...' Eden took the glass from Marc's hands first and the pills next.

'My wife is not strong enough to show you around town, Miss Lavanya, she has taken Sara's death very roughly. They were like sisters. So you can imagine ...' Then something occurred to him and he stopped and looked at Lavanya, 'Isn't your court hearing tomorrow? Do you think you'll be in the frame of mind to go ... erm ... sightseeing?'

'Just for a little while, earlier in the morning, the hearing is later in the day, I could do with the distraction ...' Lavanya said, looking at Eden.

Eden's voice, small but firm took over, 'It'll do me good to get out, Marc. I'll come and pick you up tomorrow, Lavanya.'

Lavanya got up. 'I'll take your leave then. Don't want to tire you more. Have a lovely, restful day, Eden. I'll bring you the books you wanted to read,' she kept her voice pleasant but firm.

Marc had not said a word since Eden spoke. He was watching Eden with what looked like melting concern in his eyes. She finally put the pills in her mouth and drained her glass.

Marc now turned to Lavanya and ushered her out. 'Thank you for visiting, you seem to have brightened my wife's day. All the very best for your hearing.'

Lavanya turned back to give Eden one last comforting look and saw her slumped on the sofa. Her eyes were glazed again and the tic was back.

She was glad to leave the musty dark room that stank of hopelessness.

Two visions

It was a pink dawn in Simla. Ratan shivered a little as he watched the top of Lavanya's head disappear around the corner. Every time he saw her, he couldn't help shake the thought it was going to be the last time. Last night made the thought even more desperate. He turned around and got back into the car and started pulling out of the forest cover that hid him from view.

He put his hat down and started going back up the road that took him to Nevermore. As he climbed up the mountain, two things happened. In the first ray of sunlight to pierce the dawn, through the pines, came a flash so bright that it almost blinded him. He blinked to see better and there he was. His idiot prince sitting next to him like he had on that evening of the hunting party. He was staring right ahead, eyes wild with the promise of the hunt. His mouth half-open in an excited laugh.

Ratan followed his gaze and there, in the turn of the mountain, was the tigress of Suraiah. Walking in her regal stride, belly hanging with pride. She crossed the road and disappeared into the dark of the forest. Ratan pressed his brakes, screeching to a halt, shaken. He turned to look and sure enough, the prince was gone too. Not even a leaf rustled as far as he could see down into the forest.

What had Lavanya told him yesterday? The prince was at the party that night in Wildflower Hall. The prince had seen Richard. He was overcome with a sudden longing to see the prince again. Look in those guileless eyes and believe in the world to be faultless and full of magic. He wanted to tell him that he believed him. If nobody did, he did. Not having most people believe you was the only way, sometimes, to know you were right.

To his tigress with the swollen belly, who chased him relentlessly and, at other times, benignly drifted in and out of his dreams, he had nothing to say. He liked the silence between them.

If the prince was in Wildflower Hall on the day of the party, he might still be in Simla. The king had a summer palace in Simla and his many wives would nag him to stay the entire season in the town. The prince was their favourite, they would refuse to go anywhere without him. There was a good chance.

Ratan turned his car around. He drove back towards the Ridge beyond which the king had built his palace, closer to Tara Devi to spite all the European mansions the British had built.

There was no doubt in his mind now that Richard had been at the party that night. The question was how he could expose him. Bhai had promised him he would find out if the police case file had recorded the blackmail letters. So far, nothing seemed to suggest that. If the police didn't know and Cheeni's sister could talk to them, there might be a ray of hope. Though a native servant's word was unlikely to hold much credibility. Richard would have to admit he was being blackmailed and tell the police what for. It seemed hopeless all over again.

He stopped at the local chaiwallah to pick up a cup of tea and a copy of the *Simla Times*. He gritted his teeth through the usual reports of him. He was a depraved man, a gambler, a thief, a friend of the prostitutes of Simla. He read through Lavanya's interviews, her plea to him to give himself up. Let the police do its work of proving him innocent if he wasn't guilty. What a laugh.

There was also a small piece on Surya Kant, her publisher, who was on his way to Simla for the court hearing, accompanied by Noor, a famous actress and Lavanya's close friend. Noor was coming to shoot for her upcoming movie and to provide moral support to her friend. Her quote read: 'My friend needs me and I am appealing to the people of Simla, all those who watch my films, dance to my songs, to show me the same support. Come to the court on the day of the trial. For Lavanya and her brave, fearless writing. Her voice is our voice. Don't let anybody silence it.'

That was more than half of Simla, Ratan thought. Even the Europeans loved Noor. Would they risk their reputations and come out in droves so that Lavanya's book stayed in circulation? Ratan had his doubts. There was a quote from the leader of the religious sect who had filed the case against her. 'In every religion and every race, there are those that make them look good and others that make them look bad. To help them succeed in their evil game is a disservice to our society. I appeal to our people to support our case. Ban the book. Make our society clean and pure. The way our ancestors had imagined it.'

He stubbed his cigarette and turned around to go back to the car when he saw two policemen get out of their jeeps. He kept his face expressionless and looked the other way. He was unrecognizable. His hat down, his coat collar up, a muffler covering his face to keep warm against the icy wind. He was safe. As long as his eyes didn't give anything away.

They were walking his way and as they passed him, one of them stopped and asked for a cigarette. Ratan removed the cigarette from the pack and offered it to the policeman, his hands shaking. It was Player's, a brand only the Europeans smoked; there were cartons of them at the bungalow. The policeman looked at the brand then at him with a gesture of thanks. Ratan walked on, passing the other policeman asking his partner to get him a cup of tea. Ratan almost missed a step. It was the police boy from Shyam's farm. The one he thought he had killed with his own gun. From the corner of his eye, he saw the boy leap over a puddle and go to his partner. Not only was he alive, but he was also fit, this boy. Ratan felt an almost paternal swing in his still uneven heartbeat. Like he had seen his child take his first step.

The church bells rang in the distance. Ratan said a hallelujah in his heart and walked out of there to turn into the street where his car was. There was hope in the cold mountain breeze that tugged at his flapping collar.

In that hopeful moment, Ratan looked back to get one last look at the boy he had *not* killed. In that very moment Ratan looked back, the police boy happened to be looking right at him. Right into his eyes. His partner, the one who had borrowed the cigarette, was leaning close and saying something to him. Ratan quickened his step and turned into the corner of the street, away from their view. Then he ran. Ah tigress, bitch, you knew this was going to happen, didn't you? As he ran, Ratan's mind scrambled to plan his exit from there. Getting into the car was an option but that meant, even if he did manage to get away, the car number would give him away. He would have to abandon it soon enough. What would he do without the car? If he didn't take the car, he could lose himself in one of the narrow winding streets of the cluster of houses here. Give them a chase along the roofs, losing himself at the first chance he got.

Hope still lingered. He could hear them right behind him. Their footsteps were gaining. Ratan gave his legs one last push and closed the distance between himself and the car, jumped in, hands reaching for his keys to start the ignition. But no keys touched his shaking fingers. Thinking he had dropped them, he scanned the floor, there was no sign of them. Instinctively, his hand went to his trouser pocket and found the familiar jangle of metal. The ignition caught at once and he sped before the two of them caught up with him.

They got into their police jeep. Ratan stepped all the way down on the accelerator. Ratan had to avoid the main roads. There were many police checkpoints on those roads. He had no choice but to go deeper and deeper into the town, through Lakkar Bazaar, through Victory Tunnel.

His head hurt as he hurtled here and there, wherever he saw a road leading away from the centre of town. Soon, he found himself in the middle of a street full of people. It was a marketplace of sorts, with hawkers and street-food stalls, next to a bustling mosque. He kept going, hooting his horn as people jumped out of the way. Looking in wonder at the big

Cabriolet and how it contrasted with the smallness of their street. Then the car made up his mind for him. It sputtered and slowed down, running out of petrol. It had to happen, sooner or later, but now?

Ratan jumped out, ran into the street and merged with the crowds. Unable to give the car even a goodbye nod. Keeping his head down, his shoulders down, he walked. The swell of humanity all around him made him uneasy. It had been a long time since he had been amongst so many people.

He could smell life, that once familiar clamour of noises he knew so well. Babies crying, utensils clashing, food sizzling, frying masalas, loudspeakers blaring with prayer. He was back among his people. He could lose himself here. He picked up a child's fallen prayer cap, turning into an even narrower street. Women and children, all dressed in beautiful festive wear, walked by. They were going to meet their husbands and fathers outside the mosque. Midway, he looked back to see if he was being followed. When he took his next step, a flying fist slammed his jaw.

The sudden violence in the street full of festivity felt like a gun had gone off. Everybody began to run amok. Women lifted their children and ran. Food plates fell, clattering down from nervous hands. Children wailed and the dogs barked louder than before. Ratan turned to look at his nemesis, the police boy. He seemed to have grown up in a week. A couple of stitches was all he could see glinting on his forehead, and Ratan had thought he had killed him. What delusions of grandeur. He would have laughed if another fist wasn't coming flying at him. The police boy shouted obscenities as he hit Ratan.

Gandu, Saaley, Randi ki aulad. Haraamzaadeyyyyyy rang out in the cold and crisp December air. Ratan dodged one blow, but the next one he took on his jaw. His teeth rattled, he could feel his mouth full of blood. Yet he couldn't bring himself to raise an arm, a leg, nothing. The boy now launched himself at Ratan's throat and, shouting for his partner, tightened his grip, squeezing harder and harder.

Unable to breathe, Ratan too waited for the boy's partner to arrive. It was the end, no doubt. Little by little, everyone had cleared the area. They were alone in the street. There was no sign of the partner. Then, only then, did Ratan's hands move. Catching the boy by his neck and tearing him off his throat. The boy staggered and fell away as Ratan got up and turned to walk away. The police boy again launched himself on his back.

Something shifted in his head. Ratan, turned around and hit the boy and saw him fall. He went to hit him again and continued to hit him. Till the boy, crumpled in a heap, put up his hands to protect his face. But Ratan couldn't stop. He wanted to kill this boy, once and for all. It was tiring, and it refused to end. The boy had stopped shouting obscenities a long time back. Only Ratan was shouting now. They were unintelligible sounds, more like roars, from deep within his stomach.

'Ratan! Ratan, stop! It's okay, it's okay. Leave him, let's get out of here now!'

It was Ali and Deven, Bhai's men, dragging him from there. There was a jeep waiting and they flung him into the back of it and sped away.

Out of the corner of his swollen, bruised eye, Ratan saw the boy. Crouched on the empty street, his hands still covering his face. To think he had felt hope when the morning began. Paternal stirrings on seeing the boy alive. Now it all felt like a cruel joke.

The boy's partner, the one who should have come to the boy's rescue, was sitting in the back of the jeep, staring at him. He was one of Bhai's men who must have tipped off Bhai, who had sent Deven and Ali to get Ratan. The ways of the web, weaving and weaving all on its own.

Divine justice

Lavanya's head buzzed as Eden's staff ushered her out. Flanking her from the front and the back. Feeling like an imprisoned queen fallen out of favour in a ghastly fort, about to be shown into a dungeon with a solitary three-barred window high up in the wall, Lavanya sidestepped the flanking and walked through them the first chance she got.

No wonder Eden felt spooked by them. They were too many for their own good.

Amrit Singh, waiting, looked sullen. He had been left out of the action too long.

'Where can we find the superintendent, Amrit Singh?' Lavanya whispered to him, not waiting till she was inside the jeep and out of the driveway.

Tight-lipped, he held the door of the police car open. Would she care to get in first?

Only when she was inside, the door bolted and checked, five minutes into their journey, did he speak. Telling the driver where to go.

Simla had only recently got its own spanking new intelligence headquarters. For a new building, freshly painted, the apparent squalor inside was disorienting. Old files in old almirahs, old files on old, worn-out desks, old files lying unattended on empty, rickety old chairs.

Donald Harper's room was nothing like the one in Bombay. It looked like someone had left the windows open on a stormy night. Stacks of papers lay around with no paperweight or string tying them down. Files open and flung as if in a fit of temper, all over the table. No picture frames too, Lavanya noted. Donald Harper seemed to have left his solitary personal article back in Bombay.

He walked in just as she was framing her argument in the most coherent way in her head. Determined not to let her excitement get in the way.

'Ah, Miss Shriram. There is good news. Your young man is no longer going to be a threat to this charming little hill station and its good people.'

Lavanya looked at him, not understanding. They had Ratan?

Donald Harper sat and swivelled in his chair. He rubbed his hands again and again, all his restless energy consumed in that action.

'Divine justice, you could call it. The very lad he almost killed got him in the end. They should be bringing him in anytime now.'

Lavanya tried to catch Amrit Singh's eye, who was standing right next to her. He refused to meet her eye and looked straight ahead at his boss.

'Sir, I have also received word that there was a gun in the car Ratan was driving,' he now said.

That's why Amrit Singh was so tight-lipped in the car. Lavanya's heart hammered inside her chest. Donald Harper was looking at her with something akin to glee in his eyes.

'... and you wanted to see me about?'

'I have good reason to believe that Richard Davenport was present at the party the day Sara was murdered. A person, well-known to Sara, saw him at the party and is willing to put it on record,' she blurted out.

'... and this person is?' Donald Harper looked at Amrit Singh before he turned to fix his ice-cold gaze on Lavanya. Amrit Singh looked stricken.

'I'm not at liberty to tell you now but you can meet this person tomorrow. Here. With me.'

'... and why is this person willing to talk to us now and not before? Do you know, Inspector?' Donald Harper's voice had lost its breeziness.

'I am not aware of what Miss Shriram is talking about, Sir.' Amrit Singh hated her at this moment, she could sense it. After all their recent camaraderie, she had made him look like a sympathetic native policeman in front of his boss. The worst kind there was.

Lavanya pressed forth.

'I'd like to tell you, Superintendent, this is liable to change everything you have about the case. If Richard was at the party and he hasn't told us, not only is he lying but your investigation is riddled with holes.'

There, that made her feel better. Even if they had Ratan, with Eden's testimony, Ratan could prove he was not the only suspect with a motive.

'I don't believe you, Miss Shriram. You are a desperate young girl trying to conceal a serious crime committed by a despicable man. You can pack your bags, though, his game is over. And once you have your day in court, your game will be over too. That filth that you call writing will be in the garbage, where it belongs. Now if you'll excuse me, I have a busy day on my hands. Also, Sir Richard will be glad to know that you have enjoyed his hospitality only so that you could implicate him in his own wife's murder. Ha! Isn't that typical of how native thinking works in this country? I would like to be present when he accuses you of the same.'

Lavanya shook with rage inside. He had made up his mind about her.

'I'll see you tomorrow, Superintendent. And you're right, I am desperate. Desperate to prove you wrong, which I will.'

She got up to leave as a still panting policeman stood at the door, waiting to speak. Amrit Singh gave him a sharp look and went over to have a word with him. She saw his face register momentary panic as he glanced at the superintendent. Donald Harper had gone back to finish his report.

Amrit Singh saw her looking at him and he tried to mask his fluster. But he had given himself away. She knew it, without being told. The Simla Fugitive had run away! Did she have a small part to play in his escape, considering she had come up with the name of their cocktail? Suddenly gleeful, she sat back down. She was in no hurry to leave.

Donald Harper looked up from his report to see her still sitting, looking wide-eyed. Lavanya had the pleasure of seeing his face as Amrit Singh bent down to whisper something in his ear. A muscle in his jaw worked overtime, his eyes bulged. His good-looking face had lost all its symmetry and looked at home in the room with the scattered papers.

She was ready to go now. Her cup was full. As long as you manage to keep getting away, Ratan, you can keep getting into trouble.

Don't hide

RATAN AND BHAI SAT ACROSS FROM EACH OTHER IN HIS office while Deven and Ali flanked Bhai. On the gramophone, Kesarbai Kerkar was singing *Jaat kahan ho*. Ratan sat with his head slumped down on the table. When he did look up, Bhai was looking at him, a familiar gleam in his eye.

Something came sliding across the table. It came so fast, it was a blur. It was the police boy's gun that he had left in the car boot. The boy's partner must have returned it to Bhai.

'It's time to use it,' Bhai said, his eyes bulging from the emphasis he laid on each word.

By now, they would have all the details on the Cabriolet, on the Summers, on Nevermore. Which meant he could not go back. No borrowed car, no borrowed bungalow, no borrowed freedom. He held the gun and let it spin. It stopped and Ratan could see the nozzle pointing at him. He looked up at Bhai, letting a small smile escape his tired face. It felt good to play victim.

'Use it on myself?'

'Don't waste my time, Ratan. I didn't snatch you from the jaws of death to hear you talk drivel. Now listen to me. The person who killed Sara and Shyam has you by the testicles. You may think you've stopped running but actually, you haven't. Hiding is running too. Fate is trying to throw you in the open, expose you little by little so that you act, do something. Understand?'

Ratan could sense wisdom in Bhai's words and he was sure it would dawn on him soon. Not immediately, but soon. The gramophone boomed with Kesarbai's voice calling out, like a mother would to her daughter, asking where do you go alone girl, do your feet not know? Ratan knew these feet like he knew his own.

Bhai played with his moustache, exasperated. He clenched and unclenched his hands.

'They're getting away with this. We don't matter to them, don't you see? One more brown-skinned man in their jails means nothing to them. Whoever is behind this is playing a very clever game.'

'It's Richard. Her husband, Richard,' Ratan said.

'Tell me why you think it's him,' Bhai said, as he motioned for Deven and Ali to come closer.

Ratan outlined his reasons, listening to the conviction in his voice get stronger and stronger. Sara was blackmailing Richard. Number one reason for killing her. She had something on him that was explosive. Richard had their photographs in her drawer. He knew about his wife and him. He had not given these photos to the police, even though he was being blackmailed. Why would anybody do that? Especially after your wife ends up dead. He said he was going to Mashobra on the day of the party but a guest swears they saw him at the party. The guest's testimony was not included in the police files as a key witness account. Only Richard could have engineered that.

Shyam had taken the reward money but had failed to deliver Ratan to the police that day at the bus stop. That's why he died. Richard knew Ratan would go back to the farm to confront Shyam. Ratan finding Shyam too was well-timed. It was he who tipped off the police to storm the farm at the exact same time. Richard and the police were in it together.

'Wait, go back. Who was the guest who saw Richard at the party?' Bhai asked.

'The prince of Suraiah.'

'Who is, well, an idiot? I know the king and the prince well. No wonder the police won't put that in the files.'

Bhai twirled his moustache some more and then gestured for Deven and Ali to lean in even more.

'Find out who in Mashobra vouches for our man Richard. Then find out how we can corner him.'

'Also, one more thing. The maid who you said was delivering the blackmail letters? She can be useful. Yes, I know she doesn't want to talk to the police but what if the police want to talk to her?'

'Keep her out of it. She's terrified enough as it is. Did I tell you she is Cheeni's sister? Shyam's wife, Cheeni. That's the other thing. She said Cheeni has lost her voice since Shyam's killing. I think Cheeni saw the killer and the killing.'

'You mean, Cheeni saw Richard?' Bhai asked, his eyes narrowing.

Ratan nodded. Bhai looked at Deven and Ali who nodded back, they would find out.

'One Indian maid, one Indian wife of a slain driver, one Indian idiot prince. Three people, if they were people in the eyes of the law, that is, can help you. But they are not. They are invisible. They may as well as not exist. That's why like it or not, you have to take the law in your own hands,' Bhai summed up.

Ratan knew what he had to do next. What Bhai had said a while before now made sense. Hiding and running, running and hiding, it didn't matter. Both kept you away from facing anything head-on.

Right now, the only person he needed to face head on was Richard. He needed answers. Only Richard seemed to have them.

Bhai looked at Ratan now. 'I'm going to deliver Richard to you. Then it's your call. You want to end your misery, do it. Or I'm out. You can't come to me anymore. Clear?'

'You tell me when, I'll be ready.' Ratan knew there was no going back now.

'The maharaja is organizing a hunt, as royal as they come. There will be entertainment planned, a thousand lavish acrobatics to lure the goras. Lure them into ignoring the gross mismanagement that is going on in Suraiah. Everybody will be there. The season has begun. The town has been in shock since Sara's murder. Hardly any parties, it's been hush-hush, everybody is on their guard. This is going to be a hunting party to end the pall of gloom that has fallen over the town. That's the maharaja's claim and if I know him, and I do, he won't leave any stone unturned to make sure that happens. Now here's the important part: Richard will be there too, his main man Marc will bring him. Marc too wants Richard to get back to living his life. So, to cut a long story short, it is the perfect place to corner him. You know what I mean.'

Ratan now reached out for the gun. Something to hold while his head throbbed with old familiar images. *Not the hunt again.* It had taken him what seemed like a lifetime to forget the fear he had felt all those years ago. In all his nightmares he was still running through a forest with the tigress in hot pursuit. The idiot prince on top of the car beating his chest and howling at the moon. Also the regret that he had not stayed and confronted the king. He had walked away. Instead of exposing the king and his pathetic plan to sacrifice his only son. Simply to look good in the eyes of people who already knew the secret he was trying to hide.

The cold steel in his hands gripped him back. That's why the day had started with the two visions. The idiot prince and the tigress. Everything was already in motion. The hunt was on. It was always on. He was the last to know, that's all.

Lavanya returned to find a telegram from Noor waiting for her and a package from Richard. The telegram said simply that Noor would meet Lavanya at the court hearing tomorrow. Surya Kant was travelling with her on the same train.

She had sent it from the train. They were on their way. Lavanya felt like she could waltz around the room to a Sehgal song, such was the gladness coursing through her. Noor, you fabulous creature, you have no idea how much I want to see you. Hear your stupid ideas and have you hold my hand through this mess. Even if you are more anxious than me and your long manicured nails dig into my hands and leave bloody gashes. Tomorrow, the day she was dreading, was upon her. The day of the hearing. Her day in court. But tomorrow, Eden would help reopen the case for Ratan. She would walk into the court lighter, she would get through the hearing, no matter what they said about her stories.

Uplifted by the telegram, she sat on the bed, tucking her feet under her as she opened the package from Richard. There was a little note inside.

Dear Lavanya, here's a peek into my Sara's mind and heart. Look forward to reading what you write ...

It was a love letter of a package. Books Sara loved, random scribblings of poetry on slips of paper. Little notebooks with quotes, swear words in Hindi and Punjabi, letters for school authorities to take in more girls. Letters to government bodies to make scholarships available for underprivileged girls. Sketches of the countryside, a diary of her days on the ship, her first experience trying opium with a 'close friend' and how good it was.

Richard, who are you? The devoted and grieving husband or the conniving murderer? Lavanya had never been more confused and torn.

She picked up a notebook and flipped through the pages. Titles of poems and stories with very few lines below. She wasn't a finisher, just like her. The titles ranged from descriptions of nature to those not so scenic. 'The Champa', 'Under The Moon' to 'The Butcher's Daughter'. She had many interests. She was interesting. She had underlined 'The Butcher's Daughter' emphatically, she must have really wanted to write that story.

Lavanya spent the day devouring everything, every scrap of paper, every letter. Making notes as she read through the diary, the books.

All the while hoping Ratan would make a surprise appearance. He didn't. She didn't know when she fell asleep, her notes sprawled all around her.

The next day, Amrit Singh reported on time but was in no hurry to start any conversation. He knew she was expecting Eden. They would proceed for the hearing later.

An hour went by and there was no sign of Eden. Lavanya paced up and down her room, going over what Eden had said. She was to wait in her room, Eden would come to her. She was sure Eden had said that.

Another hour later, she wasn't so sure. What if she had said that Lavanya should come to her?

She couldn't have changed her mind about talking to the police, could she?

Lavanya went to the almirah and opened the locked drawer in which she had kept the package, the tickets and the money. There was no doubt that Eden wanted to be on that ship. She shut the locker, grabbed her coat, put the ticket and the money in her purse and was ready to go.

Amrit Singh glanced up from the paper as she appeared all ready at the door.

'We have to go visit Eden. Will you hurry, please, because we are very late,' she said, as she walked ahead.

He continued to look displeased as the driver of the jeep was missing. Finally, he took the wheels and Lavanya got in beside him.

As they drove up to the Easton's driveway, they could see a small group had collected outside. About twenty servants stood in the driveway, hands clasped looking down the road. Had Eden sent them out to receive her? It was such a strange sight that even Amrit Singh started slowing down long before he needed to.

As they got closer, the faces looked stricken. Amrit Singh stopped the car and got out. Lavanya got out too, even though he gestured for her to stay inside. She knew something was wrong, something was very very wrong.

In a babble of Hindi, they spoke one on top of the other. Madam fell down the stairs. She took many of her meds all at once. Madam was lying there when they woke up in the morning. Sir was out hunting. He had left the previous evening after Madam had gone to bed. Madam had been taken to the Rippon Hospital. Was Madam going to die? What would happen to them if Madam died? Madam cannot die, they would pray for Madam. The babble became indecipherable from that point on.

Amrit Singh looked at Lavanya and they both asked almost at the same time.

Who took Madam to Rippon Hospital if Sir was not there? No please, could one of them speak and not all together, please.

It was clear as the colour of the sky, the name that they uttered. Sir Richard. They had called him in a panic, not knowing what else to do. Sir Marc always said if he was not available, to call Sir Richard. He had come to the house and taken her to the hospital.

Lavanya looked at Amrit Singh and her panic now matched the staff's, who were clasping and unclasping their hands feverishly.

The hospital corridor

THE RIPPON HOSPITAL WAS A MAGNIFICENT, TIMBERED structure with gothic spiral stairs and corridors. It was difficult to imagine it was built to provide care for natives who lay languishing, surrounded by wooden splendour.

Amrit Singh led the way through the crowds holding his police badge in front of him. Ailing patients with their anxious relatives reacted to the badge like it was a blinding torch, shrinking and stepping back, so they could pass. There were guards keeping a close watch on the corridors leading up the curving spiral to the new wing. Lavanya could feel the hot breath of patients as she passed them by in the ornately pillared corridor. They called after her, asking questions that burned her back.

Where are you going?

Up the stairs? Down *that* corridor?!

Could you take us with you?

How is it possible to ignore the plea in our eyes?

Do you even see us? Have you become numb like the guards?

Are you white-skinned inside?

Do you feel no allegiance to your people, your *own* people?

On and on they went, spurred on by each other. Lavanya could feel her legs getting slower and slower. This was Simla *too*. The heavenly hill station inside the hospital was a lot like the hell described by the nuns in her school.

Her father had put her in a convent school after a British client of his had offered to speak to the principal on his behalf. She had lasted three months. Waking up every night with nightmares of this hellish place they had said sinners go to. In her mind, even as a child, she had been a sinner.

She looked up to see she was alone. Amrit Singh seemed to have disappeared down the corridor. Lavanya found herself stuck between an old lady and her stricken son. The lady held on to her hand, refusing to let go. Lavanya tugged at it, what was she to do? Her son was unconscious on the floor. She tried again, to free her hand but the old woman was not as frail as she looked. Lavanya's legs felt heavy, her head swam and she was ready to slump down on the floor next to the old lady's son, when she felt an arm tug her with just enough force to disengage her from the old woman. She looked up to see it was Marc Easton. Her bag slipped from her shoulders. He put it back and strode past, one glance at her to say she should do the same. Lavanya summoned all her strength to look away from the woman and rushed after him.

The laments of all the people she was leaving behind followed her down the corridor, up the spiral. Then she was in an orderly, ivory-coloured corridor, as distinct from the one she had passed as black from white. It was cheerless but empty, dotted with nurses manning their desks. So this was where the English came to recover from their finer illnesses. Here, you could heal just from the peace and quiet.

Amrit Singh was waiting for her, looking impatient. Lavanya saw how his eyes changed expression when he saw Marc.

Marc seemed to know exactly where he needed to go and Amrit Singh followed him, shooting her a look to do so too. Marc stopped outside a closed door in a long series of doors. On it was a placard with the name, Eden Easton. He pushed it open. It was a sunny, well-aired room, white and empty. Marc walked in and went over to the window and looked out. Behind him, a door handle turned and Lavanya watched as Richard stepped out. His face was dripping wet. Marc took a step towards him but Richard asked him to stop right there, with his palm in front of his face. Blocking the light or his vision or the concern on Marc's face, Lavanya couldn't tell.

'Where is Eden?' Marc asked softly.

Richard looked up at the empty bed for a long time as if trying to focus.

'Eden is missing. She is missing. But not dead like Sara. Not dead.'

Marc looked at the inspector, who brushed past and opened the door Richard had emerged from.

Amrit Singh left the door open as he went in and Lavanya could see the washbasin with the tap running. He came and stood outside, shaking his head at Marc. Nobody inside.

'Richard, where did Eden go? Is she all right?' Marc asked.

'Oh, Marc, Marc. All I know is I got her here safely. Marc, you have to believe me. She was coming in and out of consciousness all the time. Oh, the things she said. The nurses settled her in. The doctor came and took a look at her. Gave her a pill to sleep. I went out to find a way to let you know about Eden and when I came back, she was gone. Gone.'

Richard looked at his wet hands as he spoke, as if fascinated by them, shaking and glistening at the same time.

'She couldn't have gone far. Donald Harper is on his way here. We'll find her. Are you okay?' Marc moved closer to Richard.

'She's gone. Oh, the things she said, Marc. Splendid for her she's gone, you know.'

'Why do you say that, Richard? Why is it splendid for her?' Lavanya asked, fearing the worst. Was Richard sedated? He sounded like his mind had shifted.

Richard looked up to see her and his eyes actually smiled. He looked pleased to see her.

'Ah, Lavanya. Aren't you glad you came to sleepless Simla? So much going on, don't you think?'

She was about to repeat the question she had asked when Marc's voice cut through the room, cold and sharp.

'That's enough, Richard. Let's go. We'll find Eden. The police have been briefed. We're going to get cleaned up and we're going to the hunt. The maharaja is waiting.'

Richard continued to look at his wet hands in dismay.

An obscene hearing

'PLEASE PLACE YOUR LEFT HAND ON THE BIBLE AND RAISE your right hand. You do swear that the testimony you are about to give in the cause now before the court will be the truth, so help you God?'

Lavanya looked at the Bible solemnly and tried her best to be sincere, placing her hand and swearing the oath. The court was overflowing with people, it seemed like the entire town had come to see her disgraced and publicly humiliated. Yet it mattered least, her mind was on matters more urgent, on one question entirely: where was Eden? She caught Surya Kant's eye, he was watching her intently. He had briefed her before she had taken the stand. She was not to speak out of turn, she was to simply answer questions, he would take care of the rest. Lavanya was certain that she had jeopardized Eden's safety in some way, that it was she who was responsible for her breakdown and subsequent disappearance. Thank God Ratan was safe, by that she knew how precariously safe he was. But safe was safe.

The judge, an extremely preoccupied man in his fifties, looked mild-mannered but impatient. He kept calling both counsels closer to whisper into their ears, his eyes on the big clock in the courtroom. Lavanya wanted to tell him she shared his sense of urgency. Surya Kant had told her Judge Saunders had a hobby that was bordering on an obsession: gardening. He was loathe to preside over cases unless they were absolutely necessary. Anything and everything was time away from his precious roses and geraniums.

Now he looked pointedly at her and asked the question that could end this hearing and give everyone the day off to pursue their hobbies.

'Miss Shriram, do you or do you not wish to apologize for the obscene content in your collection of stories found next to the murdered lady, Sara Davenport?'

It was more a plea than an ask. How she wished she could say the word and be out of here, to wait for Ratan in her room or look for Eden, she had to find Eden before the day was over. Then her eyes fell on Donald Harper standing in the corner of the room, in rapt attention. Nothing was worth pleasing him.

'I do not wish to apologize. I am proud of my stories.'

In that precise moment, there was complete silence in the room and her voice rang out loud and clear. The next second, the uproar began. It was a mixed crowd, Europeans and Indians both, men and women, literate and the hardly literate, journalists and religious representatives of various sects, she could see some known faces, poets, writers, actors and actresses too. You are more famous when you are notorious, Lavanya concluded to herself. People had travelled to witness this hearing.

'You do realize that by not apologizing, you are risking your book being banned. No reader will ever read it again without doing something unlawful and inappropriate?'

'I realize, Your Honour,' she said.

Judge Saunders sighed audibly, luckily he had been prepared for the worst, but it had been his duty to try. Now he was determined to be efficient with the speed at which the day progressed. He would not compromise with that. One glance from him and the prosecution lawyer, Satyapal Tripathi, rose to give his opening monologue appealing to the good sense of the jury, claiming aloud, in many intricate, elaborate sentences, that he would soon prove to them that Lavanya Shriram had the most nefarious reasons to have written the book of stories that had led to Sara's murder. The absconding suspect had read her sexually explicit stories and had been provoked to outrage Sara's modesty, failing which he had to kill her. Therefore, the contents of the book had the power to erode the moral fabric of society and serve as an insidious invitation for engaging in inappropriate acts resulting from lust.

Surya Kant appealed not just to the jury but Judge Saunders as well, by keeping his opening brief but sharp. He asked the jury not to be swayed by powerful forces that had come together to attack a young girl and her only published book of stories. Which incidentally, had not sold a single copy till it had been found next to the scene of crime. He asked them to focus on the only matter at hand: was the book obscene or not? And depending on that answer, did it deserve to be banned or not? Did they want to go down in history as the jury that allowed freedom of expression or disallowed it? This hearing was not about what Ratan Seth did or did not do, it was about what Lavanya Shriram's book of stories did or did not do.

The prosecution was the first to interrogate her.

'Miss Shriram, have you penned this collection of stories found on the scene of the crime?'

'I have.'

'Would you tell the court what the story of Sitara is about, in as few words as possible.'

'I would, but it's very likely they have read it?'

There was a swelling murmur from the crowds spilling all over the court house. How audacious! For a girl! The judge rapped the desk with his gavel.

'Miss Shriram, you are to answer the question please and not waste the time of the court henceforth unless you want to be punished for contempt of court.'

'Yes, Your Honour,' Lavanya said, meekly. 'Sitara's story is about a girl married too early to a much older, ailing man who looks at her as his helper and nurse, duties which she performs till he dies, at which time, she's supposed to immolate herself on her husband's funeral pyre. There, she decides to pleasure herself one last time, remembering her only lover, an Englishman.'

The court erupted. It wasn't in response to the story, much as she would have liked to flatter herself, but rather the appearance of Noor that caused the commotion. Dressed in a clinging sari glittering with intricate embroidery. The police did their best to control the packed court but their attempts only added to the growing pandemonium. The gavel came down repeatedly till everyone had quietened down and gone back to staring at Lavanya. Noor winked at her, as if to say, see what I did? Lavanya raised an eyebrow, the corners of her mouth wrinkling just a tiny bit to let her friend know, nothing she did ever went unnoticed, by her or anybody else. In response, Noor looked at the jury in complete and utter admiration. What a fine body of people and how noble, to tear themselves away from their daily lives to come to court and help decide if a girl may persist in believing she had the freedom to write, the freedom to express herself, at least. Lavanya completely missed the question directed at her by the already frustrated lawyer.

'Were you aware that you were writing things that could arouse the basest instinct in man and set him on a journey he would regret for the rest of his life?'

'What detail are you referring to, please, if you could clarify? The fact that she was forced to sit on a burning pyre or that she pleasured herself?'

'Miss Shriram, she pleasures herself in public, is that appropriate behaviour, according to you?'

'A woman about to die, for no fault of her own is least worried about the public and what it thinks, so yes, it is perfectly natural for her to do so.'

'What about the obscene words used to describe how she pleasures herself?'

'Such as?'

'Such as "breast" and "nipples"!'

'What would you have liked me to call them? I know no other words to describe those parts of the female body. Do you?'

It had become difficult to speak or be heard in the court, everybody was discussing and holding forth on what they thought was right or wrong, despite the judge urging for order in the room. At least the freedom to discuss was alive and kicking. The lawyer kept raising the pitch of his voice, till she could see him going red in the face, exasperated with it all. A glance at Surya Kant told her he was pleased, then her eyes wandered and rested on a face that was anything but. Donald Harper sat rigid, eyes blazing with cold fury. Thank God Ratan had managed to escape his clutches.

Then she was being told to step off the stand. Surya Kant did not want to question her. She had done well. She went and sat next to him, Noor sat right behind. She felt safe. One by one, there was a parade of witnesses called to take the stand. They all agreed with Tripathi that the story was obscene. When Surya Kant asked them to prove what exactly about the story was obscene, they lost their eloquence entirely. They had heard how the 'breast' and 'nipples' question and answer had gone. Still, they came to the box, morally wounded and righteously motivated.

'The phrase "she had eyes only for her Angrez lover ..." is obscene.'

'Which word is obscene, "Angrez" or "lover"?' Surya Kant asked.

'Lover, of course,' the man said, looking at the judge indignantly, as if his dignity had been hurt by merely repeating the word.

'My Lord, the word "lover" has been used by great poets since the dawn of time. It is also used in naats, bhakti poetry, that is, poems written in praise of God, or the Prophet.'

Surya Kant placed before the judge some examples of famous, world renowned poetry with the word 'lover' encircled. He had done his homework.

'But a woman having no shame, having a lover, that too an Angrez, which decent woman would do that?'

'Is it okay for a decent man to have a lover? If so, why not a decent woman?' Surya Kant persisted.

The witnesses thundered but it was clear, their storm had very little fury. The judge had lost his mild-mannered stance and was now visibly agitated at how the case was progressing. The 'evil plan' was debated at length, cross-examined by Surya Kant and proved to be a harmless inside joke that must not take any more precious time of the court. The judge quickly ruled that any more mention of the note in the book would not be entertained, it had no relevance to the words inside the book. That was matter for the murder trial, not this one, which was purely to rule on whether the book is obscene or not. This was such a relief to her that Lavanya, for the first time, let herself hope that she might make it out of this court in one piece, triumphant even. By the time Donald Harper was called to the witness box, the spectators were calmer, the furore was dying down.

'Brace yourself and whatever you do, don't speak out of turn,' Surya Kant had warned her.

'Superintendent Harper, will you tell the court why you consider Miss Shriram's book unsuitable for this country and its people?'

'It is more than just unsuitable, it is dangerous. Just the fact that it was found next to a scene of crime should tell the court everything it needs to know; symbolically and literally, it will lead to more crimes if allowed to circulate freely.'

'What about the stories, do you find them particularly obscene?'

'The fact that they were written to titillate. The language is frustrated and filthy, written by a heathen, a sick mind, no doubt.'

Lavanya was finding it difficult to focus on her hands. If she looked up, she might not be able to follow Surya Kant's instructions. He was up on his feet, at once.

'Objection, Your Honour! The witness has no right to deride the writer in this court!'

The judge glared at the superintendent, who stared right ahead, his stance absolutely undeterred. Tripathi quickly reframed his question to distract the judge.

'Superintendent, in your opinion,' Tripathi began placatingly, 'what is dangerous about the story the book was found open on?'

'The entire story is shockingly objectionable. Sitara represents everything base in Indian society, everything its women must not be. The custom that it brings centre stage, has been ruled illegal by this government, yet the writer, purely to titillate, brings it up, to turn the heat and hate up. Further, it is abhorrent that the publicly performed sexual act involves an Englishman, the very people responsible for putting an end to the practice.'

When it was Surya Kant's turn to cross-examine, the court had ceased all chatter. The jury was listening, for once. Lavanya caught his eye, letting him know she had absolute confidence in him. Inside, her heart was a hollow beating drum. She was also certain, if she looked around, Sitara was somewhere in this court, blending with another woman just like her, listening just like her.

'Superintendent, if you don't mind, would you tell the court a little about your childhood in England? Do you, for instance, come from a religious family?'

'I do, I was raised in Stinsford, a village and civil parish in Southwest Dorset, England. My father was the local pastor and my mother taught in the local school as well as looked after us, we are three brothers and one sister.'

'Thank you, Superintendent. What did your mother teach?'

'Her subject was "An introduction to the Bible".'

'Wonderful. As per my records, you have been in India, deployed in the police force for the last ten years, is that correct, right after you were married?'

'Correct.'

'Do you like to read, Superintendent? Have you read, say, Thomas Hardy, Jane Austen or Flaubert?'

'No, I do not have the time to read, if you must know, this country does not allow a law enforcement officer much time to pursue such edifying hobbies.'

'If you have not read much, then how would you know for certain if Sitara's story is "filthy" as you say?'

'I was educated, I come from a literate family, I can read, that should be enough for anybody to know filth when they see it.'

'Educated, yes, but the only book you may have found the time to read would be the Bible?'

'Growing up, yes, you could say that.'

'It has been said, that the Bible has many passages considered "obscene" by some parties? Would you agree?'

'It is considered "the good book", so no, I have heard no such thing.'

Surya Kant picked up a copy of the Bible that had been marked for just such a moment.

'I have the greatest respect for all religious books, Superintendent, I read these words out only because you mentioned language and how some words have caused you to consider Sitara's story "dangerous". I am going to read out just some sentences and if you recognize them or the passages, if you would perhaps like to read the entire page aloud, just like you made Lavanya read at your police station, you are most welcome to. For now, let me just read the words I have marked.'

Lavanya noticed the jury lean forward, not one of them looked relaxed, this was a tense moment for them. She hoped Surya Kant knew what he was doing.

'"You also took the fine jewellery I gave you, the jewellery made of my gold and silver, and you made for yourself male idols and engaged in prostitution with them." From Ezekiel 16:17.

'"If two men, a man and his countryman, are struggling together, and the wife of one comes near to deliver her husband from the hand of the one who is striking him, and puts out her hand and seizes his genitals, then you shall cut off her hand; you shall not show pity." From Deuteronomy 25:11-12.

'"Yet she increased her whoring, remembering the days of her youth, when she played the whore in the land of Egypt and lusted after her lovers there, whose members were like those of donkeys, and whose issue was like that of horses. Thus you longed for the lewdness of your youth, when the Egyptians handled your bosom and pressed your young breasts." From Ezekiel 23:18–21.

'"A loving doe, a graceful deer—may her breasts satisfy you always, may you ever be intoxicated with her love." From Proverbs 5:19.

'"My beloved put his hand by the hole of the door, and my bowels were moved for him." From Proverbs 5:4.'

Lavanya had to look up. Surya Kant had stopped, the judge had brought down the gavel, indicating that was enough. Donald Harper was looking at Surya Kant like he was seeing him for the first time where before, he had not been worthy of his consideration. Surya Kant was looking at the jury, who were blinking and looking at each other.

'Yet the Bible remains a book of colossal social significance for the world, does it not, Superintendent?' Surya Kant finished. 'I have no more questions for the superintendent, Your Honour, but I do have one final witness.'

Surprised to learn of this new witness, Lavanya turned to look back at Noor, but she wasn't there. She saw her entering the courtroom with another woman, a familiar face, such a familiar face. Noor nodded at her with a gentle raise of an eyebrow as the woman Noor was escorting went to the witness box. Lavanya's hand flew to her face. It was Donald Harper's wife, the woman from the unruly frame on his immaculate office table! The woman who had left him and taken their only child with her. Donald Harper, back among the spectators, was staring at her like she was back from the dead. She was trying her best not to look at him.

Surya Kant introduced Judith Wilkins to the court, her marriage to Donald Harper, her passion for theatre, which she had discovered only after arriving in Simla and meeting the wonderful people at the Gaiety Theatre, and her subsequent decision to leave the marriage, taking her son Thomas with her, to travel with her theatre group.

'If it's not too personal, Miss Wilkins, would you please tell the court why you chose to leave Simla with your son?'

'I had to take that decision because my husband forbade me to leave the house after I gave birth to Thomas. He did not want me to have anything more to do with the theatre. I tried to stay home at first and then found that my unhappiness with leaving what I loved was greater than my ability to obey and stay in a joyless marriage.'

'Before my good friend and fellow counsel, Mr Tripathi, interjects to ask what this has to do with Miss Shriram's book of stories, would you please tell the court why you agreed to be a witness for this hearing, Miss Wilkins?'

'My husband read parts of the play we were about to stage at the Gaiety and forbade me to leave the house, from thereon.' She was finally looking up at the man she had found the courage to leave. But there was only love and a silent plea in her eyes. All she wanted from him was to be understood.

'And what play was that, will you tell the court?' Surya Kant asked softly.

'The play that we were about to stage at the Gaiety Theatre when I was locked up and told not to leave the house, was an adaptation of "Sitara's Story" by Lavanya Shriram.'

The courtroom erupted once again, like they were watching a cricket match and someone had sent the ball flying and no one knew yet if it was six or an out. Lavanya closed her eyes, there was too much welling up inside her.

'Thank you, and my last and final question, who introduced you and the Gaiety Theatre in Simla to "Sitara's story"?' Surya Kant raised his voice so he could to be heard over the noise.

Lavanya knew who it was before Judith Wilkins said her name. It had to be and it was.

'It was Sara Davenport,' Judith said.

Finding Eden

LAVANYA CAME OUT OF THE COURT HOUSE IN A DAZE TO A flurry of camera flashes and a stampede of questions. Surya Kant had refused to say anything, asked her to keep her head down and led both of them, Noor and her, into a car waiting outside. Where Lavanya found an oddly familiar boy waiting for her with a note in his hand. He didn't have to tell her. In her heart, she knew this was a message from Eden. He was the same boy she had seen holding down the blinds for his Eeyan memsahib at the Eastons' home.

The note said 'Hari will bring you to me. Tell not a soul, Lavanya. I'll tell you why, when I meet you.'

She handed the note to Noor, who read it and handed the note to Surya Kant.

He was the first to speak, 'Let's go, Lavanya. You better fill us in on the way.' He saw her look surprised, and laughed, 'All right, we can fill each other in.'

Surya Kant, with a lot of help from Noor, spoke fast. He had tracked down Amrita Sher-Gil in Lahore and found her feeling curiously inert. She had refused to divulge any details on the day in Simla but when he had asked if she knew anything that could help him defend Lavanya's book in court, she had given him a name, just when he was at the door, on his way out: Judith Wilkins. She had been difficult to trace as she had no fixed address but his theatre friends in Bombay proved to be a tight circle. Before he spoke to her, even he had no idea she would be so crucial to the hearing. But if it wasn't for Noor, she would have never agreed to take the stand.

Lavanya reached out for Noor's hand but Noor rolled her eyes, wanting her to cut the histrionics. 'Will you please tell us now, how have you been tormenting this sweet little town?' Laughing after what seemed like a lifetime, Lavanya finally exhaled. 'I'm finding a new way every day. The police almost got Ratan yesterday. I know by now, oh thank God, he is innocent. He didn't kill Sara or Shyam. We found out Sara was blackmailing Richard, her husband, but we don't know why. I was so close to reopening the investigation today. But Eden, Sara's best friend, who was going to help me do that, went missing from the hospital and I had to come to court for the hearing.' Lavanya looked at Surya Kant and then Noor to see if they were following her, but she could see she needed to slow down. She didn't know if that was possible, anymore, to slow down. Luckily, Noor was in no hurry to grasp it all at once.

'Lava, I have no clue what's going on. If you think you made sense a while back, you didn't. But for once, your life is more interesting than mine so don't even think I'm going to let you out of my sight. Also, you're coming with me to the Nawab's hunting party. I'm going to be shooting a dance sequence and before you roll your eyes, let me tell you, it involves snakes. Yes, yes, you heard me right. I thought it was a brilliant idea, deep in a forest, where the big wild beasts should be, I dance with snakes! It has never been done before!'

As the car sped, Lavanya knew Noor would keep talking till she calmed herself down.

They followed Hari up and down a steep lane till they came to a *basti* of houses clustered together. From here, the boy, on his bicycle, bounded into an even narrower lane. The lane was completely covered by clothes hanging to dry. There was a strong wind and the sarees and bedsheets whipped around their faces. The car could go no further. Like Hari, they too lifted the flapping clothes to see the path ahead.

He took them inside a house full of people, out into a courtyard and up a flight of stone steps to a wide open terrace. There in a corner, half-lying, half-sitting on a charpai was Eden, a familiar glass of Solan No. 1 spiked lemonade next to her. Her twitch was gentler and there was some colour in her cheeks. She wore a coat the colour of dried red roses, tightly belted around her impossibly thin waist, her stockinged legs stuck out over the charpai, restless, swinging. She could have been at the club, sipping a martini if her wild eyes didn't give her away.

Eden's story was slow as she had to keep stopping to take long sips from her glass.

After Lavanya left that evening, Marc had tried to wheedle out of her why Lavanya had come to visit. As much as she tried, she could not make him believe it was nothing but a polite visit to enquire about her health. That night, she did not take her pills. She stuffed them under the mattress. She knew they would make her groggy and something told her she would need a clear head for the next few days. She had a ship to catch and she needed her wits about her. She would manage the pain somehow.

She pretended to retire to bed early. She heard noises around midnight. All the servants had left the house for their quarters, so where were the noises coming from? Curious, she went down on tiptoe to see. Richard was in the living room pacing up and down, wringing his hands. Telling Marc again and again that he had not slept for days. He was swaying on his feet. Marc tried to get him to sit down but Richard kept pacing the floor, he would not be still.

She gathered in dribs and drabs what had driven him to come home so late. Some man in Mashobra called Satbir Singh had called him. Satbir Singh had earlier told the police Richard had been in Mashobra the night Sara died. He called to say he was going to change his statement or he would have to lose his life. Then he had abruptly cut the connection.

Marc kept reassuring Richard he would take care of it. He would fire Satbir Singh immediately. Richard said Satbir Singh didn't care about a job because he would still have his life.

Eden now stopped and looked at Lavanya shaking her head.

'They know, Lavanya, they know …'

She downed her glass, her eyes going hazy.

'Finish, Eden, what happened *next*?' Lavanya said.

'Then Richard stopped pacing up and down and said, Marc, is Eden going to talk to the police? And Marc had his back to me and I heard him say, you have nothing to worry about. Let me go and see Satbir Singh now, then I'll see about Eden too. Eden isn't going anywhere. Nor is she going to talk to anybody, I'll see to that.'

Eden looked at Lavanya, shaking. 'He's never going to let me out of his sight. I know too much. I'm scared like I have never been before. Give me the ticket, Lavanya, let me go now, while I can.'

'What happened then, Eden? How did you land up at the hospital with Richard?' Lavanya wanted to shake Eden hard.

The last bit came out of her slowest. Like she was using her last reserves of energy to tell it.

Eden had crept back up to her room, with one thought on her mind. She had to get out. Before Marc came back from Mashobra the next morning. So she faked a fall, muttered to the servants about taking all the pills at once, and asked them to call the hospital for an ambulance. Instead, to her surprise, Richard arrived. Once in the hospital, Eden took the first chance she got and walked out without anyone stopping her. Luckily for her, Hari was waiting for her outside and had brought her here. The house belonged to Hari's grandmother who is well-known to the locals in Simla. 'Do you know Lavanya, she is the Congress Party's main person in Simla. She organizes all state visits, sitting right there.' Eden gestured to where a hefty woman sat with Hari, looking their way with great concern. She reminded Lavanya of her own mother who, when concerned, had looked sinister too.

'Marc would never think of looking for me here,' Eden finished. The glass was empty now and Lavanya saw Hari get up at once.

'Can you trust them?' Lavanya had to ask.

'Strangely, I feel safe here,' Eden said.

Lavanya nodded. Lavanya introduced Noor and Surya Kant, who now stepped closer. Surya Kant muttered something about it being a pleasure to meet her and Noor reached out and gave her a hug, clasping her to her chest and holding her there for an extended second. Eden held on to her, her body shaking for several seconds, clearly moved. Eden wiped a tear and looked at Noor like she had found a kindred soul.

Clearly, I don't give good hugs, Lavanya thought.

'Eden, keep the ticket and the money if you want but I need you to talk to the police. You need to make a formal statement or Ratan will go to jail. They need to know Richard was at the party the day Sara was killed. Also about the blackmail, Sara's plan to leave the country for good, with you …'

As Lavanya spoke, she looked in her bag for the packet with the ticket and the money. There was a chill spreading all over her. Her hand could find no packet inside her bag. The packet was gone.

Lavanya felt sick to her stomach. How could she lose the packet? Panic-like bile was rising up in her throat. She wanted to throw up, except she couldn't let Eden know that she had lost the packet.

She saw Surya Kant looking at her, he seemed to have guessed something was very wrong. He held her gaze, it was going to be okay, he seemed to be saying. They would figure it out later. Right now, all she had to do was compose herself and leave.

Lavanya looked up and forced herself to smile at Eden.

'… so please Eden, trust me, I will see you on that ship myself. All you have to do is record your statement, please. Stay here, rest. You are safe here. I'll bring the police here for your statement.'

'Hurry, Lavanya, hurry. Please. Marc can't know, he can't …' Eden slumped down on the charpai, her face in her hands.

The Begum

'I CAN'T BREATHE, ALI' RATAN SAID, TRYING TO SEE through the burkha Ali was helping him wear.

'Shh, Begum, shhh!' Ali adjusted the veil, his eyebrows furrowed.

Ali's wife, Isra, came behind him and slapped his hand. 'That is all you can do, shush your begums, kindly step away.'

Eyes flashing, she took the burkha fabric billowing around Ratan and patted and tucked it in various places to settle it down.

It had been decided Ratan would be going to the hunt disguised as Isra. Bhai was a special invitee to the hunt and he was taking Deven and Ali with him. The maharaja wanted all his guests to bring their wives too, as he was making special arrangements for them to have a good time. The bonanza that no one could resist was the famous actress Noor, performing with her troop of dancers. Ali's wife, Isra, had been nagging him for not taking her all day. All her life, Isra said, she had wanted to go on a hunt. See Noor Ahmed perform one of her unforgettable shows. Now that she was invited, Ali was not taking her. Deven's wife had talked of nothing else all week.

Isra was going to miss the town's most talked-about hunt. It was reason enough to drown herself in a spoonful of water. Ali muttered that a spoonful of water would never do for Isra as he took a few steps back.

Ratan smiled at Isra, his eyes apologetic. She gave him an understanding wink but kept up the pretence of being irate with her husband.

Ratan's thoughts wandered to Lavanya. Was she all right? Was she wondering what had happened to him?

The hunt was an hour away from Simla. Ratan insisted on driving and keeping the burkha on as he looked at the road. Just gripping the steering wheel steadied him. He missed Nevermore deeply. Sometimes, borrowed things are more yours than your own, he thought to himself. Deven sat next to him, keeping the conversation going.

As they approached the edge of the forest, they traded places and Ratan got ready to play his part. When Ali opened the door to his side, playing the gracious husband, Ratan got out as Isra would. Keeping his gait demure, his head down. He felt silly, none of the women he knew walked like this. Trumpets and dhols rang out for them. The villagers of Suraiah had carpeted their path with tiger skin. It made Ratan queasy to think of how many tigers and tigresses had been killed to put up a show like this. All to please the bored British officers. Or in the name of avenging the many innocent villagers killed by the tigers. Who was the bloodthirsty monster, really?

As he walked, keeping his head low, making sure Ali was walking alongside, he saw a familiar car parked up ahead. It was the car from all those years ago. No, as he got closer, he saw it was a brand new Rolls Royce Phantom but fitted much the same. More spotlights for night hunting, not one but two mounted machine guns. And an impressive gleaming new Lantaka cannon. Ratan shivered as he remembered the moment with the prince next to the cannon that didn't work. The tigress picking up the scent of fear—Ratan's, of course. The prince had been on top of the world, on top of that car. Eerily on cue, he saw the prince striding out in Jodhpurs and boots, a spring in his step. He was whistling a popular film tune from one of Noor's movies. His prince! It took him all his willpower not to call out to him. The prince looked well, rotund even. His cheeks had filled out, he had a not-so-slight paunch too. Ratan smiled thinking of how the prince loved his sweets. All the queens took turns making him his favourite sweets so that they could get him to spill the gossip. The prince said what he saw and what he heard, without understanding the gravity of the scandal he was narrating. The difficult part was sitting him down and keeping him still. That's where the sweets helped.

Ratan felt a familiar ache in his heart for the prince as he saw him disappear, flanked by his attendants. His jaw clenched at the thought of who would be given the responsibility to drive the prince on the hunt, today. Ali squeezed his elbow to call his attention to the maharaja walking up to them. Bhai, Deven and his wife had caught up with them. Bhai twirled his moustache, nodding at Ratan and getting ready to meet the maharaja with his customary bear hug. The maharaja was beaming. Ratan felt his fists clench and unclench themselves at the sight of him.

'Welcome, welcome Bhai. It is indeed a pleasure to host you and your guests today. My greetings to the ladies! We have a special programme of entertainment for you, you will see. Please allow my men to escort you to your tents. In a few hours, we will commence the hunt. A small one, just to whet our appetites for the night ahead. In the evening, we will celebrate …'

As the maharaja continued speaking, Ratan watched the man he had seen often in his nightmares. A father willing to sacrifice his son to save face in front of all his British guests. Seething with anger at the memory of that night, he looked away. The maharaja was not the reason he was here today.

Now they were being walked to their tents. Bhai had arranged for their tents to be opposite Sir Richard's. It was a well-known fact that the British did not mind mingling with the Indians during hunts. For some reason, it was the only time they felt they were on equal ground. A hunt was a sport and somehow they were good sports about not playing rulers and subjects during the game of hunting.

Ratan and Ali were shown into their tents and told to rest. They would be sent word when it was time to begin getting ready for the hunt. Ratan removed his veil, glad to be able to breathe freely.

Bhai came into their tent soon after. Ratan had seen from the windows of the tent that he had been in deep conversation with the maharaja. A man of extravagant gestures, the maharaja kept throwing his arms around. Sometimes holding them to his heart, at other times taking them over his head, flinging them open, pointing at the skies. Theatrics, Ratan knew every gesture was empty and meaningless. The maharaja was a born performer.

Bhai sat on the edge of the bed and twirled his moustache before he spoke.

'So the maharaja is in a dilemma, I say this because we could use this to our advantage. His people are up in arms rebelling against him and what they're calling his autocratic ways. My reading is he has used up all his funds in living the grand life. Putting on all kinds of shows for the government and not his own people. He is going broke with this hunt. It will be grander than anything the British have seen and you know how delirious these hunts make them. At the celebration this evening, he is preparing to ask his British friends in the government for an even bigger loan. Using his son's coronation as an excuse.'

The bastard, the bastard, Ratan thought.

'Ratan, here is an idea. We need a significant commotion during the celebration. If the villagers intercept the celebrations with their demands, the maharaja will have to stop the show, see? Send the Britishers back to their tents till he can calm his people down. That is when you sneak in. Get your time with that English bastard and we come later and finish the job.'

Ratan nodded. He only wished he could shake off the feeling that the maharaja was going to put the prince in harm's way again.

'Did the maharaja say anything about the prince killing a tiger tonight? To mark his upcoming coronation?'

Bhai looked at him, not expecting a question not connected to the plan he had put forth.

'As a matter of fact, he did. Why do you ask?'

'Nothing. It is the custom in most princely states like Suraiah. I was curious. And it's a good plan, Bhai. I will be ready.'

'Ratan, focus. I'm here for you today, I will not be there tomorrow, do you understand? You asked for this. A meeting with the man who has you by the testicles, yes? I am going to make it happen, if you don't make the most of it, I will. And then I will not ever help you again, clear?'

Ratan nodded. He understood. It was personal for Bhai too. No man of his was going to prison for crimes committed by the British. It was a big enough crime to rule a country by force and treat its people as second-rate citizens in their own country. Must they fill up their prisons too? Not on Bhai's watch.

Deven walked in and Bhai told him to go speak to the village head. He should go with all the money they had come with. Pay him to get the villagers to storm the evening celebrations. Ali joined them as they left the tent; they had little time and it was an ambitious plan.

Ratan decided to close his tired eyes for a while. He had not slept the previous night at all. He covered his head with a bedsheet and lay down.

Outside, not too far way, the idiot prince was playing with his new toy. A yellow plane that could be wound to jump out of his hands and fly, before it needed to be wound up again. Once the plane flew, he ran after it, chasing it to pounce upon it and key it up again. His attendants watched, amused, glad he was chasing after the plane and not asking them to. The prince whirled round and round with the plane in his hands before letting it fly again. Like it was a bird he caught and was setting free. This time, a gust of wind made the plane fly longer and it took a turn. The prince ran after the vanishing splash of yellow among the grey green flapping tents. The wind picked up speed and the plane flew into a tent with the prince running after it.

Ratan woke up to an object land on his face and rest there. It had been a short but deep nap and it felt like someone had slapped him and let the hand stay on his face. Ratan, groggy but enraged, grabbed the plane and flung it. When the prince entered the tent in search of his plane, he saw Ratan picking it up to get a better look at it.

Ratan stood in his burkha holding the yellow plane as he turned around to see who had entered the tent. He remembered too late he didn't have the veil covering his face. The prince grinned wide—he had recognized him.

'Ratan!'

Ratan took a step in his direction but the prince was too excited to be still. He darted this way and the other saying his name again and again. Then before Ratan could stop him, he had turned around and run out of the tent, shouting out his name.

Ratan! Ratan! Ratan! Ratan!

Ratan cursed, grabbed his veil, adjusting it along the way, and ran after the prince. His heart was beating hard against his chest. He knew the prince was going straight to his father, the maharaja. He was the first person the prince wanted to announce Ratan's presence to. Once the maharaja found out Ratan was in his camp, he would have the perfect gift to serve his British guests. Even better than the hunt.

The prince was weaving in and out of the lanes with tents on either side. Ratan tried to keep an even pace, remembering what he would look like if he broke into a run to catch up with the prince. Nobody was paying the prince any attention but if he ran after him, they would notice. A woman in a burkha running like a man after the prince, it would get everybody's attention.

Hoping and praying he would not run into Bhai or Deven and Ali, Ratan finally saw the prince go into a tent. Ratan had no choice. He followed the prince into the tent. It was dark inside, Ratan could see nobody but the prince by the light escaping from the window flaps. He was rummaging through a trunk, flinging clothes and toys over his shoulder.

'Prince!'

Ratan removed his veil and called out to him, in a loud whisper. The prince turned around. In his hands was the same bow and arrow they would always play with. The prince would let go of the arrow and Ratan would fall over. Then they would switch roles. He held them out to Ratan, his face laughing but his eyes misty with tears, his body trembling.

'Ratan!'

Ratan held out his arms as he walked to the prince.

'I missed you too, dear prince, I missed you too.'

Behind them, the tent flap opened and Ratan turned around to see the queen mother come in. The prince's mother walked in with a companion, her eyes adjusting in the dark to see her son embracing a man. Her eyes widened on seeing it was Ratan. She entered and gestured to her companion to close and fasten the tent flap behind them.

The show must go on

Lavanya left Eden on the charpai with Hari and his entire family in attendance. She hurried out, walking as fast as she could. Where could she have left the packet? All that money. In pounds. The precious, precious ship ticket, Eden's ticket back to England, for God's sake. She had run away, left her home with all its comforts and servants, left her devoted husband, only for that ticket. Lavanya felt sick with fear. Ratan would have to go to prison after all. Donald Harper, who probably hated her more than ever had before, if that was even possible, would have the last bitter laugh. Her words meant nothing, spoken or written, he would say.

'Lavanya, do you know where you're going?' Noor hissed behind her. There was the tiniest daintiest huff in her voice. It was the huff that broke Lavanya's train of thought.

She looked up to see the twisted gully they had come out onto. Following a line of neon-coloured saris drying, the same ones she had parted as if they were curtains, like Hari, a while back. Now when she looked around, she saw the string of saris stretching way behind. In every direction too. Rows and rows of them. The same colours, the same pattern. She stopped. She should have asked Hari to show them the way back. It was a maze, the lanes, all branching here and there, narrowing more and more as she looked ahead.

'Where is Surya Kant?' Lavanya said. It was his car that was waiting somewhere beyond these saris. In a bigger, wider gully, nothing like these ones.

'He stayed back when he saw you walk away too fast. I followed, to bring you back. He thinks the car is the other way. Let's go back.' Noor said.

'Let's go back,' Lavanya repeated. Not liking the maze of gullies, the string of saris blocking the light, not letting them see any way out. Also the eerie silence. She reached out for Noor's hand.

Her hand flapped in the air. There was no Noor beside her. Lavanya looked around, she couldn't see her anywhere. Had she started walking back? Which way but?

'Noor? Noor?'

There was no answer. Something was not right. She could feel a familiar dread growing inside her. The next moment, her head slammed with the force of something heavy and sharp. She reeled and all the colours of the saris on the washing lines swam in front of her eyes. The pain hit a moment later, blinding her as a hand came over her mouth, stifling her scream.

She hit out at whoever was behind her but her hands were pinned down. She was being pulled back. Somebody snatched her bag from her shoulder and she heard the sound of running feet. There were two of them, Lavanya remembered thinking, and they had Noor, before another blow knocked her out.

In the evening mist, Sitara was among the clotheslines, full of sarees. In contrast, she was in a flowing white gown. Spinning, her arms stretched out, hands like buds of flowers, opening and closing. The clouds hung dark and low above her, following her where she went. Lavanya watched her like a drunken kotha guest would watch a bewitching dancing girl. Her head swam and she wanted to call out to her, get up and go and dance with her. But all she could do was watch her.

Then the spinning became slower and slower. She came closer, still swirling, and her face breezed within inches of Lavanya. She whispered to her, like she was passing on a secret no one else could hear.

Love is a crime, love is a crime, love is a crime.

The whisper, laced with bitterness, began like a slow storm. Picking up speed till every word boomed in her head. Before a sliver of light shone through.

Surya Kant was peering down at her. Her head ached, she raised her hand to feel the back of her head and her fingers touched something thick and damp.

'Where's Noor?' she managed to say.

Surya Kant looked relieved and distressed both at the same time.

'Thank God you're okay. I don't know where Noor is. I was waiting for both of you and then when you didn't appear, I came looking … and found you here.'

Taking Surya Kant's help, Lavanya got to her feet. They walked for a while when they heard a sound, a low moan. It wasn't too far away. Surya Kant left her and rushed towards the sound. Lavanya limped behind.

Slumped against a wall, was Noor. There was blood trickling down her face. Surya Kant wiped the blood as he looked around for help. Noor was mumbling something. Lavanya slumped down next to her.

'Noor, darling, are you okay? Look at me …'

Noor looked up at her, bloody but still beautiful. Gone was the mischief and the playfulness. She could only see alarm there now. It had all gotten too real.

'The hunt … the maharaja is waiting. I have to go …'

Lavanya held her friend close. Her delicate, porcelain face had blood all over it and Noor was thinking about her show. It had to go on.

'We've got to get you both to a hospital. Come with me, hold onto my arms,' Surya Kant said.

Noor whispered into Lavanya's ear, 'Lava, don't listen to him …'

Lavanya couldn't focus. Her head ached. It was all swimming again. The hospital. She was in the hospital. All those people lying everywhere, the old woman holding on to her hand, looking at her beseeching. Her son, dead in his own eyes, lying in a heap next to her. She hadn't been able to move. If it hadn't been for Marc. He had held her by the arm and pushed forward. *Her purse had slipped from her shoulder and he had put it back.* He had put it back. He had taken the packet. It had to be him. But why? How could he have known what she had in there?

'My bag …'

She looked for her bag. She remembered it being wrenched away from her when she was struck. She couldn't see it anywhere. She held on to Surya Kant's arm as she tried to think. Did they want money, these people who had attacked her and Noor?

It was all getting so muddled up, she no longer knew what to think.

Then, as they kept walking, she saw it, lying in a corner. Surya Kant got it for her and she rummaged through it, knowing it would be empty. What had they been looking for?

They found the car. The driver was waiting and when he saw them, shook his head in a tragic way. He looked at Surya Kant to say he had warned him, this was not a safe place to come alone. Surya Kant nodded at him to start the car.

'The hospital, as soon as possible.' He kept glancing at Noor, whose head had slumped on his shoulder. Noor looked up.

'There's no time for that, Surya. To the hunt. My crew is waiting. I'm resting.'

Then her head slumped down again.

The driver started the car. When they heard the sound of running feet, the front door opened and Eden got in. Her eyes glassy, her twitch working, she looked back at the three of them and tried to smile.

'Lavanya, please … I'm much safer with you. I'll keep my head down, I promise. I need to be close to you, my ticket is with you, I can't leave you … I'll be quiet, I won't bother you at all.'

Lavanya didn't know what to say. She looked at Noor. She didn't feel up to all this at all.

'Let's take her to the hunt. She can be one of my background dancers. I'll give her a veil …' Noor said.

Lavanya caught a movement behind the car. It was Hari. Faithful, gnome-like Hari, on his bicycle. Carrying a bottle of Solan No. 1, no doubt. He would follow his memsahib to the ends of the earth, his determined face seemed to say.

A blow in the head is a blessing, Lavanya thought. When everything is as muddled up as this, it didn't make sense to have a clear head. She would have to go to the hunt. Richard was at the hunt with Marc and Marc had the packet with Eden's ticket and money inside. She knew he did. There was just one thing Lavanya wanted to clear up with Eden.

'Eden, before you decide to come, you should know this. I don't have your ticket. Or the money I promised you. It was in my bag today when I came to your house. Somebody took it from my bag at the hospital and I'm pretty sure it was your husband, Marc. He's at the hunt. That's why I'm going there now. You still feel safer with me?'

Many veils

LAVANYA SAT HUDDLED WITH A HOT CUP OF TEA WARMING her hands as she watched Noor get ready for her show. Once her crew had seen Noor and Lavanya, they had taken over. They had cleaned and disinfected the wounds with lotions and ointments. They had bottomless bags. Now Noor's wounds were being expertly covered with makeup.

Eden sat in a plush armchair in the crew tent, glass in hand. She kept looking over her shoulder. Hari was loitering outside, waiting for anything else she may need. Every now and then, Eden shot Lavanya a hopeful look.

Damn that ticket. The money. Lavanya had to find it but she had no idea how. 'Loot', the Hindi word for plunder, was among the first Indian words to enter the English language.

She had managed to leave word for Amrit Singh at the guesthouse. The receptionist had seen Lavanya and her hand had flown to cover her mouth. She had no time to ask why.

'Tell the inspector, please, I am going to the hunting party with my friend from Bombay. He and the superintendent have to meet me there. It's very, very important.'

Surya Kant had dropped them to the hunt and said he would be back. He needed to look into something, he would tell them more when he got back.

There was a flurry outside the tent and a tall, stately woman wrapped in brocade walked in. Eden put her dancer's veil over her face in time.

It was the Rani Sahiba, someone from Noor's crew told Lavanya in a whisper. The lady had a quiet presence that made everyone feel comforted. She greeted them with a smile, her eyes sweeping over everyone.

'The maharaja sends his welcome. No, Noor, please don't get up. Thank you for coming all the way from Bombay to make our evening special. We are all looking forward to seeing you perform. The prince, my son, is a big fan of all your movies.'

Noor got up and hugged the queen. Even though she had make-up on her face and nail paint on her hands.

'It is an honour, Your Highness, to be here. I promise you it will be a performance your guests will not forget. I have a small favour to ask, if I may?' The queen nodded, charmed by Noor. 'My friend Lavanya too is from Bombay and would love to see more of your wonderful camp. Would you please have someone show her around?'

It was buzzing outside. Countless servants in royal costume running around carrying refreshments for the guests. Walls were being painted by local artists. The tents, one more lavish than the other, were being decorated with bolsters and lamps. Elephants decked up in red velvet and golden finery walked down, led by their mahouts. The other animals in their cages screeched and roared at intervals to add to the clamour of the moment.

As they walked, the queen told Lavanya about the crowning that was to take place later. Her son, the prince, was soon going to be king. The hunt was a grand celebration of the event. Lavanya wondered if the prince was the same 'idiot prince' the police would not take seriously. But if he became king, wouldn't they have to? As they passed one tent after another, she wondered how she was ever going to know which one belonged to Marc. Or Richard.

'Let's stop by my tent and have somebody fix us a saffron sherbet, Lavanya. My throat is parched, isn't yours? Come ...'

She held up the flap of her tent and stepped in, Lavanya followed. The rest of the attendants stayed out.

Inside, was a lady in a burkha with a face exactly like Ratan's.

Lavanya and Ratan sat close together holding mugs of saffron sherbet laced with brandy. The prince sat, his arm in Ratan's as he played with his mother's Benarasi saree.

The queen was an old confidant. Ratan often listened to her sing on moonlit nights when she couldn't sleep. Later, she sat on the swing-set and talked to him about her life as a little girl, how she had imagined life to be. The maharaja was not an easy man to stay married to. She had been his first but not by far, his last queen. The youngest was only sixteen. He sought the queen out only to complain of the prince and how she had cheated him of a normal heir. When she sang, Ratan heard a melodious but bitter rain falling.

'Why are you here, Ratan?' she asked, concern in her eyes.

'There's no time for that now, Rani Sahiba. But there's something I have to tell you, is it safe here …?'

She assured Ratan they were safe in her tent. Not even the maharaja was allowed without her permission. She didn't have to tell Ratan, he knew she was a powerful woman again. Her son was going to be crowned king, after all. It had been her only wish for too long.

'The prince could be in harm's way, Rani Sahiba,' Ratan said.

Lavanya listened to Ratan tell the queen of what had happened at the last hunt. He feared the prince would be expected to kill a tiger again and if he wasn't successful, it could end badly for the prince. She must make sure he was with someone dependable the whole night. Especially during the hunt.

The queen listened as the prince slept, his head on her lap. It had been an exhausting and exciting day for him. He had a long night ahead of him.

Then she settled his head on a cushion, covered him with a light quilt and left the tent.

'Stay here, I'll be back.'

Ratan and Lavanya found themselves alone. They turned to each other in relief.

'Ratan …'

'Hmmm?'

'I'm about to kiss a lady in a burkha.'

Ratan removed his veil and pulled Lavanya to him. They kissed as the tent swam around them.

'Lava …'

'Hmmm?'

'I have to tell you …'

'Not now, please … I trust you, whatever you're doing, I'm sure it's fine,' she murmured as she cupped his face in her hands. 'Right now, all I want to do is kiss you and kiss you and kiss you,' she said.

'I'm going to give myself up to the police.'

'Are you mad?'

Ratan looked at her, smiled and nodded.

'Look at you, all embroiled in this mess. All because I decided to run. It's all got to stop. I'm going to make it stop.'

'I'm not going to let you. I have it all under control. I have Eden. She's going to tell the police she saw Richard that night. She will tell the police about their plan to get away, the blackmail letters, everything. They will have to re-open the case, Rat.'

She pulled his head to kiss him again. To somehow hold on to this moment.

But it was gone.

So they held each other as well as they could.

The prince stirred and stretched a drowsy hand for Ratan to hold, before it dropped off again.

'It's going to be okay …' Ratan murmured in Lavanya's hair.

'It's going to be okay …' Lavanya said into his shoulder.

'Lava, promise me you're not going to do anything stupid …'

'Can you promise me the same?' she asked.

He pulled her hair. She bit into his shoulder.

The queen was back too soon. The prince slept on. She made sure they were both escorted by her most trusted servants to Ratan's tent. Outside his tent, Ratan gestured at the two tents across his with his eyes.

Once they were inside the tent, the guards left.

'Lavanya, stay here, don't do a thing till I'm back. The celebrations will begin any time now. Let me go and see where Ali is. I'll have him take you back to Noor.'

He left. She took a deep breath, counted till ten, and came out.

She strode across, her heart hammering. She had no idea what came next. What was she going to say when she saw them? She was going to ask for her packet back. That's it. She would say: Wasn't it enough to loot an entire country, you had to loot me?

Of the two tents that stood side by side, she picked the left one. She couldn't see anybody. But she could hear voices that seemed to be coming from deep within.

She went and crouched low by the window. The muffled voices were coming from the next tent. But she heard 'Eden' a lot.

She peered as much as she could through the window and saw Richard holding his head in his hands. Marc was standing over him and talking. Then one clear sentence wafted across to her like a gift from the winds.

'She's not going anywhere, I've made sure of that. Don't worry about her at all, Richard. She's my concern.'

This was Marc's tent then. Her packet had to be here somewhere.

As she was crawling away from the window, another sentence came floating inside and she couldn't move.

'Hari is 100% reliable. I can trust him with my life. He will not let her out of his sight.'

Faithful, gnome-like earnest Hari was Marc's boy.

Hari by Eden's side, making sure she was never without a glass in hand, never without her whisky or her medication.

Hari, putting the blinds down, shutting the light out, never out of reach, always a whisper away. Hari, waiting outside the hospital, taking her to his house, keeping her there, guarded by all his family members. On his bicycle, following their car, watching out for his memsahib, no matter what. Outside her tent right now, waiting for orders.

Eden was not safe at all.

She had to go and warn her. Eden had to know. She would come back for the packet later.

An unlikely confrontation

THE CELEBRATIONS BEGAN WITH THE LOUD BEAT OF THE drums. The royal bugle came next, playing the maharaja's personal musical insignia.

Everybody was to gather in the central courtyard, a short walk from the tents, at the edge of the forest. The stage was set and Ratan had to admit, it was a stunning setting. The daintiest lights in blue and gold lit up the giant trees that framed the gigantic stage. He had not planned to walk this far out. Unable to spot Ali or Dev, he had followed the lights here. Where were they? It had gotten dark and his burkha gave him a freedom he hadn't had for days. Any moment now, according to Bhai's plan, the villagers were to interrupt the proceedings. He was to follow Richard back to his tent. Ali would distract Marc. There was no sign of Ali. He should hurry back. Lavanya was waiting, he would escort her to Noor's tent himself and come back here. Ali would find him.

Ratan had only taken five steps when he heard Noor welcomed on stage. How long it had been. All three of them had spent many evenings on his balcony, trying out smokes.

Talking about what they would do when they grew up. He longed to stay and watch her perform. She would break into impromptu songs and dances even then. Now she had a stage to herself. He had not known then what he wanted and wondered if he ever would.

He had to rush. Lavanya was missing all this. He turned to walk away back toward his tent when he saw the villagers come in brandishing lathis. They were coming from all sides, silently and stealthily. He ducked into the shadows and took a different path. It was all happening and he was ill-prepared. Luckily, he could see his tent in the distance and decided to make a run for it. Everybody was at the performance so a lady in a burkha running was nobody's problem. He reached his tent and even before he went in, he knew Lavanya wouldn't be there. He looked across at the two tents and swore under his breath. He went to the almirah and rummaged under a pile of neatly arranged clothes till he found the gun. Slipping it into the back of his trousers under his burkha, he strode across to Richard's tent.

He lifted the flap, knowing there was no going back from here. Blood pounding in his head, he looked down at his feet covered in the prince's green shoes. He found no reason to retrace his steps. If Lavanya had gone in, it wasn't safe. He was going in too. He lifted his veil, felt the cold December wind take a biting lick of his face, and went in.

There was nobody there. They were out watching Noor perform. Maybe Lavanya never came here. He walked further in, getting bolder. Only the tent flaps made a curious slapping sound outside. He looked around, everything was in order. Clothes folded, a towel, and a pair of slippers next to an overnight bag. His eyes skimmed over the top of the only writing table in the room. A handwritten letter lay under a paperweight on the study table.

Ratan walked over to see what it was. One eye on the entrance of the tent, head craning to see whatever he could. The first line stopped him cold.

Nobody must be held responsible for what I'm going to do.

He walked over and picked up the letter, completely perplexed.

Life after Sara is not worth living.

I have thought this over and over and over.

It is the only way I can correct what I should have had the courage to do before.

Forgive me, Sara, I should have done better by you.

Forgive me, Marc, only you know what is in my heart.

I am sorry to leave you, please believe me.

Richard was going to end his life? Why? Wasn't it all going his way? Why kill your wife, frame her lover, kill his friend and then take your own life?

The bloody coward. The letter shook in Ratan's hands, his whole body shook with an anger he had not felt before.

'Ratan?'

Hearing his name said aloud in that familiar voice made the blood rush to his head.

It was Richard Davenport, looking at him like he had seen a ghost.

Ratan flung himself at him, pinning him to the ground, frothing at the mouth.

'You bastard. You bastard,' was all he could utter, over and over again.

Richard tried to speak but Ratan had his hands on his throat. He tried to get Ratan's hands off his neck as he gasped and tried to breathe.

One hand still on his throat, Ratan whipped out his gun and pointed it at Richard's head.

'I know what you did, you bastard. You were there that night at the party. You killed Sara. Now you plan to kill yourself? It's that easy, is it?'

Richard shook his head, tears streaming down his eyes.

Ratan loosened his hold on the throat, the gun still boring into Richard's head.

'You didn't kill her?' Richard managed to say, his eyes wide and surprised.

It was impossible. Ratan had imagined a confrontation very unlike the one he was having. Where he would put all the evidence in front of Richard, then turn himself in to the police. Ask him why, that's all. No violence. Now he wanted nothing more than to pull the trigger on him. Get it over with. If he was going to go to jail for the rest of his life, he might as well do it. Richard could see his frustration as he tried to speak.

'Ratan, listen to me. I was there. I came back from Mashobra early, reached the party knowing Marc was going to speak to Sara about the letters she was writing. I saw them together and couldn't bear to face her. I left at once. I thought nobody saw me. I didn't kill her, *I couldn't*.'

'You're lying. Somebody did see you. You killed her and ran. You bastard.' Ratan could barely say the words without trembling.

'*I killed Sara*. Get off him, Ratan.'

Marc was standing there, gun in hand. A .577 double rifle meant to take down a dozen tigers was pointing at him.

Ratan stared at him, trying to make sense of what he had heard. Marc, it had been Marc. He had done it for Richard.

Both of them were in it together. He kept the gun on Richard's head.

'Go ahead, shoot me. Richard goes too.' This was it. No more backing off.

Nobody moved.

Then he heard Richard whisper with a sob 'Marc, no! You promised me you wouldn't hurt her.'

'Richard, I can explain. Once I do, you'll understand,' Marc said, then turned to Ratan.

'Get off him. He had nothing to do with it. It was me. I'll tell you everything, if you…'

'Ratan, no, finish it off. Pull the trigger,' Richard said holding the gun and urging Ratan to shoot him in the head.

'Richard, have you lost your mind?' Marc said. Ratan saw Marc's hands tremble and the Double Rifle shook, its aim wavering.

'Oh he doesn't know, does he, Richard?' Ratan said, gesturing to the letter lying on the table.

And just like that, he knew what the blackmail had been all about.

Sitara by the tree

Lavanya ran as fast as she could. Her lehenga and dupatta wrapping themselves around her legs, as she kept trying to free herself. Finally she picked up the beautiful fabric, crushed it in her hand, lifted it as high as she could, exposing naked legs as she ran. The drums were deafening. She couldn't hear herself think. The animals in the cages were getting restless. Their sedatives were waiting. There was time.

She reached the crew tent only to see everyone trooping out. The announcements had begun. Eden too? She scanned through all the dancers, she couldn't see Eden. There were veils over all their faces.

Noor was performing, her melodious onstage voice welcoming her fans. Promising them an evening of unbelievable entertainment.

Hari, she would look for Hari. That little bastard. She looked all around the tent, went backstage. There was no sign of Hari anywhere.

Looking at the dazzling stage with the glittering trees, was Sitara. Sitting on the branch of a tree, as if watching the show from her perch. She seemed to have eyes only for Lavanya though. Smiling at her, hands beckoning her closer and closer. Lavanya started walking towards Sitara. Soon the stage was behind her and she was walking into the dark forest. Leaving the glittering trees and the tumult of voices behind her.

As she got closer, Sitara slipped off her branch and landed on her feet. They walked together. None of them spoke.

They were by a pond now and the early moon shone its light on the shimmering water, it seemed like another world. Finally, Lavanya spoke.

'I've come too far, Sitara, I have to go back. Ratan is here too. I have to find Eden and warn her, she too is not safe … will you come back with me?'

'Why don't you go ahead? I'll be right behind. Whatever happens, remember to look up, listen to the trees. People lie, trees don't.'

'They don't speak to me the way they speak to you,' Lavanya said.

'They will. You wait and see … now go.'

Their hands lingered and then Sitara was gone. Lavanya walked back, taking the path Sitara had shown her. Coming closer and closer to the voices from the stage. All her restlessness returning, her heart beating unevenly again. She longed for the calm she had felt with Sitara.

As she neared the stage, still in the shadow of the forest, she saw Hari. He looked like he was resting against the tree, asleep. His small body curled up, knees almost touching his chin.

Something was not right. Suddenly, she felt no fear, nothing but the inevitability of it all. She knew he was dead. She looked up at the tree under which he lay. It looked down at her in all its wisdom. Its branches spreading and spreading all around her. The leaves fluttering, fanning her. Lavanya looked down at Hari, his eyes open, surprised, with a glint of amusement still in them. He had known something was not quite right too. Always. Now it was too late but he was glad in the last moments that he had known something was not quite right. Paharis have good instincts. He was a good Pahari. He had known. That's all he could cling to, as he slept never to wake up again.

It was all too clear. By the light of the moon, the trees had told her all she needed to know. What Hari had only suspected.

Surya Kant was waiting, pacing up and down outside the crew tent. There was no time to tell him anything, which was just as well. Lavanya couldn't yet bring herself to say what she had seen, what she knew. Surya Kant was in a state of discovery, consumed by what was before him. He was carrying files of papers and he spread them out on a trunk. He bade Lavanya sit next to him as he handed her the papers one by one. His journalist friends had done their homework.

Richard and Marc went way back. They had met during the war. Richard was leading the battalion and Marc had been his direct subordinate. Except Marc was not called Marc then. Surya Kant handed her a black-and-white newspaper photograph. Two laughing young men, their arms around each other, flexing their muscles. Lavanya recognized both Richard and Marc immediately, but the names under the photograph read: Lieutenant Charles Simmons and Major Richard Davenport. There were pictures of them with the rest of the battalion too. Richard looking boyish and handsome and 'Charles' looking at him with open adoration.

There were various reports of how the battalion had performed, changes in assignments, transfers to and from the unit, signed by Charles Simmons. One report stood out. Marked 'highly confidential', it was an internal communication to the Army General in chief. It informed him that Lieutenant Charles Simmons had relinquished his title and been sent on immediate leave, awaiting further instructions. On account of 'having been caught in shameful acts with Private Gary Falkland, from another battalion.'

There were confessional reports by the soldier admitting to the act, in which he claimed he 'was seduced' by Lieutenant Charles Simmons and had merely been 'obeying orders'.

'Do you see?' Surya Kant looked at Lavanya reading the reports.

'Marc Easton is Charles Simmons. In India, he is Marc Easton. Aide to a very high-ranking man in the army. The same army that had once stripped him of his badge and sent him on indefinite leave,' Surya Kant said.

'And Richard knows because Richard was responsible for bringing him here. And Sara found out. That's why the blackmail letters. She almost got away with it and then something she didn't expect, got her killed,' Lavanya said.

Surya Kant looked at Lavanya and nodded. 'The journalist who found these reports in the archives also found Private Gary Falkland. He agreed to speak to him under conditions of strict confidentiality and a considerable amount of cash. He said he was threatened with criminal proceedings if he refused to comply. He said Charles Simmons had been set up. The army had information Charles was a homosexual but no evidence. They forced the private to give a statement. They had nothing to connect him to Richard Davenport, so Richard was never in the eye of the storm. Charles disappeared after that. Nobody had heard of him since. Marc Easton, meanwhile, exists only in India. The journalist could not find any history or file on him,' Surya Kant finished.

'That's why they couldn't go back. In India, Richard was powerful and through Richard, Marc was powerful,' Lavanya said. 'Please find Superintendent Donald Harper, Surya Kant. I would come with you but I have credibility issues with the police. Will you ...? They'll listen to you, you have the facts and, well, you're a man. They're more comfortable believing men.' She got up.

'Ah Lavanya, contrary to what you think, it's no longer enough to be a man, that's why I studied law. Not to practise it, but to make sure others did. Don't worry, they will listen to me. I know what I've got here. After his day in court today, he will be glad to have this,' Surya Kant said. Lavanya got up.

'Where will you be?' Surya Kant called after her.

'With Ratan ...' Lavanya said. Like it was the stupidest question ever.

Kill the tiger

THE PRINCE WOKE UP, RUBBED HIS EYES, PICKED HIS NOSE and yawned.

He craned his ears to hear the music in the distance. The celebrations had begun.

It was pitch dark in the tent. Not even a lantern burned to disturb his sleep. His mother had made sure. He shook his head. He didn't want to think about his mother right now, he wanted his friend, his brother, Ratan. Had he left him again? Any moment now, his father's men would come to drug him like the other animals, take him into the forest and it would begin. The low swelling chant of 'kill the tiger, kill the tiger.' He knew the drill too well. He didn't want to kill any tigers. Not today. Not ever.

He had seen the truth in Ratan's eyes even before he had heard Ratan tell his mother. Now she knew what he had known in his heart forever. His father wanted him dead more than he wanted to see him crowned. It's just that he was a gambling man, the game had to play out. Everybody had a part to play. So do you, dear prince, so do you, he told himself shaking his head from side to side.

He strapped on his boots, just like the ones Ratan was wearing. Those were his too, he knew. When he would become king, he would gift Ratan a dozen more.

All his fears and hopes were known to Ratan that night he ran in those shoes. Had the same shoes led him here so many years later, to pick up the story where he had left it?

He went to the trunk and found the gun his father had given him to practise with. He must have been hoping he would shoot himself with it, one day. The prince laughed as he swung it around, threw it in the air and caught it. It was time to leave, the guards would be here any moment.

But he had miscalculated how eager they were to carry out his father's wishes. The guards came in, talking to each other. Useless, stupid things about the dancers and who would lie with whom later that night. He saw how surprised they were to see him up and ready. They looked down to see the laces of his boots strapped in two correct bows. Looked up and saw the prince grinning, his eyes twinkling. There were three shots. One for each of them. Practice session, dear papa, practice session. The prince strode out of the camp, taking big gulps of the delicious night breeze.

He wondered why the breeze had never tasted this good before.

All the animals in all their cages saw him walk past them and walk back up again. Opening each cage, snap, snap, snap. It would be a while before the animals realized they were free. Till then, he would go find Ratan. There was something he needed to tell him. About another night at a ball at Whiteflower Hall. Where he had seen a golden-haired woman fall, blood gushing out of her mouth, on a moonlit night like this one.

He had seen two people come and go as she smoked her last cigarette out there among the trees. One of them visited his father often at the palace in Suraiah. Then he had seen the person who had appeared out of the shadows striking her again and again, just to be sure. Then they went back in again without a drop of blood on them.

He had told Papa, who had bundled him in a car and taken him back home and drugged him for many days after. The drugs were nice, he didn't mind them one bit. What he minded was being told he had imagined it all. It had been real. His urine-soaked silk pants were proof. He had shown Papa, who had wrinkled up his nose and told him what a curse he was.

Ratan would believe him. He had to tell Ratan.

The prince walked towards the tent he had found Ratan in. Then stopped. A tigress stood in front of him. The prince looked at the tigress for a long moment. Then grinned and turned back. The tigress was right. Ratan could wait. He would find him later. Right now, he must pay a visit to his father. Papa must always come first.

Papa, there's something I've been wanting to tell you for a long time now. I didn't know how. But I do now. Please listen. It's going to be a little loud.

The tigress walked a few steps behind him. Till she saw him enter his father's tent.

Open cages

LAVANYA CAME OUT TO SEE PEOPLE RUNNING IN ALL directions. The music had stopped. Noor was no longer on stage. The villagers had replaced her, shouting their demands, thumping their fists. She hurried, cursing her lehenga again. She saw the bewildered animals in their cages with their doors open. The doors swinging wide, back and forth, back and forth. Yet they didn't move. Only stared, disbelieving, at the people outside.

The people, on their part, saw the open cages and didn't know what to make of it. They broke into cries of panic, running into their cloth tents only to run out again. There is going to be a stampede, Lavanya thought, holding up her lehenga. She had better hurry.

Ratan saw Marc read the letter, crumple it and put it back. He wished he wasn't here. His grip on his gun was slipping from all the sweat in his hands. His calves ached from all the squatting. He was afraid, quite afraid, he would end up pulling the trigger without even meaning to.

The rage was all gone. He was miserable but not as miserable as the two men in the same tent as him. He looked away, he didn't want to see the pain in Marc's eyes as he looked at his lover, weeping.

'Would you do this, would you take your life, Richard?' Marc asked.

'No, I wouldn't.' Richard lied through his tears.

This is what Sara had known. She never had or would ever have his heart. Not the way she wanted it, she was promised a lie. All her own lies could console her for only so long. She had to go away. Taking whatever she could from Richard before she left.

'Once a Fishing Fleeter, always a Fishing Fleeter,' she would say often. 'We travel the world looking for suitable men to find our own place in a world that will not value us, otherwise. It's more than men have ever done. Wars are easy to fight, try doing what we do. We can't ever let our guard down, not even when we die.'

She was taking her share by blackmailing him. If Richard had known, he would have willingly given her the money. Marc had not told Richard to protect him, no doubt. Marc had wanted to *handle* it for Richard. He had killed her, that was his idea of handling it, the bastard. He wished his gun was at Marc's head.

He looked at Marc to tell him he was dropping his gun, he should follow, when he saw Marc's eyes go from pain to fear. There was somebody else in the tent with them.

Ratan tried to turn on his haunches, his calves refusing to budge. From the corner of his eyes, he saw the flutter of a long skirt and a woman in a dancer's veil come in, smeared in blood.

'Oh Marc, look what a mess I've made, darling,' Eden said, completely oblivious to the guns pointed in different directions. She had removed her veil and sat down, looking weary, warming her hands by the fire. 'I never get blood on my clothes. I'm a butcher's daughter, I was taught never to do that. I must be tired, it's been an endless day.'

The last time Ratan had seen Eden was at the club with Sara, when she had told Ratan he could take the evening to babysit his neighbour's daughter. She didn't need him that night. The Eastons had offered to take her and bring her back. Only to get a message from her an hour later that she did need him, after all. He had hurried but he knew he was late.

Nervous, fragile Eden. Looking to Sara forever to tell her what to do. Except that night when he was dropping her home and the car had broken down in the middle of nowhere. She leaned forward, cupped his face in her hands and kissed him. Shocked when he hadn't responded, she had broken into tears and begged him not to tell Sara. He had not. Among the many things he had not told Sara. It had always been awkward between them since that day.

'Hello Ratan, you clever dog. Nice burkha, there. Sara would have enjoyed that. Poor, poor Sara ...'

'Eden, what are you doing here?' Marc cut in.

'Oh you know only too well, Marc, my darling, I need my ticket and my money. You took it from Lavanya, remember?'

'Of course you can have it, dear. It's in my tent, do you want to go get it now?' Marc said, holding her gaze.

Eden laughed, 'No darling, I want *you* to go get it.'

Richard was looking at Eden in a strange way. Like he had never seen her before.

'Stop it, Eden, leave now. Take the ticket and go while you can. Is Hari out there, tell him to …'

'Hari is not there, is he?' Richard was beginning to understand.

'Clever, clever Richard. It's sad how much you loved Sara, you know. She thought you were a silly old coward though. Oh Marc, don't look hurt. Everybody loved Sara, you see. Me, most of all.' Eden smiled.

'Oh and Marc, did you think I wouldn't know Hari was not mine but yours? Were you fornicating with him as well, darling?' Eden said, trying to rub a blood stain from the glove in her hand.

'You didn't love Sara, you resented her. You killed her. I was foolish to have tried to protect you. I should have told the police about you …'

'Listen to me Marc, you would never. You, darling, are a snivelling, useless coward too. You would have to tell the police about the blackmail, your strange, wonderful past! It would all come tumbling out of the closet, wouldn't it now? Then? Then both of you would be history … this blessed life in India amongst the slaves that you feed on, would be history. So don't be telling me about protection, it was me protecting both of you. You owe me! Now put down the gun and get the ticket and money, please.'

'That would be this, then?' the familiar voice, Ratan whipped around to see, was Lavanya's, she had the lost packet in her hands.

Lavanya had been in a daze since she had found Hari under that tree at the edge of the forest. It could only have been Eden. Nervous, twitching Eden was not at all nervous with a knife in her hand. Not a knife, not an axe, something in between, isn't that what the forensics had said to Amrit Singh?

'The butcher's daughter' the title of a story in Sara's diary, came to her. She had started the story—or was it a poem—but had found it difficult to go beyond the title. She had begun to suspect Eden was getting dangerous. She had never imagined she would turn on Sara, her only friend.

The attack in the saree-laden street, the vicious blows. It had been Eden sending Hari and his family to steal the packet from Lavanya. Marc had taken it from her bag that day at the hospital because he had known it was for Eden. Hari had been his informant, lurking in the shadows, listening in on them the previous day in Eden's house.

The only way Marc could control Eden was to keep her medicated and penniless. He knew she was getting increasingly unstable and even dangerous when provoked.

'What a cosy foursome this is!' Eden said, looking at Lavanya holding the packet. She sounded flippant but her eyes were blazing hatred. She wasn't expecting Lavanya here. That too, in a position of power.

'Eden, you can have this. I have no use for it. But tell me, all this mayhem, only to get on a ship?' Lavanya wanted to keep her talking. Surya Kant would be here with the police soon.

'Ah the porn writer-detective! You're going to write about this, aren't you? Hilarious. How transparent you are, Lavanya! Asking me questions, thinking I'm going to spill my guts and you can write it all down without *feeling* any of it. You're despicable, that's what you are,' Eden said, hissing the last part out.

Lavanya could see Eden's whole body convulse with emotion. Much as Eden didn't want to spill her guts, like she said, it was a physical need. She was going to. She was a talker. Especially where there was an audience. She saw Eden turn towards the fire, evaluating if it was easier speaking to the flames. It wasn't.

'Do you even know what it is like to feel trapped in a country that is not your own? To have no money? To have no love? To have a friend who has it all? Do you? Sara had not one but two countries she felt like she *belonged* in. She could have any man she wanted, any woman she wanted, oh I knew about her and Miss Sher-Gil. Once Sara was gone, I left her a cake I baked with my own hands. I also improved a painting her ugly hands made of my Sara. Did you see that one? Now that belonged in an exhibition, it did,' Eden clicked her tongue, and tried once again to remove a smear of blood from her gloves. 'So I was saying? Sara had Ratan, she had Richard doting on her, she had books, teaching, poetry, *she had me too*. And me, all I had was her.' Eden's voice broke.

Was there anybody in this tent who was not traumatized? Ratan thought, as he kept his eye on Lavanya. Who said it was an unequal world? Everyone seemed equally disturbed.

'So it wasn't you, Marc, oh thank God it wasn't you,' Richard said. There was no gun to his head any more. Ratan had let his gun drop many moments back. Marc was looking at Richard and shaking his head.

'No, it was never me but I could have stopped her … and I didn't.' Marc brought his hand down over his face, as if rubbing from it what it had seen.

'That night, we were going to drive Sara home. She had told Ratan not to come but unknown to me, Eden sent him a message that Sara needed him. I took Sara aside that night at the party, into the palace grounds and convinced her to stop the blackmail. Told her how much I loved you, Richard, that I would go away if she needed me to. She backed off almost immediately. She said she had no evidence, nothing. She said she would speak to Eden and tell her to back off too. Eden had put her up to it. She had seen us together once, kissing. Eden had convinced Sara this was their chance to blackmail us. Take all the money they could and go back home to England and live as independent rich women. They never planned to tell anybody on us. I left her there smoking a cigarette and went back in to talk to Eden. I couldn't find her anywhere'.

'... it was you I saw running across the grounds?' Ratan asked Eden, in disbelief. It still didn't make sense.

'Much as I would love to chat like my cheating husband here, I must be getting on. Lavanya, throw me that packet, will you?'

'Eden, Sara was going to stay back, wasn't she? She had changed her mind about leaving. She told you the evening before and you wouldn't have it. That's what drove you over the edge. That's when you sent that message to Ratan. Picked up my book that she had given you to read for the play you were staging with Judith Wilkins at the Gaiety Theatre. You found Sara later that evening, right after Marc had spoken to her. She must have been happy to see you, her one true friend and co-conspirator. Before you slit her throat ...'

'Shut up and throw me what's mine!' Eden screamed, shaking with anger.

Lavanya spoke fast but she was thinking even faster. 'It is yours and you can have it, I don't need it, but before you go, admit you made a mistake, pinning it on Ratan, won't you? When he didn't stay to get caught by the police that night you killed Sara, Ratan made sure your troubles had only begun, am I right? Much as you hate Marc, he shielded you, he had little choice, but he did. He hoped like you, that if the police suspected Ratan and caught him, all your problems would be over. You would get better, you would stay, everything could be managed. There was no need to tell Richard, who could barely get over Sara's death. Let him too, think it was Ratan who had killed Sara, but when Shyam didn't want to give his friend up ...'

'Eden, why did Shyam have to die?' Ratan asked quietly. He realized what Lavanya was doing.

'Oh I don't know, Ratan!' Eden said, beyond exasperated. 'Could it be because the poor bastard thought he could give us the wrong information about you and get away with it?' Eden hissed.

'Eden, it wasn't Shyam, it was his wife Cheeni who told the police that Ratan was hiding at the farm. That Ratan would be leaving for the bus station at dawn, I was going to tell you it wasn't Shyam but by then ...' Marc interrupted, inching towards Eden.

It had been Cheeni. The face at the window that night Ratan was leaving their farm. Plotting. Scheming. Little did she know how horribly wrong it would all go. He remembered the shock of finding Shyam following the trail of his own blood. Then he remembered how Shyam had seemed to hold on to him. How he had opened his tightening fist to find a gold button, the flash of which he had seen in Sara's study too, the night he had gone in to look in her desk drawer. On Marc's shoes. As Marc took another step to go towards Eden, Ratan knew it was Marc who had killed his friend, not Eden.

'GIVE ME MY PACKET! NOW!' Eden screamed, red in the face. Marc took another step.

'Eden, who killed Shyam? I know it wasn't you.' Ratan said as he gripped his gun again. Eden stopped, she looked at Marc, daring him to speak. Marc looked at Richard who too, was looking at him, disbelieving, wanting to be reassured. Marc closed his eyes.

'Oh darling, are you going to let this august gathering here believe it was li'l ol' me again who took Shyam's life? Richard, I may be a butcher's daughter, I may have learned how to use a cleaver. I did kill Sara, there is no denying it, but the love of your life isn't innocent either, he is a liar, he is the one who …'

'Eden! Stop, please, stop, let me. Richard, it was me, I killed Shyam. I had no choice,' Marc was looking desperately at Richard. 'When the police did not find Ratan at the bus station, I went to the farm to talk to Cheeni. Shyam was completely unaware of what Cheeni had done. Cheeni denied it all, said she had never taken any money for the information and I had to threaten to kill her when the fool threw himself on me …' Marc said, 'and the gun went off.'

'Right then, this is all very touching but I have a ship to catch,' Eden looked at Lavanya, her teeth set in a snarl. 'Lavanya, are you giving me my packet or do you want to die too, love?'

Give it to her, Lavanya, Sitara said. She spoke from behind Eden. From the fire that had engulfed her, cleansed her, given her the freedom she had now.

'You can have it. I don't want to hold it any longer.' Lavanya walked a few steps towards Eden and threw it at her. And into the fire.

Eden turned to see the packet curling into thick black strips as the flames began to engulf it.

Then she lunged at Lavanya, whipping the knife axe from behind her.

And both Ratan and Marc fired their guns.

Outside the tent, a tigress, waiting, pacing up and down the open cages, with the animals still inside them, started walking away into the forest.

Acknowledgements

ROY DANIELS, MY FRIEND IN THE SKIES, WHO GLUTTED MY shelves with books and kindled that odd bookish ambition.

Ramesh Srivats, who read an early awkward draft and drove in the Bangalore rain to sit in my terrace and talk about it.

Paritosh, who did re-reads in between scrubbing for surgeries, and made regular check-ups on my word count for the day.

My pad in Bangalore, where the light slanted just right, where I could prowl around at odd hours, unquestioned, where the writing came easier.

Anuja Chauhan, who talked me into finally letting go and so warmly introduced me to her publisher.

Swati Bhattacharya and Sumita Kaul, my cheerleaders, who listened with great responsibility to numerous renditions of the amorous night.

Anu Menon, who not so gently pushed me into infusing into the story some much-needed legal drama.

Manisha, who spent a holiday in Greece reading and then sitting by the phone answering long probing questions.

Pia, who gave her wise and often hilarious counsel when I was stuck and didn't know one word from the other.

Ravi, who passionately championed the book without letting anyone know he had not really read it.

Jiya, who listened uncomplainingly as I read aloud (but offered unsolicited advice on my pronunciation).

Doggess Nuri, for just being there, sometimes warming my feet and at other times flipping my laptop shut.

Aashi, Rachita, Divya and Paarth, who were endlessly encouraging.

Raaja Bhasin, author of *Simla, The Summer Capital of British India*, who met me at the Gaiety Theatre and so generously gave his time to talk to me about Simla in the 1930s.

Harper Collins India CEO Ananth Padmanabhan, editor Swati Daftuar and her team, who believed even in the early drafts and made the book better with every edit.

I'm grateful beyond words.

About the Author

Sonia Bhatnagar grew up in Calcutta, Goa and Delhi, graduating in English Literature from Delhi University. She is currently the National Creative Director of a global advertising agency.

She's been scribbling stories on every available surface since she can remember and started writing *In Your Blood I Run* in between shoots and PTA meetings, on flights and in vanity vans. Inordinately fond of travelling and discovering new places, she believes her spiritual home is in the mountains, but she is yet to find it.

When she's not writing, she can be found napping, reading or watching movies at home with her now YA daughters, her miracle rescue doggess and her long-suffering husband.

Allergic to tube lights, mansplaining and middle seats, she thrives in unconfined spaces and believes there's no therapy like girlfriend therapy

Keep in touch with Sonia on facebook.com/sonia.bhatnagar.96

She is @soniasofar on Instagram and twitter.

30 Years *of*

HarperCollins *Publishers* India

At HarperCollins, we believe in telling the best stories and finding the widest possible readership for our books in every format possible. We started publishing 30 years ago; a great deal has changed since then, but what has remained constant is the passion with which our authors write their books, the love with which readers receive them, and the sheer joy and excitement that we as publishers feel in being a part of the publishing process.

Over the years, we've had the pleasure of publishing some of the finest writing from the subcontinent and around the world, and some of the biggest bestsellers in India's publishing history. Our books and authors have won a phenomenal range of awards, and we ourselves have been named Publisher of the Year the greatest number of times. But nothing has meant more to us than the fact that millions of people have read the books we published, and somewhere, a book of ours might have made a difference.

As we step into our fourth decade, we go back to that one word – a word which has been a driving force for us all these years.

Read.